Redneck's Revenge

The Second Isabel Long Mystery

Also Available:
Chasing the Case

Joan Livingston

CROOKED
CAT

Discover us online:
www.crookedcatbooks.com

Join us on facebook:
www.facebook.com/crookedcat

Tweet a photo of yourself holding
this book to **@crookedcatbooks**
and something nice will happen.

For Fred Fullerton,
a reader, writer,
and dear friend.

About the Author

Joan Livingston is the author of novels for adult and young readers. *Redneck's Revenge*, published by Crooked Cat Books, is the second in the mystery series featuring Isabel Long, a longtime journalist who becomes an amateur P.I. The first is *Chasing the Case*.

An award-winning journalist, she started as a reporter covering the hilltowns of Western Massachusetts. She was an editor, columnist, and most recently the managing editor of *The Taos News*, which won numerous state and national awards during her tenure.

After eleven years in Northern New Mexico, she returned to rural Western Massachusetts, which is the setting of much of her adult fiction, including the Isabel Long series.

For more, visit her website: **www.joanlivingston.net**. Follow her on Twitter **@joanlivingston**.

Acknowledgements

I extend my appreciation to anyone who encouraged me to write. You know who you are.

Also, I offer special thanks to Laurence and Steph Patterson, of Crooked Cat Books, and my editor, Miriam Drori.

Praise for Redneck's Revenge

"The second book in the Isabel Long Mystery Series bounces along with humor, plot twists, colorful voices and rich character development. Redneck's Revenge is also a human story, a well-crafted tale of small town secrets, complicated relationships, life changes and lies. A romantic storyline adds spice and warmth to this cozy mystery."

Teresa Dovalpage
Author of *Death Comes in through the Kitchen*,
A Girl Like Che Guevara,
and *The Astral Plane*

"Set in the frozen Northeast, author Joan Livingston's spellbinding descriptions of small town America and classic Yankee characters weave humor and a love story with murder. The story sweeps us along and there are enough plot twists and turns in this deftly written work to satisfy the most hard-core mystery fan. A great choice."

Brinn Colenda
Award-winning author of
Homeland Burning and
The Callahan Family Saga

"I particularly like Joan Livingston's folksy, no frills style. I think that's a nod to her years as a newspaper editor (something her main character, Isabel shares with her). She knows how to turn a phrase. The reader has a sense of the setting. One can see it, feel it and smell it. I have the itch to go explore Western Mass. because of her writing. The characters are colorful and entertaining. It is almost as if I know them somehow, and you will too."

Joseph Lewis
Author of *Author of Caught in a Web and the Lives Trilogy*

Praise for Chasing the Case

"The story unfolds in a small town in New England at the onset of winter, a community so vividly depicted you can hear the snow fall. Written with meticulous attention to the details mystery readers relish and a welcome playfulness, this novel zips along like a well-tuned snowmobile. I can't wait for the next installment in what promises to be a great series."

Anne Hillerman
Author of the New York Times bestselling
Chee-Leaphorn-Manuelito mysteries.

"Joan Livingston has delivered a smart, fast-paced mystery, with a savvy and appealing protagonist who knows her way around the backwoods of the New England hilltowns. I can't wait to read more about journalist turned private investigator Isabel Long."

Frederick Reiken
Author of *Day for Night,*
The Lost Legends of New Jersey, and
The Odd Sea

"Lurking beneath the surface in small town, Back East life, there is always a mystery. In *Chasing the Case*, Joan Livingston, as only she can do, digs down into the underbelly of a small town to solve a crime. Take a trip to the land of pot roast and murder with Joan. I did, and I liked what I read."

Craig Dirgo
Author of The Einstein Papers,
The Tesla Documents, and
Eli Cutter series

Redneck's Revenge

The Second Isabel Long Mystery

Franklin Pierce

Isabel Long. The man's greeting was more of a statement than a question, but then again, Franklin Pierce is expecting me. He's a private investigator and I need his services. It's not what you think. I don't have a case for him to solve. I want him to hire me for three years, so I can be a bona fide P.I. We are meeting at his office, which is just a narrow storefront between a Cumby's – that's Cumberland Farms to those who don't live in New England – and a pizza joint. The sign on the window says:

FRANKLIN PIERCE

LICENSED P.I.

FRAUD, DIVORCES, LOST PEOPLE.

Franklin Pierce is on the pudgy side, pushing seventy or more, maybe, with glasses and a double chin that hangs loose like a turkey's wattle. He's got to be about five-foot-two or shorter because I tower over him. Get this. He's wearing a cowboy hat and a long canvas coat as if he's a cattleman out West. But when he opens his mouth, he's pure Yankee with those missing Rs and added Rs, plus a twang that says his folks have lived in this part of the world, that is, Western Massachusetts, since the white folks found it and the people who lived here before them.

He clutches a set of keys as I make my approach to the front door. Naturally, I was ten minutes early, my M.O., and waited in the car with my mother before he arrived. Yes, Maria Ferreira, my ninety-two-year-old mother, soon to be my ninety-three-year-old mother April 2, is with me. But when Ma saw Cumby's, she hightailed it out of my car. She says she'll go to the pizza joint afterward to get something to drink. She could have stayed home, but it's February, and like the rest of us, she's got a bit of cabin fever from the seemingly endless winter that began in October.

I smile and extend my hand to Franklin Pierce. I feel a bit self-conscious my skin is colder and rougher than his. I'm curious why someone would name their kid after one of the worst presidents so far although I can think of a few other contenders. But now isn't the time to bring up that observation. I need to win this man over. So, what will it be: Franklin or Frank although I seriously doubt Frankie. I play it safe.

"Mr. Pierce, hello."

"Please call me Lin. And you? Is it Isabel or Izzie? Which do you prefer?"

I shake my head.

"Never Izzie," I say.

"I'll remember that."

"Okay, Lin. How do you spell that?"

"L-I-N."

Gotcha. I follow him inside. For a man who makes money investigating private cases, this office is a bit of a joke, or maybe he doesn't make much. Someone could easily move in one of the cheapo dollar stores or a salon where they fix blue hair for old ladies. A cracked vinyl couch is set near the entrance along with a coffee table stacked with magazines I bet aren't current. The only art on the walls are a print of Norman Rockwell's "Runaway," the one in which a cop talks to a boy inside what looks like a diner, and framed newspaper pages that are yellow and faded. We're moving too fast toward the back of the office for me to read what they say. A desk piled high with papers but no booze bottles or ashtrays, I'm relieved to see, is semi-hidden by a partition along with two chairs for guests, a file cabinet, and beyond them a door I presume leads to a bathroom. I smell pizza through the walls from the joint next door.

Lin places his cowboy hat on the desktop and throws his long canvas coat over the back of his chair before he sits. He wears a dark suit, a bit frayed in the cuffs. His striped tie has a stain, perhaps coffee or a drop of grease. He shaved this morning. And he's almost due for a haircut. Yes, my observation skills are getting sharper. I will need them if I continue to investigate cases.

I take Lin's cue and choose one of the chairs opposite him. He studies me as I unbutton my coat and slide it away. I came dressed for this interview in a blouse and skirt. I pulled my silver hair back into a twist, now that it's long enough. I haven't dressed this fancy since I got canned from my job as the managing editor of the Daily Star. Now that I'm not sitting at a desk all day, I've lost some weight, a welcome development. My cheekbones are even more pronounced.

"Nice work on the Adela Collins case," Lin says. "I was impressed. It's tough to solve a missing person's case after so many years. How many was it?"

"Twenty-eight."

He repeats the number.

"Yup, that's a long time."

"I read the stories in the Star. I'm familiar with Jack Smith and his sister, kind of a tragic situation. I hear she's on permanent house arrest. I suppose that was the compassionate thing to do, uh, given her mental capacity."

Eleanor Smith may not have gotten enough oxygen at birth, but she managed to fool everybody, well, except me. But I admit I figured out she killed Adela purely by accident, or as I used to say when I was a journalist, a reporter's good luck.

"That was Adela's father's doing," I say. "Andrew Snow."

"Yes, I'm familiar with him, too. Jefferson is just down the hill from Conwell after all. I've spent some time up there."

"Business or pleasure?"

His lips form a slight smirk.

"Both. Actually, Andrew Snow hired me to investigate his daughter's case shortly after her disappearance when it appeared the police had given up. I focused on whether Adela could have just walked away and started a new life somewhere else. I came up empty." He bows his head for a moment. "You did a much better job even after so many years."

I recall Andrew Snow telling me he hired a P.I. in hopes of

bringing some closure, mainly for his ailing wife's benefit. But there was no evidence Adela Collins had started a new life somewhere else, as Lin put it. Now I'm facing the man who Andrew hired. It's a small world, much smaller in the hilltowns, where familiarity trumps coincidence.

I'm ready to talk business, but like most Yankees, Lin Pierce needs a little more to get him going.

"I see."

"What do you believe was Eleanor's motive?"

Ah, yes, motive. He wants to talk more about the case.

"Eleanor was super attached to her brother, Jack. He's all she has, well, except for her dogs. At the time, Jack and Adela were, uh, involved. Eleanor called to tell Adela she knew she was fooling around with other men. She was going to tell her brother." I pause. "Our understanding is Adela went to see her. We don't actually know what happened next, but Eleanor ended up strangling her. You read the news story. You know how she got rid of her body and her car."

"I heard she tried to do you in."

"She didn't strangle me at least. I think she panicked. She hit me over the head in the woods and left me there. Luckily, Jack came home and found me."

"Yes, you and Jack."

Yes, me and Jack. Lin wants me to know he knows about Jack. Actually, there isn't much to say these days. We talked it all out a couple of weeks after I solved the case. Let's say things have cooled to zero although they were hot and heavy before that all broke. He's got his sister to watch and a business to run after some rotten publicity.

The Conwell Rod and Gun Club even cancelled its annual Deer Supper at the end of shotgun season for the first time ever. Jack and his murdering sister were supposed to be the cooks. It sure complicated things for the supper and Jack's business when I solved the case.

My moles in the Conwell General Store's backroom, those snoopy, old guys I call the Old Farts, say Jack's trying to get back on his feet. Having a sister who's a killer did draw a lot of curious-seekers at first. But nosy out-of-towners don't stick around. It's a long trip to Conwell for a drink and a snoop.

The whole Adela connection was bad for local business, except for the True Blue Regulars, who stuck by Jack. Besides, the Rooster is their second home, and for a few, better than their first. There hasn't been any music on Fridays yet, the Old Farts told me one morning, but Jack found a cook, one of the gals in town, the wife of a buddy, so he's back serving food on the weekends. Jack doesn't need my help these days. He told me he couldn't afford to pay me anymore. I haven't been back to the Rooster since but not because of that. Let's just say it's personal.

"We're still friends," I tell Lin.

"Is it true what I heard about your mother?"

"Depends on what you heard, I suppose."

He chuckles.

I find myself slipping back into my sassy self. It feels good. For the past few months, that part of me was buried. I was too afraid to offend anybody, everybody.

"What I heard is she helped you with your case."

"Yes, you heard correctly. I guess you could call her my Watson. I went over the clues with her. Ma's read enough mystery novels and watched enough crime shows to help steer me in the right direction. While she didn't figure out Eleanor was the culprit, she was the one who suggested Adela left her home that night and wasn't dragged out of there."

"And she's ninety-two?"

"Yes. She'll be ninety-three in April."

Ma moved in with me last year because she was tired of living alone. I was alone, too, after my Sam died. Our three kids, Ruth, Matt, and Alex, are out of the house although they don't live too far from me. It's worked out well with Ma. She's a fun companion. Who would have thought when I was younger and wilder? She's a good cook, and like the fine Portuguese woman she is, she keeps me in kale soup, a staple of our people. Yes, Long is my married name. Ferreira is the name I got at birth. I'm a hundred percent Portagee and proud that I've invaded a Yankee stronghold in the hilltowns.

All right, Lin, enough with the dillydallying. Let's get on

with it.

"As I said over the phone... "

He waves his hand.

"Yes, that. You said you want to work for me to fulfill one of your requirements to get a P.I. license."

"That's right."

"So, what would make you qualified to be an associate? Have you ever worked in law enforcement?"

I shake my head.

"A cop? No. I was a journalist for over thirty years. I started as the Conwell correspondent for the Daily Star. Adela Collins' disappearance was my first big story." I watch his head bounce in recognition. "I knew how to chase a story. I found the pieces and put them together. I believe the skills are transferable, except I'd never carry a gun or wrestle anybody to the ground."

He squints as he thinks.

"I recall reading your stories. Didn't you used to run the paper?"

"Uh-huh, for fifteen years until it got bought out," I say. "As I explained over the phone, I'm not looking to take your cases although I'd be willing to help if you need it. I'll find my own."

"Well, I've never hired anybody and frankly, I couldn't afford you if I did." His voice drops. "I'd say I'm semi-retired. I own this building, so it's convenient to keep an office. It helps with taxes."

I was prepared for this.

"How about a buck a day? Could you afford that?"

He chuckles.

"You work cheap, Isabel."

Yeah, I do. I'm doing okay moneywise because of Sam's insurance. The house is paid off. Ma chips in. I did like it when I brought in a little spending money working at the Rooster. Twenty, twenty-five dollars a month from Lin isn't going to amount to much, except lunch out with my mother.

"You could say that, Lin. And if I get hired to work a case, I will give you a cut, say ten percent."

Lin Pierce hums as he ponders my proposal. I got a visit from the state cops after I solved the Adela Collins case. Without any show of gratitude, the sergeant informed me I needed to get a license if I planned to do any more investigating. He didn't even know Adela's father, Andrew Snow, paid me. Cash. That's a secret between us two. Could there be other juicy mysteries to solve? Sure. The hilltowns may seem like sweet little spots with their quaint homes and maple trees, but they have country-style darkness. Some real nutcases live here. I've seen bad feuds and bad blood. Cheating. Thievery. Fights. Grudges. Revenge. They just don't take pictures of that stuff and put them on calendars. Norman Rockwell didn't paint them either.

The paperwork the sergeant left me says I have to be honest and of good moral character, which strikes me as amusing. Plus, I have to find three citizens willing to testify that's true. Really. They can't be blood relatives. I may ask the Old Farts to vouch for me. I bet they'd get a kick out of it.

I also can't have committed a felony. Check on that one. The sticking point is I must have been a cop, no thanks, or work for a licensed private investigator for three years. I didn't want to work for a P.I. in the city. I do have my mother to think about. Lin Pierce's office is in Jefferson, the last hilltown before the closest city, Hampton, the county seat actually. Jefferson is rural but not as rural as Conwell and the other tiny towns around it with populations of a thousand and under.

When I told Ma about Lin, she asked, "What did he sound like over the phone?"

"Unsure."

"About himself or you?"

"Oh, definitely me."

"Did you check him out? What's it say on that Google thing?"

I smiled. My mother has never touched a computer, but she's picked up on Google.

"Better than that. I asked the Old Farts."

"Oh, them," she said with a bit of scorn in her voice. "What did those fellows have to say?"

"Well, the Fattest Old Fart said Franklin Pierce used to be an ambulance chaser, but he hasn't been doing much of that these days."

"That doesn't sound too promising."

"The Serious Old Fart said he did insurance cases, like catching somebody who's faking he's hurt. He also spied on cheating husbands and wives. But I got the feeling the Old Farts were leaving something out. I even mentioned it, but the guys were tight-lipped. Now that's a bit unusual. Maybe he's kin to one of them."

My mother frowned.

"You're going to do things like that? Spy on people?"

I shook my head.

"I'm not planning on it. All I want is for Franklin Pierce to say I work for him. If I get paid for a case, I'll give him a cut."

"You think he'll go for it?"

I tip my head forward. I believe I'm about to find out.

Lin clears his throat.

"All right, Isabel, I'll take you on as an associate. If you're not working a case for me, I'll pay you a buck a weekday as a retainer fee. If you are, I will up that to twenty an hour. And if you get a case, I'll take fifteen percent, not ten. Let me get you the paperwork for the state and IRS."

I smile to myself as he rifles through a desk drawer. I was figuring fifteen percent but decided to lowball him, a suggestion from my mother, who played her share of slots and Bingo at the Indian casinos in Connecticut before she moved in with me.

"Sounds like we have a deal."

He winks.

"Do you have any prospective cases?"

"After I solved the Adela Collins case, I did get a few calls from people, but nothing that grabbed me like that one. I'm not about to search for missing dogs or treasures that somebody's grandfather was supposed to have buried in his backyard. But now that I'm an associate, I'll spread the word. I'm not planning to be a P.I. fulltime. It's more like a paying hobby."

"Okay."

The office door opens. Lin leans way over to his left.

"Can I help you, ma'am?"

"I bet that's my mother." I turn. "Yes, it's her. She was shopping next door at Cumby's. Let me introduce you. Lin Pierce, meet Maria Ferreira."

Sweeten the Deal

Ma and I don't stay in Jefferson once my business is done. She informed me this morning another snowstorm is on its way. My mother is the official weather watcher in our household. It's part of her late-night routine. She plays solitaire on a tablet one of my sisters gave her while the TV is on. She has her shows. I'm in bed long before her, but then again, I'm up at the crack of dawn, a habit I acquired when I worked at the newspaper and just can't seem to shake even though it's been nine months since I got the heave-ho. You might've heard the story. After a corporation bought the Daily Star, we were supposed to reapply for our jobs. Like hell, I told the publisher, who ended up getting canned later even though he did what the new owners asked.

Besides, I like the quiet that time of day. The dog, Maggie, and cat, Roxanne, hang out with me like we could be best friends, as if that were true. They love Ma better, but, honestly, that's okay.

"What did you think of Lin Pierce?" I ask her.

"He did what you asked him for."

"That's not really an answer, Ma."

She pauses.

"I was expecting somebody a little more hard-boiled."

"You mean pickled?"

"No, no, more like Philip Marlowe or Mike Hammer."

I laugh.

"I think you're dating yourself there, Ma."

"I am ninety-two."

"Almost ninety-three."

"Don't remind me." She's laughing. "I think he'll be all

right. You just need to be a part of his business and not take any of his cases unless he really needs you. From what you say that doesn't seem to be a possibility anyways."

"That's right."

"Now that it's official, how are you going to get the word out besides telling those Old Farts in the back room."

I grin hearing Ma call them that name.

"Actually, I believe that will be sufficient to get the ball rolling. I'm not looking to do this full time. As I told Lin, this is more like a paying hobby than a business. I gotta do something to keep me out of trouble."

My mother snorts.

"Out of trouble, I like that," she says.

What have I been doing since I solved the Adela Collins case? That happened a few weeks before Christmas, so I got busy with everything that goes with the holiday, buying gifts and getting together with the family. I used to go a little bit nuts decorating the house when Sam was alive. We'd get a tree from one of the local farms. The kids would come over. Christmas the previous year was a somber affair. Sam had been dead less than two months. I didn't bother with Christmas at my house. Ma wasn't living with me then. This year, we split the holiday between my house and my daughter, Ruth's. She took Christmas Eve. I took the day. I put up a tree and baked lots of cookies, a personal request by my sons, Matt and Alex. Ma made a couple of Portuguese dishes: bread pudding, favas beans, and bacalhau, which is salted codfish.

I now have a granddaughter, Sophie, so that's worth celebrating. My son-in-law's parents drove up from Connecticut. His mother got a little smashed and asked a whole lot of questions about the Adela Collins case. I just couldn't get away from it. Ruth was a bit annoyed, but it isn't my fault her mother-in-law can't hold her liquor or her mouth.

I skipped New Year's. Sam and I went a few times in the past to the Rooster, but I heard from a reliable source, the Old Farts, of course, Jack didn't have anything going. Besides, it would have definitely been weird if I'd showed up.

Then winter hit us harder, except for the thaw in January,

which always gets our hopes up spring will be early. But the thaw only breaks people's hearts, except for the rednecks who love driving their snowmobiles and the cross-country skiers, those newcomers in tights. I dodged storms to take Ma into town to go shopping. We did the Conwell triangle on Saturdays and sometimes Wednesdays, going to the dump, store, and library in that order. I politely greeted winter-weary residents and was relieved not to run into Jack just yet.

What else? I shoveled snow and carried more firewood into the basement. I went snowshoeing with Matt and Alex. I remembered when I did that with Jack in November, his first time actually, and how we kissed, again for the first time. I couldn't bring myself to park at the Rooster lot, so the boys and I started on a trail at the town park.

I wrote a couple of freelance articles about life in the sticks for a magazine, but my heart wasn't in it. I read books from the town library and watched crime shows with Ma. We figured out who did what before the characters. Ma joked we had to keep our detective skills sharp for the real thing.

I did take a cursory peek at the boxes of notebooks from my old reporting days I have stored in a closet upstairs and decided to let them be. I was told reporters should get rid of their notebooks pretty damn quick, so some lawyer couldn't subpoena them. I'm glad I held onto mine. They were helpful with the Adela Collins case. Maybe they'll help with another. I'm not ready for that big backyard bonfire just yet.

Yeah, I visited the Old Farts in the backroom a few times just for jollies and to keep up with the news not fit to print.

Mostly, I moped.

Ma noticed it, too.

"When are you going to find something to do?" she asked me one day.

"What do you mean?"

"Like when you solved that mystery."

"You heard what the state cop said about getting a license," I reminded her. "I need to find a licensed P.I. to take me on."

"What's stopping you?"

Ma had a point. I have a hard head and an iron will. I

suppose I'm generalizing when I say it's because I'm a full-blooded Portagee. But I'm descended from people who went all over the world in tiny wooden ships. My grandparents came over from the Madeira and Azores islands in them.

When I checked online for private investigators in the area, I eliminated the ones who were too far away. My mother is in great shape, but I don't want to leave her alone too much although she does have the dog and cat, who are absolutely devoted to her and pretty much ignore me, except when they want to eat. I went down my list of possibilities. They all had heard about my success finding Adela Collins' killer. After all, the story went national: a reporter, whose first big story was a woman's disappearance, solves the mystery twenty-eight years later. One P.I. wanted me to work fulltime, but I turned him down nicely. Then I heard about Lin Pierce, from one of the Old Farts, actually.

"Isabel, are you listening to me?" my mother says beside me in the car. "You're not daydreaming again, are you?"

"Sorry. What did you say?"

She points.

"What are those tubes hanging from those trees?"

We're past the Jefferson town line and into Penfield, where two guys decked out in coveralls are hanging line off the maple trees. I did enough stories about maple sugaring to give my mother a complete rundown on the process, from hanging line and tapping trees to boiling the sap in flat evaporators. I can tell you the difference between Grade A and B, and why. I've written about good seasons when there was a long enough stretch of freezing nights and warm days to make all the work worthwhile, and I've written about bad ones, that is, when spring came too darn fast and the trees started budding. One sugarer told me the season is done for when the peeper frogs start chirping. I always think of that when I hear them in the woods.

I tell my mother, "When the time's ready, sap from those maple trees will flow through those tubes into a big tub. At the end of the day, the sap gets pumped into a tank on the back of a truck. Then the sap gets boiled down into syrup back at the sugarhouse. It takes forty gallons of sap to make one of maple syrup. Real maple syrup. Tasty stuff. I'll take you some time to a sugarhouse."

"I'd like that."

"When the season is in full swing, they'll stay up all night boiling."

"Sounds like a lot of work."

"Uh-huh, but that's true about a lot of ways people make their living up here, like Charlie who brings our firewood. How much do you think he makes? I bet not a lot after you factor in the equipment and fuel. It's called sweat equity."

As we head up and west, the snow comes down harder. It's already sticking to the road. I slow my Subaru. Traffic is light. Anyone who works in the city is already there and hasn't left for home yet.

Ma watches the scenery. Everything is still locked in snow. The guys on snowmobiles must be living it up. Maybe that'll help Jack get over this strange turn of events.

So, what did happen to Jack and me? He came to see me, and like I said, we talked it over and out. He stayed a couple of hours. The man cried about his sister and Adela. I cried because I care a lot for him.

The next day he called.

"Maybe we should take a break for a while," he told me.

I am well aware of what taking a break for a while means. I should have been ticked off he couldn't say it to me in person, but then again these were unusual circumstances. I agreed only because I didn't want to beg or try to reason with him. There are moments when I wonder if that was the right thing to do. Uh-huh, I've been doing a lot of second-guessing these days.

Besides, I hadn't been with a man other than Sam in decades, a time span that includes having three kids and a move from Boston to the hilltowns of Western Massachusetts. I wasn't expecting romance when Jack hired me to work two nights at the Rooster, but one thing made its way to another, and we had fun flirting, dancing, and, yes, having sex. He was easy to be around. He made me laugh. But that was before I found out his sister killed his former girlfriend, a scenario that sounds like one of my mother's crime shows or novels, but the God's honest truth, it happened. Jack said he doesn't hate me for finding out. But I don't know if he could love me in spite of it.

I will admit losing Jack has a lot to do with my moping around these past few months.

Beside me in the Subaru, my mother speaks, "Isabel, you all right over there?"

"I'm fine, Ma. Just paying attention to the road," I lie.

She hums. She knows my tendency to go off somewhere in my head. I was a big daydreamer as a kid. I still am as an adult.

"I heard the Rooster is serving food again," she says.

I glance her way. Ma doesn't venture out in town without me now that it's winter.

"Where did you hear that?"

"Mira, the librarian, told me when we were in there yesterday."

"I missed that part of the conversation."

"Anyway, it might be nice to go out for dinner soon. Mira says the new cook is better than the old cook."

"I presume she hasn't killed anybody either."

"Isabel."

"I don't know, Ma. It might be a bit awkward with Jack and all."

"It's about time you got over that. This is too small a town not to run into him. And I would be there with you."

"If that's what you want." I sigh. "Hey, I've really got to pay attention to the road. This snow is getting messy. Oh, there's a highway truck, thank God."

I beep the car's horn in gratitude.

Back at the Rooster

The jukebox is playing something by Willie Nelson when my mother and I enter the Rooster Bar and Grille. It's a little after five, of course, because I still haven't gotten my mother to eat later than that. I'm not a fan of early dinners, but it makes Ma happy, and really, it isn't too much to ask of me. Coming to the Rooster may be pushing it, however. Three months ago, I would've been stationed behind the bar, popping the caps off Buds and chatting with the customers. Jack and I would be carrying on a friendly banter, flirting, and dancing a little. It was strictly fun for adults. I did try to stay clear of his sister, which tells me my instincts were right on.

In the Rooster's parking lot, I gave Ma a chance to turn back. I even offered to drive her to the city if she wanted to eat out so badly.

"That's not what I had in mind," she said, and then she tried to distract me with, "Oh, look at all those snowmobiles."

Snap out of it, Isabel. You ain't in junior high, and Jack's not your first crush.

Ma chooses a window table. I'm helping her with her coat when Jack hustles from the kitchen with a plate of food in each hand. He notices me, I'm sure. I know from firsthand experience you see everything and everybody from behind that bar. Jack keeps moving toward a table at the other end of the room. He's working solo. Even with this early crowd, he's super busy. That's why he hired me. Four hands are better than two in a busy bar.

Would I come back to work at the Rooster? What do you think? In a heartbeat, but only if Jack and I could continue where we left off, without his nasty sister, of course.

I glance around the place. It isn't as full as I recall for a Friday, but then again there's no band tonight. I recognize all the True Blue Regulars who come here straight from work if they have jobs in the middle of winter. For the most part, they're friendly guys who'd rather be drinking here than at home. I've already gotten a few waves and a lot more curious stares.

I spot a hand-written sign tacked to a post that says the Cowlicks are playing next Friday. Beneath the words **MUSIC IS BACK** someone scribbled, "It's about fucking time." Before that whole mess happened, the Cowlicks were the unofficial house band at the Rooster, playing that crowd-pleasing mix of country, rock 'n' roll, and a bit of blues once a month. They had every danceable Lynyrd Skynyrd tune in their repertoire. On the other weeks, Jack managed to draw other bands, most with the same repertoire. They got one shot to impress him and the Rooster's music fans. The last band to play here was called the Hunters and Gatherers because it was the middle of shotgun season, an irony I enjoyed.

Then all hell broke loose two days later.

My mother leans forward.

"You look nervous, Isabel," she says.

"I am nervous, Ma."

"Do you want to leave?"

I glance behind her as Jack walks our way. I bite my lip.

"Too late for that, Ma," I mutter. "Incoming."

"Jack?"

"Bingo."

My mother takes the paper menus stuck between the napkin holder and the salt-and-pepper shakers. Her head bobs down. She studies the menu as if she's cramming for a test.

I study Jack instead. I can't help it. He squints like he's staring at the sun, but that's impossible since it's already dark outside and Jack keeps the lights inside the Rooster on the dim side. He's got a grin I'm trying to read. Is it a happy-to-see-me grin? Or is it a why-in-the-hell-did-you-come-back-to-my-place grin? Remember that line from Casablanca about all the gin joints? Well, the Rooster is the only gin joint in Conwell and the hilltowns around it although I would say it is more like a beer joint.

Jack hasn't dropped the grin.

He stops in front of me. He doesn't say anything. Neither do I. But the air between us is thick and heavy like something is about to break although I don't know what at this point.

"Nice to see you, Isabel. You, too, Mrs. Ferreira."

My mouth keeps up a smile. I can't help it.

"Same here," I say. "How've you been, Jack?"

"Better, thank you."

"Glad to hear."

"Business is pickin' up." He hooks his thumb behind him. "Did you see the sign? We're gonna have music again on Friday nights. You should… "

I finish the sentence in my head. The missing word is come. I let him off easy.

"The Cowlicks, eh? I like those guys."

He turns his attention toward the bar. He's got customers. He tips his head.

"Why don't you look over the menu? I'll be back to take your order."

I study the menu. It's mostly burgers, sandwiches, and fries. The day's special is meatloaf, I kid you not.

"Do you know what you want to get?" I ask my mother.

"I liked his sister's menu better. I guess I'll go with the tuna fish sandwich and French fries. You?"

It's Friday, and tuna fish is the only non-meat dish on the menu. Ma holds onto that Catholic thing of no meat on Friday. I don't eat much meat since I'm one of those natural food nuts, but more meat now that Ma lives with me. I was almost going to make a bad joke that I'd kill for Eleanor's cooking but decide against it. I shove the menus back in their place.

"The same," I say.

Jack returns with a beer for me, my usual brand from the tap, and a Diet Coke for Ma.

"Here you go," he says. "Ready to order?"

Jack scribbles on a pad as I tell him what we want.

"How's your sister?"

20

"Eleanor's okay. She misses workin' here and goin' places. At least she's got her dogs. We do have a hundred acres." The bell rings from the kitchen. Jack sticks the pencil behind his ear. "Gotta get that."

I'm halfway through my sandwich and beer when I realize the place is filling up. As my mother mentioned earlier, a lot of snowmobiles are parked outside. People get thirsty for beer or something else driving those machines along the trails in the woods. Dale Collins, Adela's son, and Bobby Collins, her rather unlikable ex, sit at the bar and talk. I guess eliminating Bobby as his mother's killer made Dale more receptive to his father. Both give me a nod and a smile when they spot me.

My interest is on Jack, naturally. He's serving and chatting. He's collecting empties from the tables. I feel like helping him, but I can't. Once in a while, I catch him glance my way.

My mother leans forward.

"Isabel, stop making goo-goo eyes at Jack."

"Goo-goo eyes? What's that?"

"Like you're in love with the man."

I suppose I am, or at least an extreme like.

Instead I say, "Sorry."

"Don't be sorry."

My attention turns toward the woman who approaches our table. It's Marsha, who my mother and I nicknamed the Floozy although we keep that to ourselves. She was the person who gave Bobby Collins an alibi the night his ex-wife, Adela Collins, disappeared although nobody believed him or her, myself included. It turned out she was being honest all along. Let's say Marsha is a little rough around the edges.

"Hey, Marsha, how are you?"

Her dry bush of brown hair swings around as she checks behind her. I catch a whiff of cigarette smoke, booze, and B.O. Oh, dear.

"Can I talk with you for a minute? It's kinda important," she says.

"You remember my mother, Maria? It's okay to talk in front of her."

"Sure."

Marsha aka the Floozy nods as I scoot over, so she can take the space beside me. Yowser, I smell more than a whiff. I'm guessing the Floozy is in her late forties, but she's got some serious country miles on her with missing teeth and some heft she crams into tight jeans. I spot a roll of flesh beneath her loose-hanging flannel shirt. I wonder if she and Bobby Collins are still an item since I didn't hear any, "Hi, ya, honey," from either of them. But then again, Bobby and Dale are yakking it up big time.

"What's up, Marsha?" I ask.

"Heard you're still doin' that investigation stuff," she says.

I smile. Word spread fast thanks to the Old Farts.

"Well, part-time and if it's a case I'm interested in," I answer.

She snorts.

"I think you'll be interested in this one."

"Is it for you?"

"Nah, my cousin. I don't think you've met her. She lives in Caulfield."

Caulfield is a hilltown even smaller than Conwell that's north and west from here in the next county. That town wasn't part of the Daily Star's coverage, and honestly, I've never had a reason to go there. Maybe Sam and I drove through it a few times to get to somewhere else. Nothing sticks out in my mind about the place.

"Tell me more, Marsha."

"I'd rather you hear it from her."

"Fair enough. Why don't you bring her to my house? You know where I live?"

The Floozy gives me an amused smile. Of course, she knows where I live. Everybody in this nosy little town knows where everybody else lives, what vehicle they drive, and how they make their money. They know their marital status and how many kids they have.

"I can do that."

"What day works for you two?"

"How about Sunday? My cousin works Saturdays."

I nod. She's not messing around.

"Make it around three."

"I hear you're chargin'. My cousin can't afford much."

"Maybe we can work something out."

"All right then." Marsha slaps the table before she's on her feet. "See you Sunday."

I giggle as the Floozy pounds Bobby hard on the back before she heads back to the far side of the room. I wait until she's definitely out of earshot before I ask my mother for her take on that conversation.

Ma slides her empty plate forward. I only ate half of my sandwich. I'm not big into piccalilli in my tuna salad. The fries were a bit on the soggy side.

"Sure, I'm interested in what the Floozy's cousin has to say," Ma says. "The fact she wouldn't say what it is makes me curious. And then she agreed so fast to meet Sunday."

"What do you think? Money or murder?"

"Maybe both."

I laugh. My mother's instincts are usually spot on.

"You ready to hit the road?" I ask. "Let me get the check. You can just put away your pocketbook. I've got this one."

I glance toward Jack for the hundredth time this night. He's stuck behind the bar opening bottles, the King of Beers, no less, for a few customers. I see my chance when he starts wiping down the bar with a rag and dropping empties into a carton on the floor.

"Be right back," I tell Ma.

"I'm not going anywhere."

Jack grins when he sees my approach.

"I'd like to settle with you," I say.

"Sure enough." He begins searching through the stack of tickets. "Here you are."

I have several things I'd like to settle with Jack. I bet you can guess a few of them. But suddenly, I'm shy. The words stay inside me.

"You asked about my sister," Jack says as he adds up my bill. "One thing we do for some fun is go snowshoeing on our land. I bought her and me a pair like the ones you have."

"Does she like it?"

"Oh, yeah, we take her mutts with us. She laughs up a storm."

That might be something to see. I don't recall his killer sister ever laughing up a storm. Maybe a giggle or a snicker. Mostly grunts.

"I'm glad," and then I manage, "It was nice seeing you again," and feel foolish for it.

Jack raises his eyes from my bill.

"I'm… "

But whatever else Jack was going to tell me stops abruptly when his creepy cousin, Fred Lewis, wraps an arm around me and, no fooling, kisses my cheek.

"Hey, Isabel," he says. "If this lunkhead won't see you anymore, I'm ready to take over."

"Take over what?" I say.

Jack is red-faced. I am, too.

Fred hoots.

"I like sassy women," he says.

"Well, this sassy woman says you can let her go. I'm gonna pay Jack."

He drops his arm.

"Sure. Sure. But the offer still stands."

"I'll remember that if I have something that needs taking over."

Thankfully, Fred loses interest and finds somebody else in the bar to terrorize. He's joshing with some buddy who's got a stool at the bar.

Jack hands me the ticket. I reach for my wallet. I have enough to pay cash.

"Sorry about my cousin," he says.

"It's not your fault he's a jerk."

Jack nods. He's not grinning or smiling.

"I wanted to say before I'm glad you came, too," he says softly.

"Oh, Jack."

On the drive home in the car, Ma and I discuss Marsha the Floozy, the Rooster's new menu, and our meal in that order. We both agree we are intrigued by the Floozy's proposal. The new menu needs some tuning up, and the food was so-so, but it was good not to cook tonight.

We are a half-mile from home when Ma throws this at me, "He still likes you."

Of course, she's talking about Jack, and I feel my face must be getting red again, but I decide to downplay her observation.

"Sure, Ma."

"Yeah, I saw the way he kept staring at you."

"Was he making goo-goo eyes, too?"

"No, men don't do that. You should've seen his face when you went up to pay that bill, especially when that cousin of his grabbed you."

"Aw, come on, Ma. You've been reading too many romance novels lately. Stick to mysteries."

My mother makes a low laugh.

"Isabel, you're such a funny girl."

The Floozy's Cousin

Marsha and her cousin show up around three Sunday in the Floozy's rusted clunker of a car I hope will be able to make it back up our snow-covered drive. I should have warned her to park at the top and walk down. But being local gals, I bet they've handled their share of steep driveways in the winter. I do have buckets of sand in the Subaru's cargo hold. Anyway, it wouldn't be the first car I've had to push out of here.

My mother announces the cousins' arrival from her chair in the living room, where she's reading the cozy mystery she picked up at the town library yesterday. Football season is over, so the TV is off. Ma's not a basketball fan. She'll watch the Red Sox even when they stink. She did inform me which day the team's equipment truck leaves Fenway Park for Florida.

The kitten, Roxanne, is on her lap. The dog, Maggie, is curled near the woodstove, her spot these days when she's not begging for Ma's attention.

"Your company's here," she says as she parts the drapes. "You want me to go somewhere else?"

"Nah, you can stay right there. I'm going to meet with them in the kitchen, so you can listen in. You're welcome to join us."

"This chair's just fine."

Both women appear uncertain about where to go until I open the front door and give them a friendly holler. I hate keeping the door open, it's still so damn cold, but it'd be rude to shut it. Of course, the dog runs outside to greet them. She's got her tail wagging, and I like it that the cousin reaches down to give her a pat. Marsha takes the lead up the walkway. Her cousin isn't as tall or as heavy. Her hair is stuffed in a knit hat

26

but what sticks out is dark. I'm guessing she's younger than Marsha, maybe in her late thirties. She's got one of those tight faces that make you think she might snap if she doesn't like something somebody says, or maybe she's just tired, or maybe she's unsure about meeting a nosy newcomer. Let's be clear. I will be a newcomer even if I live to be older than my mother and die here.

"Come in," I tell the women as they stomp their snowy boots on the porch. "Don't worry about that. Maggie, go lie down."

Marsha and her cousin give my house the once-over as I shut the door behind them. I don't know about the cousin, but it might be the nicest house they've been inside. I'm not being a snob. I've seen the trailer where Marsha lives, at least from the outside. But maybe the cousin is better off.

"This is Annette. I told you about her," Marsha says.

I reach out my hand. It takes Annette a while to offer hers. I'm betting she's one of those women who aren't into handshaking. I wasn't either until I got into journalism. I liked how it threw men off when I extended my hand for a shake, especially in the hilltowns. Annette's hand is colder and its skin rougher than mine. I wonder what she does for a living, and I suppose I'm about to hear. I introduce my mother before I ask her last name.

"Waters," she says. "I live in Caulfield."

"Why don't we go into the kitchen? You want coffee? Tea? Water? Can I take your jackets?"

Both shake their heads as they follow me into the kitchen. Perhaps they'd rather have a beer, but this is supposed to be a business arrangement and not a gabfest in my kitchen. I have a pad and two pens on the tabletop. Always have a backup pen. I learned that rule the hard way as a reporter when I was stuck doing an important interview without one. I thought to record our conversation today on my phone, but it might spook them. I'm still learning my way around this P.I. business. I expect to for a while.

I started investigating Adela Collins' case purely for personal reasons. I understand what happens when someone

27

disappears and what that means to the people who love them. My little cousin, Patsy, went missing when I was a kid. They found her remains years later when a wooded area was cleared for a subdivision but not her killer. I haven't forgotten the feeling of losing Patsy or wondering who took her. They say it's often people close to the victim and not some stranger danger. I hate to think someone I know killed my cousin and got away with it.

The women take off their coats and bunch them over the tops of their chairs. Annette slides her black, knit hat off her head and into a jacket pocket.

"Marsha says you're hoping I could help you," I tell Annette.

"Yeah, catch the bastard that killed my father," she blurts.

Whoa. I reach for a pen. A father killer for my second case? She's definitely got me interested. Ma coughs from the other room. She's interested, too.

"Okay, first things first. I'm gonna need some basic information about you and your father. Then we can get into the details about his death. That all right with you, Annette?"

Annette glances at her cousin, who gives her a nod.

"Isabel's all right," Marsha says. "I didn't think so at first, but she proved my Bobby didn't do it."

I smile at the Floozy's glowing endorsement. It definitely appears she and Bobby are still together. That pound on the back at the Rooster was more like a love tap, I suppose. Besides, the night was young when I saw them. My mother and I were gone before it got older. Who knows how long Bobby and his son, Dale, talked?

To get business out of the way, I get Annette's address and contact info. What does she do for a living? She's a mechanic. Is she married? Used to be, but now divorced. Kids? One, a son named Abe who's nineteen. Siblings? Two brothers, well, three, but one died when he was a baby. They're still in the area. What about the mother? She died years ago. Cancer.

I wish I could be recording this or typing it on my computer. I'll have to make a strong effort to write everything down neatly, so I can read it later.

28

"That's good." I speak in a soothing voice. "Please tell me about your father. I don't believe you said his name."

"Chester A. Waters. Everyone knew him as Chet. I kept my family's name after the divorce. I know what you're gonna ask next. He was sixty-nine when he died."

Marsha pokes her cousin.

"Tell her the date."

"Oh, yeah, yeah, three years ago in January. It was Jan. 15."

"Three years ago?"

"Is that too long?"

"It depends on how much information you can give me and other stuff. I also don't know anybody living in your town, so I'd definitely need your help with that. And other members of your family." I have my pen ready. "What did your father do for a living?"

"He ran a junkyard. He called it Rough Waters Garage and Junkyard."

"That's a clever name. Was it at his home or someplace else?"

"Home."

"How big was it?"

"Huge. He took in wrecks and sold the parts. If they weren't too bad, he fixed 'em up. Once in a while he'd get a crusher when a car was down to its bones."

"Is the junkyard still there?"

"Yeah, it's mine now. I run the place. You can add junkyard dealer to what I do to make money."

I manage a straight face. I learned that trick when I was a reporter and listened to people share the most outrageous things about their lives, all off the record, of course. Now that I'm no longer in the news business, I might let loose a few of those stories. But a woman owning and operating a junkyard? That's a new one on me.

"What happened to your brothers?"

"None of 'em wanted to own a junkyard and a garage. One of my brothers, Chester Jr., is a school principal who doesn't like to get his pink hands dirty." She holds up her own, which are dry and blackened beneath the nails. "My other brother, Mike, drives truck. We divided up the land as equal as we could make it. I had a small house built right where my father's used to be on the same slab. That's where I live."

I put down the pen. I just don't meet too many junkyard owners and like I just said, never a woman. The newcomers hate junkyards and make rules to ban them from opening, but probably the one Chet Waters owned was grandfathered or the town of Caulfield isn't so particular. When I was a reporter, I saw two neighbors, a newcomer and a native, almost come to blows at a meeting over a proposed junkyard. The board of selectmen turned down the request, and the guy didn't contest it.

By the way, Conwell only allows one unregistered vehicle on a property. That's how the town took care of that problem although I personally know several people who buried junks they no longer wanted in their backyard. I never understood that. Why not have them towed to a junkyard instead?

"What was your father like?"

Annette grins. So does Marsha, who has been amazingly still.

"He was nice if he liked you, a son of a bitch if he didn't, which was most people. Wouldn't you say, Marsha?"

"Yup, I was glad he liked me. He sure didn't like my parents, but I didn't either."

I met a lot of men like that when I was a hilltown reporter, but I keep that information to myself. Remember what I said about Yankee men being the strong, silent types? They're like old lawnmowers that need a few cranks to start running, and then they talk your head off. What about grumpy men? Of course, I met them, too. They were a bit trickier, but I found most came around if I didn't back down and was honest about my intentions.

"Why don't you tell me about the day your father died?"

Annette raises her chin.

"It was night. His house caught fire and he didn't get out in time. They said he was drunk and probably set the place on fire with a cigarette. They said it was an accident. His place, well, it's my place now, is way out on a back road. No real neighbors. It was late, the middle of the night, actually, so nobody called in the fire. I'm the one who found Pop's body the next day. It looked like he tried to crawl out. He was badly burned and... " Her voice cracks. She stops for a moment. "There wasn't much left of him or the house. It used to be a camp."

FYI, a camp is a cabin, typically small and rough. While Annette talks more about the experience, I try to recall if I ever heard anything about the fire. Like I said, the Daily Star didn't cover Caulfield, but we might have run a wire piece, something short, with a headline like: **Caulfield man dies in house fire.**

"I'm sorry about your father," I say. "I'm curious though. How did they know a cigarette started it?"

"Beats me. There was hardly anything left. But that's what the fire marshal said. I don't think he tried that hard if you wanna know the fuckin' truth. He probably thought my father was just some dumb redneck. He asked my brothers and me if Pop smoked, and so he decided that's probably it. Everybody knew he drank heavy."

I write while I listen. I don't even glance at the paper, so it's going to be dicey later on if I can read it. But then again, I've got Ma listening in the other room. She's got a mind like a steel trap. She may be up there in years, but if you met my mother, you'd understand.

"What makes you think it was murder and not an accident?"

"I just know."

"Annette, if you want me to take on this case, you're gonna have to do better than that."

She checks Marsha, who gives her an encouraging nod.

"He found somethin' in one of the junks."

"Go on."

She presses her lips together before she continues.

"Drugs and some money in the trunk of a Toyota Corolla. It was shoved inside the spare where somebody cut it. He showed it to me before he died. It was a month before, maybe less."

"And?"

"It wasn't there later on. I didn't think to check until a few weeks after Pop died. I was too worked up about his dyin'."

"That's understandable."

"And it kept snowin'. It dawned on me about the Corolla when I was plowin' out the junkyard. I dug out the car to get inside the trunk. The tire was there, but everthin' in it was gone."

"Could he have brought the stuff inside his house for safekeeping, and it got burned up?"

Her head swings back and forth.

"Nah, he told he was gonna leave it in that car. He figured it was safer. He didn't want anybody breakin' into the house. Made sense to me."

"Do you think the drugs and money came with the junk? Or did somebody hide them there?"

"That's a real good question."

Marsha pokes her cousin.

"See? I told you she knew her shit."

I pause. You might think I'm nuts, but I like what I hear. I'm definitely keen on this case. Annette and Marsha may be rough and gruff around the edges, country style, but I have a soft spot in my heart for people like them. I did when I was a reporter, choosing to write stories about what the country folk did and liked such as truck pulls and pig roasts. I found them more interesting than the newcomers' idea of fun.

"I guess you couldn't tell the police about that."

"You're fuckin' right."

"But if the drugs and money belonged to somebody else, why kill your father? They could've easily just taken them back when he wasn't around."

"That what I want you to find out. And who's the fucker that did it."

I smile. Annette doesn't hold back. But now that we're talking about cops I need to set something straight.

"You should know I'm gonna check in with your police chief. It's a courtesy, and besides I don't want the chief to get

32

bent outta shape I'm snooping around and think I don't trust the local cops."

"Yeah, yeah, I figured as much."

"Besides, I'll need the cops if I solve this case. I can't arrest anybody." I note Annette's sly smile. "Online I saw the chief's a woman. Nancy Dutton. Right? What's she like?"

"Nancy's kinda new. Maybe a year. She was on the force when my Pop died though." Annette shrugs. "Nancy's okay. I actually grew up with her. Yeah, you'll need her when you catch the bastard."

"All right then."

Annette leans forward over the table.

"I know you charge money," she says. "I ain't got much."

We are at the part that's unfamiliar to me: the business end. Andrew Snow paid me that thousand out of the goodness of his heart. He says it brought him a bit of peace knowing what happened to his daughter. His only regrets were that his wife, Irma, died years ago, and, of course, that it turned out Eleanor Smith was the killer.

I've looked up what people charge, anywhere from forty to a hundred bucks an hour. That's not gonna fly with Annette. Besides, I'm green at this detective stuff.

"You do understand it'd take a lot of my time trying to figure out this case. Gas, too."

Her head bobs.

"Yeah, I got me an idea how to pay you."

"Go ahead."

"I can do all the work on your cars for free. I see you got a Subaru and a Ford. I can fix both of 'em no sweat."

"They both have low miles."

"You still gotta change the oil. If you need tires, I've got really good used ones."

"Uh-huh. I should tell you I have a business arrangement with a private investigator in Jefferson. I need to work for a licensed P. I. for three years, and Lin Pierce agreed to take me on. Heard of him? No? I'm supposed to give him fifteen percent of what I make."

"Shit," she says stretching out the word. "I can do his

vehicles, too."

I feel myself smiling. I like Annette's persistence. I can relate.

"I have one more question. What if I don't find out who's responsible?"

Her eyes lock onto mine.

"Just give it your best shot. That's all I ask." She bumps her cousin with her elbow. "Marsha told me how you solved that really old case. Mine only happened three years ago. I can tell you believe what I'm sayin' about my Pop might be true. I see it in your eyes. No one else, except for Marsha, has gotten that far."

"Fair enough. If you don't mind, I'd like to think it over. And I need to talk with my business partner about your payment plan. I'll call you tomorrow afternoon. That work?"

"Yeah, that works," she says. "Thanks for meetin' me. I hope you take me on."

As soon as the cousins leave, I sit beside my mother. She puts down her book. We both watch the Floozy gun her car and barrel it up the driveway. She turned down my offer of sand. I admire her resourcefulness and driving skills.

"Well?" I ask my mother.

"Sounds like an interesting case, but at this rate you won't be making much of a living," she says. "But then again, our cars would be running great, and we wouldn't have to spend money on that."

"Good points. But I have to ask Lin Pierce if he minds." I get up to find my cell phone. "Maybe it's time to check in with the Old Farts, too. One of them has got to have known Chet Waters and his daughter."

Calling Lin Pierce

A woman answers the phone when I call Lin Pierce's house. He warned me he only uses his cell phone for emergencies, and when he punched my numbers into its contacts list, it was one of those ancient flippers. The guy's what I'd call a fuddy-duddy, but he's my fuddy-duddy.

"Lin? It's that woman," I hear her say.

That woman, eh? I hear footsteps, and then a brief exchange between Lin and the woman I assume is Mrs. Pierce.

"Yes?" he answers.

"This is Isabel. How are you?"

"Fine. Fine. What's going on?"

"I might have my first case. A woman wants me to find out who killed her father."

"Another murder?"

"At least, she thinks so. Did you know Chet Waters? He lived in Caulfield. His daughter, Annette Waters, came to see me just now."

"Chet Waters? Not personally. Wasn't he the guy who died when his house burned down? I believe he owned a junkyard."

"That's the one. His daughter is convinced he didn't die because a cigarette caught fire and he was too drunk to get out. Her father showed her something valuable somebody hid in one of the junked cars, but it was gone when she went to look weeks after his death."

"What was valuable?"

"A lot of drugs and money."

"This sounds like it could be dangerous."

"Maybe, but that's not why I'm calling you. I haven't said yes by the way." I pause. "She doesn't have much money. She's a mechanic and wants to pay me off doing maintenance

35

on my cars. She said she would do the same for you, for your fifteen percent. Are you amenable to that?"

"Uh, Isabel, you're not going to get rich this way."

"You ever barter?"

"Sure, you should see the stuff I've got at my house. Let me know if you ever want a mounted moose head." He sighs. "Yes, she can work on my cars."

"Thanks, Lin, I'll give her a call and get started."

Back with the Old Farts

The Fattest Old Fart, and I could also call him rightly the Loudest Old Fart, announces my arrival early Monday morning to the rest of the group as I make my way between the shelves stocked with canned goods, boxes, and jars. All the regulars are parked on the benches in the backroom of the Conwell General Store. Besides the Fattest Old Fart, there are the Serious Old Fart, Bald Old Fart, Skinniest Old Fart, Old Fart with Glasses, and Silent Old Fart. Today there are no Visiting Old Farts. Of course, the Old Farts don't have a clue I call them that. I use the names their parents gave them.

"Look who the cat dragged in," the Fattest Old Fart says.

I glance around.

"What cat? I don't see any cats back here," I say, which, of course, gets them all cackling.

I choose a spot next to the Fattest Old Fart, who usually sits alone because he takes up so much space on the bench, and I'm kind of a skinny gal, actually a skinnier one these days. He nods to the Serious Old Fart, who gets up to pour me a cup of coffee from the machine and throw a few coins into the pay-up jar.

"Here you go, Isabel. Still waiting for that espresso machine to get fixed, so this will have to do," the Serious Old Fart says, pleased with repeating the joke I've been hearing for the past few months. Being he's the serious one of the group it makes me laugh, which gets the others laughing, too. "I believe I made your coffee just the way you like it."

I grimace when I take a sip. No amount of half-and-half is going to make this coffee taste better. But I thank him anyways.

The Fattest Old Fart turns my way.

"Do you have a case yet?"

"I might."

I have everybody's undivided attention.

"For God's sake, Isabel, spit it out," the Fattest Old Fart says. "Don't toy with us."

I take another sip of the store's horrible coffee just to tease them a bit.

"Any of you know Chet Waters from Caulfield?"

Their heads bob.

"He kicked a few years ago," the Bald Old Fart says. "Got burned up in a fire. Supposedly he passed out and the place caught fire from his cigarette."

"That's the one. Interesting that you used the word supposedly. His daughter, Annette Waters, came to see me. She doesn't think her father's death was an accident. I haven't decided yet if I want to take the case. What can you tell me about him?"

I see a lot of sideways glances.

"Chet could be one mean son of a gun," the Serious Old Fart says, and then he adds before I can make a wisecrack, "But when it came to business, he was fairer than most. I bought my son's first car off of him. Decent price. The car ran for years."

The Old Fart with Glasses speaks.

"I used to go to his junkyard for parts. I could say what I needed, and he knew just where to find it. That was no easy trick considering how big the place was."

"How big?"

"You haven't seen it yet?" the Old Fart with Glasses asks. "Isabel, you're in for a real treat. It's gotta be one of the biggest one around, if not the biggest, even bigger than Sinclair's in Fulton. Nearly everybody has their junk hauled to Chet's junkyard. Now his daughter runs it. Never heard of a woman running a junkyard."

"Me neither. What else?" I ask.

The Bald Old Fart snorts.

"The man could drink you under the table," he says.

"Did he ever go to the Rooster?"

"You might want to check with Jack to see if he was on one of his lists," the Bald Old Fart says. "Sorry, Isabel, I didn't mean anything by that."

The Old Fart with Glasses fills in the awkward silence that follows. I'm certain the breakup of one of Conwell's most notorious hookups was a source of discussion here.

"Yeah, yeah, I remember seeing him in the Rooster," the Old Fart with Glasses says. "A hotshot pool player, as I recall. He liked playing poker. Heard he was suspected of cheating a couple of times."

So, Chet Waters drank a lot, played pool and poker, and was a Rooster customer from time to time. He was an unpleasant guy but a fair businessman. Maybe he cheated at cards. What else?

"Can you think of anyone he might have crossed?"

"You mean bad enough to get him killed?" The Serious Old Fart snorts. "That's your job, Isabel."

The rest of the Old Farts join him.

"Thanks a lot, fellows."

"How well do you know Caulfield?" the Bald Old Fart asks me.

"I think I drove through it before. Does it have a store?"

"There's a gas station and the owners have a few things inside, beer, and coffee as good as you drink here," the Bald Old Fart says. "It's called the Pit Stop."

I glance around to make sure Jamie Snow, the owner, isn't around.

"That bad, eh?"

"Yeah, I heard their espresso machine is out, too," the Bald Old Fart jokes.

"You're all too much. I will definitely have to check it out. What about Chet's daughter, Annette Waters? I'd have to work with her."

There's a low rumble of chuckles. I glance from one Old Fart to the other.

Finally, the Fattest Old Fart clears his throat.

"Let's just say Annette is one woman who likes to work hard and play hard."

"What do you mean play hard?"

"Oh, Isabel, figure it out," the Fattest Old Fart says.

I immediately do. Annette is a floozy like her cousin. Perhaps, she is a doozy of a floozy. Now I'm even more interested in this case.

"By the way, guess who she used to be married to?" The Old Fart with Glasses offers a rare question.

Crap, I forgot to ask Annette that question. I'd better be on my A game if I want to solve this or any other cases. You can do better than that, Isabel.

"Uh, no clue."

"Fred Lewis."

Annette was married to Jack Smith's creepy cousin? Crap, I can't shake that guy loose.

"How long ago was that?"

"A while back," the Old Fart with Glasses says. "You're gonna take the case?"

"I believe so. My mother's certainly interested."

"How is your dear, sweet mother?" the Serious Old Fart asks.

"Sick of winter like we all are, but she's adjusting fine to life in the sticks. She'll be ninety-three in April." I smile at their nods. "Thanks for spreading the word for me. I'm now officially associated with Franklin Pierce, P. I., although you probably already know that."

"Yeah? He hired you?" the Bald Old Fart asks.

"Yup, for a buck a day."

"You work real cheap," the Old Fart with Glasses says.

"That's what he said, too." I stand. "Thanks for the coffee and the info. See ya all soon."

Googling Chet Waters

By the time my night-owl mother is up, I've already talked with Annette and found what I could online about Chet Waters, which isn't a heckuva lot. Yeah, I'm using that Google thing. When I checked the stats, I learned Caulfield has about six hundred people. The town is part of the coverage area for the Berkshire Bugle, but like the Daily Star, it cut back reporting on its swath of the hilltowns unless something huge happened like an old man dying in a house fire. I found three stories about Chet by the Bugle, plus an obit.

Going back few years before his death, an enterprising reporter with the Bugle wrote a profile of Chet, which is a good read as we say in the business. It appears his profile was part of a series on interesting hilltown folk, which makes me wonder who else was featured.

Here's the headline for the story: **Meet Caulfield's junkman Chester Waters.**

CAULFIELD — Chester "Chet" A. Waters IV knows how to turn trash into treasure at his aptly named Rough Waters Garage and Junkyard.

Waters' junkyard is located on a neighbor-less road in the middle of nowhere in this small hilltown. But its remoteness doesn't hinder customers from finding him.

Got a car not worth trading in or fixing? Waters will take it. Need an engine for a '64 VW Beetle? He will likely have one to sell.

Waters began his junkyard after he got out of the Army. He enlisted after he graduated from high school.

"It was great to get out of this hell hole and see a bit of the world," he said with a laugh.

Waters came home, looked around for a job and when

he came up empty, started fixing cars and taking the ones nobody wanted. He still fixes cars at age 65, but he has his daughter, Annette Waters, to help out.

"My daughter's a real solid mechanic," he says. "She takes after me."

Waters and his late wife, Gladys, raised three children, including two sons, Chester A. Waters V and Michael Waters. The couple lost a son when he was a baby. "That was a tough one," he says.

"What do the boys do? One's a principal for a school and the other's a truck driver," he says with a laugh. "I sees them when they want something fixed."

Many towns won't allow junkyards. But Waters says he started his business long before anyone started making rules about them, so it's grandfathered.

Besides Waters owns about a hundred acres bordering state forestland he inherited from an uncle. He says his parents "were good people but they didn't have a pot to piss in."

With its long road frontage, the land gives him a buffer zone from potential neighbors who might want to build on Maple Ridge Road.

About 20 acres is dedicated to his junkyard, with the wrecks and abandoned vehicles filling three long rows. He says he has to work to keep trees from sprouting in the yard. He uses a gas-powered weed whacker to keep them from taking over.

"Pop likes a clean junkyard," Annette Waters says.

The story continues. It's a sizable piece. I'd say about a thousand words, which amounts to about twenty-five inches. Sorry, I can't stop thinking like a journalist. For the rest of the story, the reporter interviews townspeople, both fans and foes of having such a large junkyard in their town. Chet takes the reporter out for a ride in his restored 1947 Ford, which he writes ran like a dream. A couple of photos accompany the story. Chet walks between the rows of junks in one. He hugs his daughter in another.

The next story is dated Jan. 17, which is the day after the

fatal fire was discovered. I was right about the headline: **Caulfield man dies in house fire**. Yes, that about sums it up. I recognize the reporter's byline. Sean Mooney was an intern at the Daily Star before the Bugle hired him. He was a solid reporter, but we didn't have a full-time opening and the Bugle did.

Here's his story.

CAULFIELD — A Caulfield man died when his house burned to the ground in an overnight fire discovered by his daughter Wednesday morning.

Officials are investigating the blaze that killed Chester "Chet" A. Waters IV, 69, who ran a junkyard and a vehicle repair shop on his Maple Ridge Road property located on one of the town's back roads.

Caulfield Fire Chief Roger Dickerson said no one called in the blaze because of the home's remote location and the time the fire apparently broke out. He said Annette Waters found her father's body when she arrived to work in his garage.

"His daughter told us she spotted some smoke when she was driving up Maple Ridge," Dickerson said. "Annette said she couldn't believe it when she saw what was left of her father's house. Then she found her father, who had managed to crawl from the house. She called 911 right away."

Annette Waters, who remained on the scene while fire officials extinguished any burning sections, declined to comment.

Waters, a Caulfield native, ran Rough Waters Garage and Junkyard, where he repaired vehicles, collected junk cars and sold parts. To many, he was a colorful character in this town of 600 people.

According to the Caulfield Annual Town Report, Waters held two town positions, Fence Viewer and Surveyor of Wood and Bark.

At the Pit Stop, the town's only gas station, Pete Woodrell, one of the owners, said Waters had been there Tuesday morning to fuel up his pickup.

"Chet was an okay guy although he could be a bit ornery," Woodrell said. "That's what I liked about him. You knew where you stood with Chet. It's a rotten shame this happened."

Lenora Ashley, a Caulfield resident who was getting gas at the Pit Stop, said Waters was "a proud man." "You wouldn't think so cause he ran a junkyard," she said. "But it was how he made his living, that and fixing cars. He'll be missed."

Funeral services are pending.

Sean Mooney was still green when he was told to drive to the sticks and find somebody willing to talk with him, not such an easy feat when you don't live in the hilltowns. People are suspicious. It was a cinch when I was the hilltown reporter for the Daily Star because I was a resident of Conwell. The firefighters even let me cross the fire line so I could get a closer look. I reported on what I could, and then I checked in with the busy chief to tell him I'd give him a call that night. It was a tactic that worked.

Here's Chet's obit, which was brief although not surprising, given people have to pay by the word for obits these days. A long time ago they were free, and I used to field angry phone calls from grieving people who complained the paper was making money off the dead.

Chester A. Waters IV, of Caulfield, died suddenly Jan. 15. He was the son of Chester A. Waters III and Anna (Pope) Waters. He was preceded in death by his parents; his wife, Dolores (Franklin) Waters; and a son, Lucas. He is survived by his daughter, Annette Waters; and sons, Chester A. Waters V, and Michael C. Waters (Lillian); and four grandchildren. Mr. Waters attended local schools. He was an Army veteran. He ran the Rough Waters Garage and Junkyard. His family has lived in Caulfield for six generations. A memorial service will be held Jan. 19, 10 a.m. at the Caulfield Congregational Church. Burial will be in the spring.

The last story about Chet was a brief follow-up, again by Sean Mooney. The headline was: **Man's death in fire ruled** accidental.

CAULFIELD — The state fire marshal's office has ruled the Jan. 15 blaze that killed Chester A. Waters, 69, was likely caused by the careless disposal of smoking materials.

Fire Marshal Phil Gallagher said considering how badly the home on Maple Ridge Road was destroyed, it was difficult to determine an exact cause, but he said Waters was a smoker. He may have passed out from drinking alcohol.

Due to the condition of the body, the state medical examiner said the exact cause of Waters' death was unknown although severe burns and smoke inhalation were likely factors.

When contacted by phone, Annette Waters, the victim's daughter, said she disagreed strongly with the ruling.

"Yeah, my father smoked and he drank, but I don't believe for one minute it's an accident. He'd never get that drunk," she said. "I don't think they took my father's death seriously enough."

She declined to comment further.

I print the stories for my mother. I've tried coaxing her to learn how to use the computer. She's happy enough playing solitaire on her tablet, but no dice on anything more than that. Sam was the same way, but he wouldn't even touch a tablet. I joked we had an agreement: he didn't use my computer and I didn't use his power tools. I believe I got the better end of the deal. I like having my fingers intact, thank you.

"Did you get a hold of Annette?" my mother asks right away in the kitchen.

"Sure did."

"What'd she say?"

" 'Well, are you gonna help me?' " I laugh. "She's a bit tough, but she's glad someone believes her. We went over a few things. I told her I wanted to visit her place, get a tour of the junkyard and the town. We need to go over every possible lead since I don't know a soul in Caulfield. At least with Adela, I knew the family and had her father's okay."

45

"When are you going to see her?"

"Tomorrow. Wanna come?"

Tuesday's usually the day I watch Sophie but not this week. My mother, the weather fan, already informed me no storms are in the forecast for the next couple of days although it's supposed to be damn cold.

"I'll think about it. Sounds like it could take hours. But I would like to see this junkyard."

"Yeah, I hear it's a whopper. Besides, I need your ears and eyes on Annette. You didn't let me down with the last case. We make a good team."

My mother smiles.

"That's right, Isabel."

At the Junkyard

My mother reads out loud the directions I wrote as I drive the next morning to Caulfield. I'm glad she decided to come. Along the way, we talk over what little we have on the case and more about family stuff. She mentions going home, which she still calls the town where she lived most of her life, to see my brother and his family for a week or so. My sisters live on the West Coast. The last time Ma left, just before Thanksgiving, I hooked up with Jack and had a whole lot of fun. That seems a long time ago although it isn't.

My mother's impression is that Caulfield is in the sticks. I agree. The town is heavily wooded, except for a few houses and mobile homes off the main road. There is the obligatory New England center: a town hall, highway garage, and a Congregational church, all named for Caulfield, no less. I don't see any schools, but this being such a tiny town, I imagine the kids who live here are bused elsewhere. There isn't a general store, but as the Bald Old Fart informed me, Caulfield does have a gas station with two pumps called the Pit Stop. The owners must be NASCAR fans, so I am anticipating real country folk. Ah, yes, I spot a doublewide mobile home behind.

The roads are clear to the pavement when we take a left onto Cutter Road, the second after the Pit Stop, then a right after two miles to Maple Ridge Road, which is snow-covered. Annette told me it's a dirt road that rides a whole lot better in the winter when the snow fills in the ruts and potholes.

"You've got all-wheel drive on that Subaru," she assured me over the phone yesterday. "You'll do just fine."

After 1.8 miles, my mother points toward a sign: **ROUGH**

WATERS GARAGE AND JUNKYARD.

"That's the place," I say.

I drive through the gate, and as Annette told me over the phone, we wait in my car because her dogs will be loose. She has four, all mixed breeds but predominately German shepherd, which circle my Subaru and bark their heads off. These are junkyard dogs, loyal to their owner and suspicious of anyone else, including two women in a Subaru.

I gesture toward a cabin with weathered clapboards and beside it, a garage. Beyond them, junk cars stretch in three long rows over the snow.

"My, this is one huge junkyard," Ma says. "I've never seen anything like it before."

Annette walks from the garage and calls on her mutts to follow her to a pen. My mother and I venture out after she shuts its gate.

"Thanks for the warning," I tell Annette.

"They're just doing their job," she says before greeting my mother.

"Did your father have dogs?" I ask.

"Uh-huh. Buster. He was one big son of a bitch, almost a pure German shepherd. Buster wasn't here the morning I showed up after the fire. I thought it was strange, but I was only thinkin' about Pop and the fire." She squints as the sun coming through the bare trees washes over her face. "I found Buster a couple of days later when I walked the yard. He was dead. Somebody broke his neck."

Whoa. She's hitting us with new information, and we just got out of my car.

"Did you tell anybody about the dog?"

She spits on the dirty snow.

"Eh, the marshal said it had nothing to do with the fire. Cops, too. They thought my Pop could've done it cause the dog was sick or somethin'. They were wrong. Buster was just fine when I saw him the day before, and my Pop sure loved that mutt. He'd never put a dog down that way. He would've given him a single shot to his head. He would've brought Buster's body into the woods cause the ground was too frozen to bury him."

"That seems odd to me, too."

Annette rubs her red hands together. She stamps her feet on the snow.

"You're damn right about that." She tips her head toward her house. "Let's go inside. I've got some coffee. We can have that talk."

"Ma, you go first. I'm right behind you."

Annette's house is basically one long room. To the left of the door is the kitchen area with an apartment-sized stove and fridge. The counter and shelves are unfinished wood. To the right is a built-in table with four chairs. A couch, woodstove, and a TV are on the other end beyond a steep set of stairs leading to the second floor, where presumably Annette sleeps. The woodwork is rustic but durable. This place won't fall down, and it's small enough that the woodstove does its job to keep the place warm. I should know. I learned all about that stuff from Sam, who was a carpenter, make that a damn good carpenter as it says on his grave's headstone.

Annette has her back to us as she stoops to feed the stove a couple of logs from a pile nearby. She adjusts the damper then turns around.

"This is nice and cozy," my mother tells her.

Annette nods.

"Built it myself," she says. "Hey, how about that coffee?"

Another cup of caffeine is definitely going to put me over the edge, but I say yes. Ma does, too. It's all part of the interview process, making the person being questioned feel as comfortable as possible.

I fish my phone from my purse and hold it aloft.

"Do you mind if I record our conversation? It's just easier that way."

"Go ahead," Annette says from the kitchen area. "I don't give a shit."

Her coffee is better than the store's but not as good as mine. I drink it anyway. It's time to get down to business. I want more details about the day she found her father's body.

"First off, do you have a photo of your father? I'll take a

49

picture of it with my phone and print it out at home. I have a wall in my office where I tack up photos, clues, maps, whatever I find. I did it with my last case."

She reaches across the table for a manila envelope and pulls out a glossy photo. It's the one taken of her and her father that accompanied the profile in the Berkshire Bugle. How fitting she is the one trying to find some justice for her father. Annette must have requested a copy. Or maybe the reporter, Sean Mooney, did it as a favor. I used to do things like that, giving a free photo or extra copies of the newspaper after a story appeared. It often helped when I made a cold call later about something else.

"Here you go," she says.

I snap a shot and check the image on my phone to make sure it's usable.

"I saw this photo online. It went with that story that was in the Berkshire Bugle about your father. The photographer took a very nice photo of you two. What else do you have for me?"

She reaches for two more envelopes.

"This one has copies of the reports from the medical examiner, fire chief, and the cops." She slides the second toward me. "This one has copies of the business records for the previous year, so you can see who owed him money. You need anything more?"

"These will be very helpful, Annette. Let's start our interview. Ready?" I fire up the memos app on my phone. "You told me the month or so before the fire your father showed you some drugs and money he found in the trunk of a junked car. Was the car a recent addition or had it been here a while?"

She frowns as she thinks.

"It was one of those Jap makes, a '78 Toyota Corolla. I believe it came in a coupla weeks before he found the stuff in the trunk."

"Could you find me the paperwork on that, too?"

She smiles at Ma and me.

"It's in the second envelope. Lucky the papers were in the garage and not his house."

"Smart thinking. Go ahead. Tell me more."

Her head swings from side to side.

"Weird though. Pop usually checks each vehicle pretty thoroughly. He figured anythin' he found inside was fair game. I guess he didn't with this car. When he took out the spare, he saw somebody had cut the rubber to hide the drugs and money inside."

"Interesting. What did the drugs look like?"

"There was a bag of pills and a block of some white powder. I don't think it was baby powder."

"Could be coke or meth."

"Pop only found it cause he needed a tire for one of the cars he was fixin' up to sell."

"Where did the car come from?"

"Some used car lot in the valley. Pop dealt with 'em all the time. People would bring in pieces of junk as trade-ins, or the dealership bought cars cheap at an auction that turned out to be in worse shape than they thought."

I nod. The drugs and money could have belonged to someone who once owned the car and doesn't live in the hilltowns.

"I hope you don't mind, but I'm gonna ask you a lot of questions today and probably more in the future as we try to solve this case."

"Shit, go ahead. I'm glad somebody's takin' this serious."

"Do you think someone could've snuck in here and stashed the drugs and money after the car was dropped off?"

"Not if Buster, Pop's dog, would let 'em."

"What if the dog knew the person?"

"That's a possibility."

I glance at my mother.

"Can you think of anybody who didn't get along with your father?"

Annette snorts.

"My Pop wasn't the easiest person to like. A lot of people in town would have nothin' to do with him. He got into it with some. He did take a shine to a few of the women in town after Mom died. Nothing serious. Just some dirty old man flirtin'.

He would've liked you and your mother." She laughs. "I made that list like you asked. He and the guy who runs a junkyard in Fulton hated each other's guts. He's on it. Let me get it."

Could this be a case of a junkyard war? Hold on, Isabel, you're getting ahead of yourself. As Annette searches through a pile of papers on the kitchen counter, my mother mouths: "Ask her about the family."

I nod.

Annette brings back a lined sheet containing the names on Chet Waters' so-called enemies list. Frankly, I was expecting more given this man wasn't the easiest person to like even by his daughter's assessment.

"That's a start," I say.

"I left out one of the old ladies in town," she says. "She didn't seem like a killer to me."

I glance at Annette. She keeps a straight face. I feel like laughing, but I hold myself back. I'll laugh about it later with my mother.

"Any family in there?"

"Uh-huh, I put one of my brothers on the list. Mike the truck driver. I don't see much of him. Who knows what he's into these days?"

"What's his story?"

"Pop was real tough on him when he was a kid."

"What about your other brother?"

"Chester? Yeah, it was the same for him, too. But he never stood up to Pop like Mike. Chester went his own way."

"Was he tough on you?"

"By time I came along, I guess he got it out of his system. Besides, I'm a girl."

I skim the list of last names, which for the most part are typically New England, that is, Anglo Saxon and French. They are all unfamiliar, except for one: Fred Lewis. Jack Smith's creepy cousin is once again connected to a case. In the last, Fred was fooling around with Adela Collins behind Jack's back.

"I recognize only one name," I say. "Fred Lewis. Weren't you two married?"

"Yeah, we were. He a friend of yours?"

"Uh, hardly. He comes into the Rooster. He's the owner's cousin. How long ago were you two married?"

"I kicked him out and divorced him about twelve years ago. We were married three. I try not to think about it. He was a real asshole to me. Oh, sorry, Mrs. Ferreira," she says. "Pop couldn't stand his guts. Besides, everybody knows he deals drugs on the side."

No, not all of us, but now I do.

I quickly read the notes beside each one. A few have phone numbers.

"I'm glad you made these notes. I'm gonna take a photo."

"Nah, just take the paper."

"Fine. Did anybody on the list come into the junkyard just before the fire?"

She's silent as she thinks.

"I'm gonna have to think about that and get back to you."

"How about giving me a tour outside? If you don't mind, my mother would be more comfortable staying here beside the fire."

Annette waves her hand.

"Mrs. Ferreira, take the couch, why don't ya?"

Annette and I put on our jackets and leave. I zip mine as she talks about building her house. She got a little help with the framing, but mostly it was her banging away. The four dogs charge the fence in their pen between the house and garage. They bark their heads off.

"Shut the fuck up," she yells. "She's okay."

The mutts quiet down.

"It might be hard, but can you describe what you saw that morning. I want to see it, too."

She stops and points toward the gate.

"I saw the smoke when I was drivin' here. I thought maybe somebody was burnin' brush until I got to Maple Ridge, and I knew it had to be comin' from Pop's place. There wasn't much of his house left. It must've burned really, really fast cause it was all wood and small, just like mine. The gate was closed but not locked. I yelled and yelled for Pop. Then I saw his body. He managed to get out and was on the ground. I don't know how he did it. Pop must've crawled. He was an awful mess. It made me sick to see him. But I checked him over anyways. I was hopin' he was still alive." Her voice catches. "But he was gone. I just hope he didn't suffer. He looked so bad."

I swallow. No daughter should have to find her father that way.

"Sounds like a tough situation. I'm sorry, Annette."

"Don't be sorry for me. Find out who did that to Pop."

"One thing. You said the gate was closed but not locked. Wouldn't your father lock up at night?"

She stops and stares at me.

"Shit, you're right. He always locked up at night."

"So, somebody else could have been here and just shut the gate behind."

She shakes her head.

"I never thought of it that way. You're real smart. I'm glad I listened to Marsha."

I smile to myself as I follow Annette to the garage's side door. There's nothing surprising inside, just a typical garage that's dark save for the overhead fluorescent lights and bars over the windows. The inside smells like the oily stuff and chemicals used to fix vehicles, about six decades worth. But it's as neat a garage as a person could possibly keep it. The hood is up on a Chevy pickup truck, date unknown. A car is parked deeper inside.

"I'm fixin' the Chevy for the owner of the Pit Stop. Needs a new water pump. The Mustang belongs to my son, Abe. That's Pop's middle name, actually Abraham."

"Your son lives around here?"

"He's nineteen. He and a few buddies rent a place in Fulton."

"What does he do for a living?"

"Right now, not much. Guess he's like his old man."

"Fred?"

"Nah, somebody else. I had him before I met Fred. You wouldn't know the guy," she says. "Seen enough?"

54

"For now. I'm just trying to get a feel for the place."

Her lips quiver. I believe she was going to smile, but she holds back.

"Wanna get a feel for the junkyard now?"

I laugh.

"Yeah, I'm ready. How about showing me that car?"

"Follow me."

We walk along a wide snowy aisle, following boot prints. From their size and the print, I believe they all belong to Annette. I get an idea.

"There had to have been a lot for you to take in when you came that morning, especially with your father. It must've been a shock. This was January, so there was likely snow on the ground. Did you see any footprints?"

Her face swings toward me.

"You know, I did. I had to wait for the cops to come. It took a while. It was too hard lookin' at Pop. He was burned so bad. I had to walk away." She pauses. "I remember the heat from the fire had melted the snow around the house. But I saw boot prints in the row where that car was. Course, they could've been there from before. I hadn't walked the yard in a while." She points straight ahead. "If we go a little more, I can show you the car."

We are about in the middle of a long row when Annette stops in front of an orange Corolla. She flings open the trunk, which contains the spare. I touch the tire's cut rubber. Annette watches as I shoot photos of the car and its trunk.

"I've seen enough for today."

"What are you gonna do next?"

"I plan to go over your paperwork and see what's what. I'll set up interviews with the people on your list."

"Who'll be first?"

"Not sure," I say, but in my head Fred is at the top of my list.

The Pit Stop

We leave the back roads of Caulfield, and for jollies, I decide to gas up at the Pit Stop. I still have half a tank but what the heck. I'm sure the people who run this joint must overhear lots of stuff that goes on in town. Certainly, that's true at the Conwell General Store, especially from you-know-who in the backroom. Besides, if I keep showing up in Caulfield, people are going to get suspicious. It's better to get the word out about what I'm doing.

"Why are we stopping here for gas?" Ma asks. "It's cheaper in the city."

"I only need half a tank. I see it as an opportunity to meet more people."

"All right then. Zip up your jacket. It's cold out there."

"Yeah, Ma."

The sign on the pump says: **PAY INSIDE FIRST**. I knock on the windshield and hook my thumb toward the sign before I head toward the wooden shack.

A bell on the door announces my arrival to a man who pops through an opening behind the counter. I scan the store, which appears to have all the necessities of life such as the cigarettes, chewing tobacco, and nips arranged on the shelf behind the counter. A coffee machine with the fixings is to the left. Oil and antifreeze are stacked in a center aisle. A cooler holds beer, soda, and maybe water and milk. The wall is decorated with NASCAR posters and an American flag.

"Howdy, ma'am, what can I do for ya?" he says.

The man behind the counter is a tall, thin guy with a hilltown-issue mullet and wide-angle sideburns. I'm guessing he's in his late forties. He's got a Jimmie Johnson ball cap perched on the back of his head. He could be a model for

Redneck Monthly, if there were such a thing, even the centerfold if he sat astride a Harley, with his flannel shirt, jeans, and NRA Life Member belt buckle. But he's got a nice smile and friendly glint to his blue eyes.

I met tons of guys like him when I was the hilltown reporter for the Daily Star. Maybe he was at one of the truck pulls I covered. What's a truck pull, you ask? That's when a guy, although there are gals, too, strips his car or truck down to pure power. Then he or she sees if it can move tons of dead weight over a line. Some make it. Some break down. It's noisy as hell and the crowd gets into it. The vehicles all have crazy names like Pulling Around and Troublemaker.

"I'd like to buy some gas, please," I say. "Ten bucks worth."

I fish for two fives from my jeans. No credit card machines at the Pit Stop. Cash or, if they trust you, a check only, as the sign says on the front of the register.

"Sure enough." He nods through the window. "That your Subaru? Just passin' through?"

"I live in Conwell. My mother and I were visiting Annette Waters."

He hums as he checks my car again.

"You the gal she's hirin' to find out about her father?"

"Yes, I am. Name's Isabel Long." I stretch out my hand. "What's yours?"

He gives me one of those I'm-not-used-to-shaking-hands-with-a-woman grips, but it's not too strong or damp, thank you.

"Pete Woodrell. I own this joint with my wife. Barbie's not here. She's drivin' her school bus route."

"Nice to meet you. You'll probably see more of me in the future."

His head swivels a bit.

"You believe Annette and her cockamamie story about somebody killin' her old man?"

"I take it you don't."

He clicks his tongue.

"Chet was a regular here in my little store. He could put the

57

booze away. Hard stuff. And he smoked like a chimney. He probably kicked from the smoke before he got all burned up. At least, I hope so. I hate to think he suffered." He clicks his tongue again. "But somebody killin' him? That sounds like a daughter that won't let go."

"Maybe so, but I'm planning to find out what I can for her," I say. "Sounds like you knew Chet well. If you wouldn't mind, sometime soon I'd like to ask you some questions about Chet. Maybe you'll recall something useful."

"Useful."

"I'd only take twenty minutes of your time tops. We can meet right here at the store."

He works a finger along one of his wide-angle sideburns.

"You wanna talk about Chet? Sure, I can do that. But it might be a complete waste of your time."

"Yeah, sometimes you find dead ends. It's all part of an investigation." I shrug. "By the way, I saw your Chevy in her garage."

"Annette's a great mechanic, 'specially for a woman. And she doesn't charge an arm and a leg."

I let the comment " 'specially for a woman" slide as I spot a stack of booklets on the counter. The cover says: **CAULFIELD PHONE BOOK**. We have one in Conwell some local group sells as a fundraiser. The phone book costs three bucks. I have just enough on me.

"I'll take one of those phone books, too. Here you go. I'd better head out. My mother's waiting in the car."

"Sure you don't need help?"

"Nah, I've pumped my own gas a million times. But thanks."

"See ya soon."

"You can count on it."

I shuffle my feet a bit as I pump my ten bucks worth of gas. Damn, it's cold, and I want to be back home before it gets any colder. I need to get a fire going.

I'm screwing on the gas cap when I notice a police cruiser pull into the lot. It has the name of the town on the side. I can recall when Conwell bought its first cruiser after the cops got sick of drunks puking in the backseat of their personal cars. It wasn't safe either hauling alleged criminals. The cops didn't threaten to quit, but the board of selectmen could read between the lines. I even wrote about the new cruiser when I was a reporter and took a photo of the proud police chief standing beside the car. Caulfield's cruiser looks almost new, so I bet it's a recent acquisition. I'm also betting having a woman police chief is another first for this hick town.

A woman is in the driver's seat. Chief Nancy Dutton has arrived. Now I don't have to track her down because I doubt Caulfield has a police station, most likely an office at town hall or a spare room at the chief's house, which is common in the hilltowns.

I tap my mother's window, jerk my head toward the cruiser, and walk that way after Ma nods. I reach the car as Chief Nancy Dutton gets out. She's wearing a heavy blue cop coat over her uniform. She's a big-boned gal with dark hair cut short, a style that makes her full face appear fuller.

The chief glances my way when I say hello.

"Yes?" she asks. "Can I help you?"

"Chief Dutton, my name's Isabel Long. I'm a private investigator working a case here in Caulfield."

That gets her immediate attention.

"Private investigator? What are you working on?" She hums. "Never mind. Annette Waters hired you."

"Did she tell you?"

Chief Dutton shuts the cruiser's door.

"No, I told her to get herself a P.I."

"Really?"

"Yeah, she wanted me to open her father's case. I was on the force when Mr. Waters died, but I wasn't part of the investigation cause the State Police took charge. They thought it was more than our small department could handle. They were probably right. We're only part-timers here."

"I understand. I live in Conwell."

She hums again.

"You're the one who solved the Adela Collins case. Nice work on that." She pauses. "Please contact me if you find anything I should know about."

"Will do. Have any hunches about Mr. Waters' death?"

"Off the record?"

"Yeah, off the record."

"Something didn't set right with me about the whole thing. I don't know what it was. Just call it cop instincts." She reaches inside her jacket and pulls out a card. "Here's how you can reach me."

I dig into my purse for a blank piece of paper and write down my info.

"Sorry, I don't have any cards yet. I just started working for Lin Pierce. He can vouch for me."

"I know Mr. Pierce. He's done some work up here." She glances at the Pit Stop. "I need to get going. I could use a cup of coffee. Yeah, it ain't Starbucks, but it'll have to do."

"That's okay. My mother's waiting in the car. I don't want her to get too cold. Nice to meet you, Chief Dutton."

"Same here."

Of course, on the way home Ma wants a blow-by-blow about my conversation with Chief Dutton, and then we're talking about our meeting with Annette.

"What's your gut feeling?" I ask my mother when we're done.

"Gut feeling? There's definitely something there. But I'm not sure what it is at this point."

"I agree. But even though this happened only three years ago, it's gonna be harder to crack this case. I don't know anybody there."

"What did you do when you had to report on a story in a place where you didn't know anybody?"

"I followed the leads I had. One person led me to another. Yeah, yeah, I hear you. I should do the same for this one. Well, I have Annette to start me off."

"Who's first?"

"Jack's creepy cousin, Fred."

"You going to talk with him at the Rooster?"

"Makes sense."

My mother makes a sniffing laugh.

"I hear they have a band playing on Friday. I bet he'll be there for that. You should go."

I give my mother a sideways glance. I can guess what else is on her mind.

"I just might," I tell her.

Annette's List

After supper, naturally kale soup and hearty bread we got from the city that's pretty close to Portagee bread, I go over Annette's list of suspects. I'll save the envelopes of records for another day. Here's the list and what she wrote.

MIKE WATERS: My brother. All he cared about was getting his share of the land.

AL SINCLAIR: He runs the junkyard in Fulton. He and Pop had some nasty fights.

GARY BEAUMONT: No good bum. Lives in Caulfield. Does drugs. Sells drugs.

LARRY BEAUMONT: His brother. Ditto.

FRED LEWIS: My asshole ex-husband. He deals drugs. Maybe the ones Pop found belonged to him.

ANTHONY STEWARD: One of the newcomers who got himself elected to the zoning board. He wanted to shut the junkyard down. Kept looking for reasons.

JOJO TIDEWATER: Ex-boyfriend. Another loser and drug user. I can sure pick them.

I show the list to Ma, who asks how I'll find these people and their phone numbers. The lack of technology is on my side for once. There's no cell phone service for most of Caulfield. That little phone book I picked up there will come in handy. Annette wrote the numbers for Mike and JoJo since they don't live in Caulfield.

"I'm going to start with Fred. I should be able to find the other junkyard in Fulton pretty easily." I hold up the phone book. "The rest? I'll start making some cold calls."

I take Annette's list upstairs to my office. Already I have the photo of her and her father tacked in the center of one wall. Printouts of the news stories, plus road maps of Caulfield and

Western Massachusetts are beside it. I add the list Annette made. I don't have much.

I pick up the phone. Lin Pierce answers.

"I'm taking the case," I tell him.

"You have a lot to go on?"

"Not really, but the client gave me a list of names and other paperwork, so that's some place to start."

"What names?"

I rattle them off. The only ones he doesn't recognize are Anthony Steward, the newcomer, and JoJo Tidewater, the ex-boyfriend.

"Beaumont brothers? Bad news there."

"That's the impression I get," I say. "Annette did give me all the official records, too, and her father's finances for the previous year. There's a lot to go over."

"Keep me informed," he says and then, "Good night."

Dance Music

On Friday night, I pace around the house until my mother says, "Enough already, Isabel, why don't you go?"

I glance at the clock on the kitchen stove. It's after nine. The Cowlicks are warming up with the first set of the night, and I'm at home, nervous as hell, not about quizzing Fred Lewis, although I don't want the creep to get the wrong idea, but, of course, about seeing Jack. Suppose he's found somebody else already? I shake my head. Shut up, Isabel. You were the first woman he'd been with in years. He told you himself. Besides, you don't have a claim on him.

I go upstairs and check myself in the bedroom mirror. My silvery hair looks good longer. Makeup? Nah, not at the Rooster. I turn around, pull off my top and get something closer fitting with a V-neck.

My mother says, "Good choice," when I walk downstairs.

I'd tell her not to wait up for me, but she'll still be awake well after last call if I last that long.

"Wish me luck," I tell her.

The Rooster's parking lot is packed with snowmobiles, cars, and pickups. I manage to find a space on the far end, tight against a snowbank, and when I get inside, I'm surrounded by music, voices, and other barroom noise. Every seat in the joint is occupied or saved with a jacket. I'll just have to get myself a beer and stand out of the way. I don't see el Creepo Fred, but he'll be here tonight. I can almost feel him making his way here from whatever hole he lives in.

I greet people I know and vice versa as I make my way to the bar for a beer. I am four back in line. Jack's behind the bar, in constant motion as he fills orders. The light is on in the kitchen, but dinner is over. I suppose the new cook has a pile of dishes to wash. The tables are filled with empties. With this crowd, I expect Jack is having a hard time keeping up.

He raises his head and grins at me as he pops the caps off bottles of Bud.

Finally, it's my turn.

"Hey, Isabel, the usual?" he asks.

"Not tonight, Jack. Make it a Bud Light, please. It'll be easier to hold a bottle than a glass in this crowd."

"Sure enough." He still has his eyes on me as he reaches into the cooler. "Great turnout, eh? Just like old times."

I hand him the bills. Damn, I'm smiling too much.

"Just like that."

The night rolls along. After a while, I realize I've never been here alone on dance night. It was Sam and me on the floor. Then it was Jack and me working the bar together. Honestly, I feel a little lost. First, I stand, and then a stool opens up at the bar. It's at the far end next to the wall for the men's room, so I can turn halfway on the stool with something behind my back if I don't mind listening to men taking a long piss and talking behind me. I watch the musicians and dancers. People just want to have fun at the Rooster.

"Want another, Isabel?"

Jack has slid over to my side of the bar. I check my bottle. It's nearly empty. One thing nice about Bud Light is I can drink more of it and not get a buzz.

"Uh-huh. This one's almost done."

I see he already has one open for me. I go for the money in my wallet.

"Put your money away, Isabel. This one's on the house."

I'm making that stupid smile again.

"Thanks, Jack." I'm searching for words and almost slap myself when I say, "Want me to clear some tables for you?"

He chuckles.

"You don't have to work off that beer."

I shrug.

"You look a bit swamped. I thought I could help."

He thinks about it for a second, and then he hands me a tray.

"Yeah, I could use an extra hand."

I grab the tray and slide off the stool.

"Just save my place."

I get busy, grabbing bottles off tables, dodging drunken dancers, and gabbing with the drinkers. The number one question I hear is: "Are you back?"

"I'm just working off a beer," I joke.

"You work cheap," one of the Rooster's True Blue Regulars says.

"Gee, I've heard that one before," I tell him.

I make four trips. Each time, Jack gives me an appreciative grin.

"You're getting good at that," he says after I drop the last tray on the bar top.

"Yup, I haven't lost my touch."

I laugh when I take my stool because there's a hand-written sign next to my beer. It says: **RESERVED FOR ISABEL**. I glance toward grin-faced Jack. He's waiting for my reaction.

"Just for you," he says.

"Thank you very much."

But my mood shifts abruptly when you-know-who arrives. Of course, Fred makes a beeline to my end of the bar. I don't mind too much because he's on the list of Annette's suspects.

"Hey, gorgeous, drinking alone?"

I shake my head.

"Hardly, with a bar this full."

Fred moves closer and over my invisible line of comfort.

"You've got a point."

"I was wondering if I could ask you a few questions."

"Sure, darlin'."

"Annette Waters hired me to look into her father's death." I watch as Fred drops his shit-eating smile. "She told me you and she used to be married."

"Don't believe a word that bitch says. She's a goddamn liar."

"About you or her father?"

"Me."

"I only want to talk about your relationship with her

father."

The smile is back.

"That's gonna cost you." He tips his head toward the band's side of the room. The Cowlicks are revving up Lynyrd Skynyrd's "Gimme Three Steps." "You gotta dance with me first to ask me that. Seriously."

I roll my eyes and drop off the stool. Fred slips his arm around my back as he leads me to the middle of the dance floor. He's got me by the hand, twisting and twirling me amid the drunks who shout the chorus. He's no Sam or Jack, but he's a decent dancer. Fred struts and smiles. Shoot, what I'll do for a case.

I slip my hand from his grip when the song ends and head back to my stool.

"Hey, wait, let's dance some more," he says.

"You said one dance."

"Shit, you're tough, Isabel."

"That I am."

But as I squeeze through the crowd, I realize there's no way I can interview Fred here. Too much noise. Too many ears and eyes. Fred is back and standing close.

"So, what do you wanna ask me?" he says.

"How about we do it tomorrow instead?"

His mouth drops open and wide. I swear he's practically drooling. His hand is on the bar's edge.

"What do you have in mind?"

"I can meet you here at two tomorrow. It'll be quieter, so I can ask you those questions."

"Oh, that."

"Yeah, that."

"Sure, I'll be there."

I finally shake Fred loose when some of his snowmobile-riding buddies arrive. A couple of the Rooster's True Blue Regulars ask me to dance, fast numbers thankfully, and I comply. It's strictly for laughs and the exercise.

I watch Marsha aka the Floozy bully her way through the crowd toward my direction. She's smiling at me, so I know she's just in a rush and not pissed off. She greets me, "Hey,

Isabel."

I respond, "Hey, Marsha, what's happening?"

"I talked with Annette last night. She really likes you and your mother. Says you didn't make her feel stupid."

"I'm glad she feels that way."

"She told me about the list she gave you."

I glance around. Too many people are too close to talk about who's on Annette's list. But I want to hear what the Floozy has to say. She just might steer me in the right direction.

I tip my head toward the crowd.

"I bet you could help me, but this isn't the place."

Marsha's eyes light up.

"Oh, yeah, yeah, yeah, I get it."

"How about we go outside?"

Her head bobs like somebody's yanking it with a cord and she's got that "Yeah, yeah, yeah" chorus going again. I eye the **RESERVED FOR ISABEL** sign next to my beer. I tap the guy sitting next to me and tell him, "I'll be right back."

Marsha lights up a cigarette halfway out the door as she leads me off the front stoop and toward a spot between two pickups. It's frigging cold out here, but this is as private as it will get at the Rooster. I try to stay upwind from the Floozy's cigarette.

"What did you think of Annette's list?" I ask.

"If I was gonna bet money, I'd put it on the Beaumont brothers," she says.

"Why's that?"

"They're in that line of business. I mean sellin' drugs. Al Sinclair, who runs the junkyard, is just some old guy tryin' to make a living. He's ancient. But I know for a fact he and Chet kinda hated each other's guts. Somebody told me when Al heard what happened to Chet, he said it couldn't have happened to a nicer guy. Really. Maybe there's somethin' there." Marsha takes a drag from her butt. "The newcomer guy? Nope." She makes a snickering laugh. "I see she threw in a couple of exes in there. That's wishful thinkin' on her part."

"Wait a minute. Go back to Al Sinclair. What set that off?

Because they were competitors in the junk business?"

"It was probably more than that, like somethin' that happened years and years ago, and they can't let go of the grudge." Marsha shrugs. "Shit happens up here. Sometimes it goes back a generation or two. People just don't forget or forgive. They like to do payback." Then her face brightens. "Wait a minute. I remember now. It had somethin' to do with Chet's sister or maybe Al's. Eh, you can find that out by askin' one of the old-timers."

I nod. I know exactly which old-timers to ask, my friends in the backroom of the Conwell General Store, yes, the Old Farts. This could be something or nothing, but I won't discount it.

"I will," I say. "What about her brother, Mike?"

"Hmm, kind of a jerk, but not sure if he'd kill his old man. But keep him on the list for now."

"What about the other brother?"

"The professor." Her lips flutter. "That wimp? He calls himself Chester by the way."

"Wimp? What does that mean? Is he a weakling because he has a desk job or is there something more?"

"Somethin' more. Let's just say he swings the other way."

Oh, so he's gay. Big deal but maybe it was with his father.

"So, the Beaumont brothers are your prime suspects. They ever come here?"

"Not anymore. They made Jack's list. He booted them out for dealin' drugs in the parking lot."

As she says it, I have one of those ah-ha moments. I recall Gary and Larry Beaumont's names on the permanently banned list posted behind the bar.

"Ah, it was those guys. Where do they hang out?"

"There's a biker bar in West Caulfield. It's on a lake. You can probably find 'em there. Guess the owner ain't so fussy about who drinks there."

"Then that's probably the place for me to find them."

"You really gonna do that?" she asks.

"They're on Annette's list of suspects."

Marsha sucks in the last bit of smoke before she chucks the

69

butt in the snow.

"You got balls, Isabel."

"I've heard that before," I say.

"I tell ya what. If you wanna, I'll go with you. I can't speak for my Bobby, but definitely I'm game for a trip to Baxter's. That's the bar's name." She leans forward. "Let me drive, okay?"

I believe I'd welcome riding shotgun with Marsha. Safety in numbers, as my mother would say. Two isn't exactly a big number, but I'd bet on Marsha over three newcomer women any day. Besides, I get the feeling this could be one of those anthropological experiences I had as a reporter when I found myself immersed in a far different world than I was used to living in. I kept my eyes, ears, and mind open as if I were some explorer. I get the feeling going to Baxter's with the Floozy would be the same.

"You wouldn't mind?"

"Nah."

"How about next Saturday?"

Her eyes light up. I believe this woman likes a bit of danger.

"I can almost guarantee the Beaumont boys never miss a Saturday at Baxter's. I can ask Annette to meet us there. We'll make it a girls' night out."

"How about we make it a covert operation?"

"What's that?"

"We'll be under cover. Like spies."

I see the empty spaces between her teeth when she cackles.

"Yeah, under cover."

"I'll get back to you, but save Saturday unless the weather's real bad," I say. "Let's head inside. I'm freezing my ass out here."

Marsha cackles and shakes her head as we walk inside. She's happy to be a part of this investigation.

My stool has been saved. The guy sitting on the next one says, "I had to fight off a few for you, Isabel."

"Well, thank you very much."

I lean back against the wall while I mull my good fortune

to have the Floozy on my side. I take in the sights. Jack is one busy man tonight. The Cowlicks are on fire. People are bumping into each other like pinballs on the dance floor. Everybody's happy to have music at the Rooster again. Me, too, and I still have half a free beer left.

It's midway through the third set when I hear the familiar opening to Waylon Jennings' "Good Hearted Woman." I half-expect to hear that cowbell ring and Jack holler the bar is closed until the song is over. And then he grabs me by the hand and makes believe he's dragging me onto the dance floor. It was our thing here at the Rooster, well until things got messed up.

But I don't, and he doesn't.

Suddenly, I feel the bottom of the floor has dropped, and I'm going with it. I don't dare look at Jack. I don't even wait until the song is over. I down the rest of my beer and slip out of the bar without so much as a good-bye to anyone.

El Creepo

Fred shows up at the Rooster parking lot exactly at two. I'm standing outside my car with my backside against the fender. It's still damn cold, but at least it's sunny.

"Hey, the Rooster's closed," are the first words out of his mouth.

I glance back. The Rooster is locked up tight. Yeah, I tricked him. I heard from the Old Farts, of course, Jack doesn't open these days until three on Saturdays, especially since football season is over. I'm not expecting my conversation with Fred to last more than twenty minutes max, so I should be long gone before Jack or his cook shows up.

"It doesn't open for another hour."

"Damn it, Isabel, how are we supposed to meet? It's fuckin' cold out here."

"We can sit in my car."

He snorts a laugh. I don't even want to venture a guess at what he's thinking.

"All right then."

We get in the front seats, and I'm glad for the console dividing his from mine. I don't want him putting his hands all over me.

"When you and Annette were married, did you get along with her father?"

"Sort of. We both liked to throw back a few."

"What do you mean sort of?"

"When things went sour with Annette, he took her side. It's to be expected. She's his daughter."

"How come you two got divorced?"

"Let's say in those days I had a bit of a temper."

"You hit her?"

72

He stares.

"I smacked her around. I admit it. I'm not proud of it. She sure could push my buttons." He raises both hands. "Yeah, yeah, that's no excuse. It pissed off Chet when he found out. Anyways I've cleaned up my act. Never touched a woman like that since."

I nod. I believe him.

"When was the last time you saw Chet Waters?"

He holds up his hands like he's stopping traffic.

"Whoa, whoa, are you suspecting me of killin' him?"

I'm prepared for this. My mother wasn't crazy about my idea of meeting Fred in the parking lot, but I reminded her there isn't any other place in town. The Conwell Town Hall isn't open Saturdays, and I don't know if I could've enticed Fred to meet me there anyway. Invite him to my house? Are you outta of your mind?

"No, I'm not," I say, leaving out the part Annette thought he could. "I'm not familiar with Caulfield at all. I know you a little. I was hoping you could help me. I'll repeat my question. When's the last time you saw Chet?"

He works his mouth.

"Actually, just a couple of days before the fire. I needed some parts for an old truck I was fixin'. I tried the other junkyard, Sinclair's, but Al didn't have them. Chet did. It was strictly business. He seemed to get over that I was a lousy husband to his daughter."

"Was Chet an honest guy?"

"Would I buy a used car off him? Yup? Would I play cards with him? Nope."

"So, he was a mixed bag," I say. "I'm going to tell you something I want you to keep between us. Just before he died, Chet found drugs and money in the trunk of one of his junks. Any idea how they could've gotten there?"

His brow hangs hard and low over his eyes.

"Annette tell you I deal drugs?"

"I'm going to be honest. Yes, she mentioned something like that."

"Don't believe a word that bitch says. She's a goddamn

73

liar. Yeah, I smoke weed and I've put stuff up my nose. But I'm not selling. You got that straight?"

I keep calm.

"See? This is why I wanted to ask you directly. There are at least two sides to a story."

He grunts.

"Shit, you're right about that. Who else is a suspect?"

"That's between Annette and me," I say. "But if you think of anything else, give me a call, or maybe I'll see you here."

He smirks.

"Too bad about you and my cousin." The smirk grows. "Course, I'd make a mighty fine replacement. I'm willing and able."

I refrain from shaking my head or making a face. I may need Fred for this case.

"I'll keep it in mind."

We both turn when Jack's pickup pulls into the lot and toward his usual space beside the side door.

"Wanna come inside? I bet we could wrangle us a couple of free beers," Fred says.

"Maybe some other time."

"Sure enough. I understand."

Fred is being as nice as possible. With a wink and "Bye, gorgeous," he's out of my car and strutting toward Jack's truck. I back the Subaru and give them a friendly toot of the horn before I leave the lot. In the rearview mirror, I see Jack watching my car while he talks with his cousin. My ears are burning.

Sunday with the Family

Today is Ruth's birthday, so we're having the party at my house. Ma roasted the chicken. I made two lemon meringue pies, Ruth's favorite dessert. Even as a kid she asked for the pie instead of birthday cake. I was happy to comply. Ruth's in-laws, Anne and Phil, drove up from Connecticut. Actually, they came yesterday, stayed at Ruth's, and will leave Monday. I'm expecting a third degree from Anne about the new case should the topic come up.

I swoop my baby granddaughter, Sophie, into my arms as I greet Ruth, Gregg, and his parents at the door. Alex and Matthew are already here, talking with their grandmother and cleaning out the fridge although they know we're having a sit-down dinner. Those boys, really men now, have hollow legs, as my mother would say.

It's the usual Long noisy gathering, which gets noisier after I start pouring wine and beer, and we do the birthday cake thing. Ruth opens her gifts and cards. We take turns holding Sophie.

I've been waiting for the interrogation, but it doesn't happen until Ruth's in-laws, actually her mother in-law, are into their second glass of wine.

"Isabel, have you started a new case?" a pink-faced Anne asks.

Ruth rolls her eyes even before I answer. The boys laugh over their beers.

"Actually, I have. A woman contacted me because she's convinced somebody who had it in for her father killed him instead of him dying in a fire. The official word is he was passed out from drinking when a cigarette started the fire. It's a small house, so it didn't take much."

"Who's the woman?" Anne asks.

75

"Annette Waters. She lives in Caulfield, a town north of here. Her father owned a huge junkyard. Now she does. Annette is a mechanic, too."

Anne's mouth drops open.

"A junkyard? A woman owns a junkyard?"

I nod.

"My mother and I went there a couple of days ago. Biggest one we've ever seen."

"It sure was," my mother says. "Annette keeps it rather neat for a junkyard. But we haven't seen Sinclair's yet."

I set down my glass.

"That's a junkyard in Fulton. I'm going Tuesday, maybe with Ma if she wants." I turn toward my daughter. "Yeah, Ruth, I know I'm watching Sophie tomorrow. I promise not to take her to a junkyard."

"That's right. No junkyards."

Anne's head swings from me to my mother and back to me.

"Who do you suspect?" she says.

"I don't know the town of Caulfield, so I guess everybody at this point, except his daughter, Annette. She certainly wouldn't be asking me to investigate her father's death if she were guilty. Annette did give me a list of suspects." I turn toward Matt and Alex. "You two ever meet Gary and Larry Beaumont?"

My sons eye each other before Matt speaks, "Aw, Mom, you don't want to mess with those guys. I went to school with the younger one, Larry, before he dropped out."

Matt, the union heavy equipment operator, graduated from the regional vocational school. I'm already getting a feeling for Gary and Larry, but my son actually knows one of them.

"Why do you say that?"

"He got busted for selling dope. He and his brother were just, uh, total jerks."

"I'm planning to meet them anyways. But I'm not going alone."

Alex hoots.

"You taking Grandma?"

I shake my head.

"Not this time. I'm going with Marsha to that biker bar, Baxter's, in West Caulfield. I don't think Grandma would enjoy that experience."

Ma laughs.

"You never know," she says. "But I think I'll stay home with a good book instead and let your mother have all the fun."

Anne's mouth drops open.

"You're not really going to a biker bar, are you?"

"Sure, why not? It's part of my legwork for this case."

"It sounds awfully dangerous," Anne says.

I lift my glass of wine.

"You haven't met the woman who's coming with me. She's one tough broad. Tougher than most men I know. Ma and I call her the Floozy."

"To her face?" Anne asks.

"Are you kidding me? I've got more sense than that." I laugh. "She'd beat the crap outta me."

"What about Annette?"

"They're cousins. She's a tough cookie, too." I laugh. "Hey, Ma, I think that'll be her nickname."

"The Tough Cookie? I like that," Ma says.

Everyone is laughing when Ruth gets up. I think at first she's fed up with all of this P.I. nonsense, her words, not mine, but then she returns with a small white box.

"This is for you, Mom," she says.

The box contains a neat stack of business cards. I lift one. It says: **ISABEL LONG, P.I.** and it has all of my contact info, including my association with Lin Pierce. Ruth is beaming. I reach over to give her a hug.

"Thanks, Ruth, these will come in handy. I could've used one of these the other day when I met the Caulfield police chief."

I pass a few cards around.

"You need a business card if you're going to do this P.I. stuff for real," Ruth says.

Anne leans across the table. She holds one of my cards.

"Isabel, what are you going to wear to this biker bar?" she asks. "You have any leather clothes?"

"Leather? Ha, nothing like that." I laugh. "Just my regular clothes. I'm going under cover."

Of course, Ruth rolls her eyes. My boys laugh while Anne opens her mouth to ask yet another question.

From One Junkyard to Another

At the last minute, my mother agrees to come along Tuesday for the field trip to Sinclair's Junkyard. She tells me bad weather's coming this evening, freezing rain, the worst, and this may be our last chance to be out and about for a couple of days. Besides, she's interested, as I am, in whether Chet Waters' death could come down to a junkyard war.

"But what about the drugs and money?" I ask her on the drive over to Fulton.

"Maybe it's just a coincidence. Maybe it was planted."

I glance over at my mother.

"See? Once again, you come up with a couple of angles I didn't consider."

My mother laughs.

"Guess I haven't lost my touch."

Fulton is just another puny hilltown in Western Massachusetts. It's almost a duplicate of Caulfield next door, with its collection of public buildings and a gas station. This one's called the Go Between. I'd tip my hat, if I could ever find one to fit my gigantic head, to the owners who came up with that clever name.

Unlike Annette's Rough Waters Junkyard, Sinclair's is on the main drag, which makes my life a lot easier. It has a high wooden fence, at least in the front, so it looks more like a fort than a place to buy used parts. After I pull the car inside, I give the place a quick once-over and wait to see if any barking dogs pounce toward my car, but none do. There isn't a house, but a small building for an office and a garage beside it. High, chain-link fencing with a roll of barbed wire at the top surrounds the rest of the yard. I would say the amount of junkers rivals Annette's.

79

"Ready?" I ask my mother.

I'm helping Ma from the front seat when a man leaves the office. He's short, almost child-sized. He has a full head of white hair and long sideburns. He walks with a bit of a jingle to his step as if he's in a hurry to see what two women want in his junkyard. I don't blame him. How many women show up here in a new Subaru?

He stands near my car.

"Somethin' I can do for you, ladies?"

I show him my most pleasant smile.

"Real orderly junkyard you've got here," I tell him.

He glances around as if he doesn't believe me.

"Thank you."

"You don't have dogs?"

"I got something better, a good strong fence and an alarm system with cameras. Don't have to feed 'em or worry about 'em bitin' a customer." He scratches the front right corner of his forehead. "Are you both lost? Need directions to somewhere?"

"No, no, we're not lost. My name's Isabel Long and this is my mother, Maria Ferreira. We'd like to ask you a few questions."

His face freezes into sharp folds.

"You're not church people, are you?" he asks, and then when I shake my head, "You collectin' money for some charity?"

"No on that one, too," I say.

"Well, what do you want?"

"I'm a private investigator. Annette Waters hired me to look into her father's death. She doesn't believe it was an accident her father died in that fire. She thinks someone might've killed him."

Al Sinclair keeps scratching his forehead. If we were playing poker, I would say that was his tell and I'd bet against him.

"If you don't mind my askin', what in the hell does that got to do with me?"

I check on my mother.

"Would you mind if we stepped inside your office? I can tell you all about it in there. It's a little cold for my mother. She's ninety-two."

He gives my mother the once-over. I try not to smile. Having a mother who doesn't mind people knowing her age is a clever way to get our collective foot through the door. Besides, Ma doesn't look ninety-two, and when you're that age, it's something pride-worthy.

"Sure, ladies," he says, and then the three of us are walking toward the office.

"My, this is nice and warm," my mother announces when Al shuts the door behind us. "Thank you."

It's actually hot as hell, but I'm not going to complain. Al sits behind a desk and slides a pile of papers to the side, so we can see each other. He sits back in one of those old office chairs, wooden, likely oak, and with a solid spring action in its base.

"What's this all about? Isabel, did you say?"

"That's right." I reach into my purse and hand him one of my cards. "Here's my contact info."

He glances at the card.

"Isabel Long, P.I., eh? Never met a real P.I. before."

"I'm an associate of Lin Pierce in Jefferson."

"I've heard of Lin." He tosses the card on his desk. "What's this got to do with me?"

"We live in Conwell, so I'm trying to get to know this area. I'm meeting with several people. Someone recommended I stop by since you and Chet owned the same kind of business in neighboring towns. How did that work out for you both?"

"I'm a second generation junkman. I inherited the place from my father. Still got a few of his old clunkers. I started workin' for him when I was just a kid. It became all mine when Dad died."

"It's my understanding Chet opened his junkyard and repair shop after he got out of the service. Is that right?"

He nodded.

"Yes, ma'am. Then he came along."

I bet if we were outside he might have spit on the ground

after saying that.

"Isn't it unusual to have two large junkyards in neighboring towns?"

He works his mouth as if he's got something loose inside. Uh-huh, he wants to spit.

"I'd say that's probably true since most towns won't allow 'em."

"Was that a problem between you and Chet?"

He nods.

"Oh, I see where this is goin'. Did Chet piss me off?" His voice has got a tight kink in it. "Sure he did. I had my reasons but not because we both had junkyards. He was a mean son of a bitch." He glances at my mother. "Sorry, ma'am."

My mother nods in absolution.

"You said you had reasons."

"It's personal." His chin juts forward. "It happened years ago. End of story."

I'm remembering what Marsha said. Whatever it was involved somebody's sister, but Al's clammed up. I'm just a nosy newcomer to him. Chet's just a mean son of a bitch.

I glance at my mother, who gives me the slightest shake of her head. She's telling me to move onto something else. We both know we can find out what did happen elsewhere. I don't want to lose this guy.

His eyes have a lock on me.

"I will say one more thing, and then we're done. Once in a while, we'd end up at the same place together. I wasn't afraid of tellin' that son of a bitch what I thought of him like the time he cheated my boys when they were playin' cards. There's other stuff like that."

"Your boys?"

"Yeah, Junior and Roy."

"How much did they lose?"

"More than they could afford. He even took my father's gold watch Junior put up. Yeah, yeah, the kid shouldn't have done that." He leans over the desk. "The worse part is I think Chet enjoyed it."

"Shoot."

82

"You're right about that," he said. "Eh, I got back at him for that. I told a dealership in the valley Chet was out of business." He makes a head-shaking laugh. "Somebody new answered the phone, so I pretended I was Chet." He laughs that way again. "Took Chet a coupla weeks to figure that out. Revenge is sweet."

I ponder that statement. I've witnessed numerous cases where somebody managed to take it out on somebody else. The locals turned it into an art, against each other sometimes, and even against newcomers. Once, the guy who put in the cellar when we were building our house got pissed off because Sam didn't hire him for a job. Sam wasn't the general contractor, but Ed didn't forgive him for that. Sam tried to make it up to the guy by having him do more work at our house. Ed strung us along for months. In the end, we both chalked it up to redneck's revenge. I'd say Chet and Al were pros at it. As for Ed, we ended up getting somebody else to do the work for cheaper. I say so much for revenge.

"I suppose," I tell Al.

"His daughter, Annette, thinks somebody killed her father. It could be true, but it wouldn't have been me. If so, I would've done it years ago when I was young and hotheaded. I've got too much to lose now. I've got family and a business."

"Your boys live around here?"

"Yup, just down the road. Both are married. One's got a baby on the way. Our first grandkid. The wife is nuts about it." He almost smiles just then. "They both work here with me. We've got a nice business. When I kick, it goes to them."

"I see. Where were you the night of the fire?"

He doesn't even pause.

"With my wife. I go straight home every night after I lock the gate. We live just up the road."

Al's wife is his alibi, admittedly not an airtight one. What wife is going to rat out her husband? Likely not Al Sinclair's.

"How can you be so sure? That was three years ago."

He makes a sound in the back of his throat.

"Hard to forget the night somebody burns up in a fire around here."

"That's true."

"You can ask my wife if you want. She could vouch for me. Want her number? Her name's Kate by the way."

"Why not?"

Al scribbles on a piece of paper. I glance at Ma. She's ready to go. She's given me the sign, which is when she opens and shuts the clasp of her purse with a loud click, just in case I miss it.

"I believe you answered all of my questions for now." I take the paper. "Oh, no, wait. One more, please. If Annette is right about her father, do you have any idea who could've done it?"

"Have you heard of the Beaumont brothers?"

"Their names have come up more than once."

"I'm not surprised," he said. "If you ladies don't mind, I've got a business to run."

"Thanks for speaking with me," I say. "Give me a call if you think of anything else. You have my card."

Ma and I talk it over as I take the back way home through Caulfield. Al Sinclair definitely remains on the suspect list for now. He's hiding something about Chet. Maybe it's something big, maybe something small, but I need to find out what it is.

And a reckoning is definitely in order with the Beaumont brothers.

"You sure you don't want to go to that biker bar with the Floozy and me on Saturday night?" I ask. "The Tough Cookie will be there, too."

"Very funny, Isabel."

I see the Pit Stop ahead. I don't need gas, but maybe we can get something to drink for the ride home. Or better yet, I'll pick up a six-pack. I'm outta beer at home. The sky is slating over. We won't stay long. I hit the directional.

Besides, I want to pin Pete down to an interview. I've called a couple of times and he's put me off, saying he was too damn busy. He won't be able to avoid me in person.

"Come inside with me, Ma. Wait 'til you see the place. You're in for a treat."

Today I get to meet the missus, Barbie, who sits behind the

register reading a magazine while hubby loads six-packs into the cooler. Pete Woodrell turns when he hears us.

"Hey, babe, this was that gal I was tellin' you about," he says, getting to his feet.

"Nice to meet you, Barbie," I say. "I'm Isabel and this is my mother, Maria. We're making our way back from Fulton, and I thought we'd stop by to say hello and pick up a few things." I glance at my mother. "Why don't you get yourself something to drink? My treat."

Ma clicks her tongue because I told her I'm paying. It's kind of a contest between us, who gets to pay, and I make sure I keep winning.

Barbie Woodrell is on the round side. She's got dyed red hair puffed up nicely. It goes with her puffed-up smile. I'm guessing she's in her early forties, a bit younger than hubby. She fingers a pendant around her neck, a nervous habit I presume. The pendant is gold with an amethyst stone, quite pretty really.

"That's a sweet necklace."

She pats the pendant.

"It was my grandmother's. It came with earrings, but I lost one, so I only wear the necklace. Maybe I'll find it some day. That'd be real nice." She smiles shyly. "To tell you the truth, the earrings were a little bit fancy for the Pit Stop. Pete and I don't go out much at night. We're usually pooped after a long day manning the store."

"Shame you lost the earring," I say.

Barbie nods.

"Pete, here, was tellin' me Annette hired you. Chet was a real nice man. And it was a shame what happened to him. But, hon, that sounds like a complete waste of money to me."

I'm not about to tell the Woodrells about my financial arrangement with Annette, so I let her comment pass.

"I believe it's important to her," I say, and then my mother is beside me with a can of diet soda. "That's enough? Want something to eat with that? Check out those muffins, Ma. They look homemade. You bake them, Barbie?"

Barbie's head bounces although her hair stays fixed. A

good amount of teasing and a heavy dose of hair spray will do that.

"Sure did, hon, this mornin' before my bus route. Banana nut. I'm surprised we've got any left."

"Go ahead, Ma. Pick one out for me, too."

"Okay, but we should get going before the storm starts," she says.

"Let me get some beer. I'll be right back."

While Ma carries on small talk with Barbie, I study the beer selection. The best I can do is the brand from Boston. No microbrews at the Pit Stop, but then again I wouldn't expect them.

Pete keeps stuffing six-packs in the cooler. I expect people will be stocking up before the storm.

"Did I hear you say you were in Fulton?"

I grab the carton's handle.

"Yes, you did. We were visiting Sinclair's Junkyard."

"For parts?"

"Just asking Mr. Sinclair a few questions."

"For that investigation?"

"Uh-huh."

"Seems like you're really takin' this all seriously."

"I sure am," I say. "When would be a good time for us to get together to talk about Chet?"

He works his lips as he thinks. He's figured out he can't get rid of me easily.

"Early afternoons are kinda slow for us. Say, uh, one-thirty, two. What day were you thinkin'?"

"Name one."

"Not sure how much damage this ice storm they say we're gettin' is gonna do. How about Thursday?"

"Works for me. I'll see you then. Barbie can join us if she wants."

He stands and slides the cooler door shut with a hard click.

"Don't know if she'll be around. She's got a bus route in the afternoon."

"Then I guess I'll have to catch her another time if she isn't."

Later in the car, I ask Ma how someone could actually cheat at cards. While not a big card player, she was a steady visitor at the Indian casinos in Connecticut for years until she moved in with me. Then there were Bingo nights at the church halls. I went a few times with her to Bingo, but I was more interested in watching the people than listening to the callers. I was terrible at it. My mother, of course, was a frequent winner.

"There are plenty of ways to cheat," Ma says. "I saw it on TV, of course."

"Of course."

"It can happen when somebody's dealing cards. The person knows how to pick out the best cards and makes sure he gets them in his hand."

"So, it's not like he's peeking at somebody's cards."

She laughs.

"If Chet was a cheater, he must've been very good at it. But then again, when people drink, they don't pay close attention to what they're doing," she says.

"Maybe Chet didn't drink or pretended to. I could see a couple of kids getting carried away gambling."

"He also probably picked up on people's tells. You know what that is?"

"Yeah, I do. I used that trick when I was a reporter. I watched their body language carefully if it was a touchy interview."

"You might make a good poker player."

"Eh, I'll stick with what I'm doing. I'm not a betting woman."

Ma chuckles.

"Well, I am."

I wait for a pickup to pass before I take a left onto the road back to Conwell.

"What did you think of the Pit Stop?"

"The store in our town is nicer."

I smile when she says "our town." I'm pleased Ma is feeling more at home living in Conwell.

"How about Mr. and Mrs. Redneck?"

"I liked her a whole lot better than I did him."

I nod. "Yeah, me, too. Well, I finally got him to agree to meet with me Thursday."

"I don't have to come for that one, do I?"

I laugh.

"No, you don't."

We are over the Conwell line and soon past Jack's house. His sister, Eleanor, is in the front yard with her mutts. She's throwing a ball. I realize this is the first I've seen Eleanor since the day she knocked me over the head and left me in the woods. She doesn't look like she's suffering too much from being in exile.

"There's Eleanor," I tell Ma.

"So it is."

Ice Storm

I didn't notice the freezing rain until I let the dog, Maggie, outside. The front porch is glassed over with a layer of ice. The dog is in and out fast for once.

"The storm's started," I announce to my mother.

"How bad is it?

"I'm sure glad I'm not driving in it."

I've driven through a couple of ice storms, manageable only because of the amount of sand and salt the highway crews laid down. We've had some storms move in so fast and bad, the highway guys drove their trucks backwards so they had enough traction to get up a hill, or their boss would call them back to the garage because it was too damn dangerous out there.

But I'm prepared. I have buckets of sand from the highway yard in the back of the Subaru. I put candles and a couple of kerosene lamps on the kitchen table because it's likely we will lose power. I warned Ma, who has a flashlight on the table beside her chair, and checked in with the kids. I have beer in the fridge and a cold one in my hand.

Annette picks up fast when I call.

"Heard you were up at Sinclair's," she says right off the bat.

"I'm guessing you went to the Pit Stop."

"Course. Had to stock up on beer. At least, all I have to do is walk a few yards to the garage to get to work."

"Beer, eh? That's why I stopped, too," I say. "I gave Al Sinclair the third degree. He mentioned that your dad supposedly cheated at cards with his sons, Junior and Roy."

"Yeah, yeah, I heard all about those crybabies. I say don't play cards for money if you can't afford to lose."

89

"Sound advice. I heard he and your father liked to give each other a real hard time like the time Al told that dealership Rough Waters went out of business."

"I remember that. Al got Pop good on that one. Really pissed him off." She snorts a laugh. "Did he tell you about the time Pop let a few skunks go in his junkyard?"

"Uh, no." I shake my head. These two men had a good run at being bad to each other. "Just so you know, I asked him where he was that night. He said he was home with his wife. Not much of an alibi I'd say."

"Shit, no."

"My words exactly. He mentioned something else, but I'll get back to you on that after I find out more. Have you talked with Marsha?"

"About Baxter's? Yeah, yeah, I'll meet you two there."

"I'm glad you're both coming and we're doing this in a public place. From what everybody says, the Beaumont brothers sound like bad news."

"You've got that straight."

"First off, I'm gonna do a little research online while we still have power. See you Saturday."

I head upstairs. I haven't touched the envelopes Annette gave me. I'll save them for tomorrow when I'll have nothing to do because of the storm. Right now, I'll do the Google thing on the Beaumont brothers. Yes, they both have records as adults. Likely they had them as juveniles, but those are sealed. Here's the lowdown: Drunken driving, breaking and entering, and assault. There's nothing about drugs, but maybe they just didn't get caught. Their mother must be proud.

I print everything and tape the paperwork to the wall. There's not a lot there.

I should talk with the reporter at the Berkshire Bugle who covered the case. Sean Mooney was on the staff still when I checked the Bugle online. He has to remember me from when he was the Daily Star's intern. I'd like to hear his take on what happened. What the heck, maybe he's at the newsroom. I dial his direct line.

"Berkshire Bugle. Sean Mooney here."

"Hey, Sean, this is Isabel Long. You might remember me. I used to be the managing editor of the Daily Star."

"Of course, I remember you. Heard there were big changes at the Star when the paper got sold. We've got a couple of your people here at the Bugle."

"I heard as much."

"What can I do for you? Sorry. I can't talk long. I've got a deadline to meet. Writing a weather story, what else. What's it like up there in the boonies?"

"Real icy." I pause. "Anyway, I wanted to ask you about a story you did three years ago. Does the name Chet Waters ring a bell?"

"Chet Waters? He's the guy who burned up in that fire. It was in Caulfield, I believe. What about him?"

"Now that I'm not in the news business, I'm doing P.I. work."

"Yeah, I heard about that, too. You did a great job on that missing woman case. Adela Collins. Thanks for taking the call for that story we did."

"No problem. Now I'm looking into Chet Waters' death. His daughter, Annette, doesn't believe it was an accident. She thinks somebody with a grudge against her father killed him."

"I recall the official ruling. You think she's onto something?"

"She might be. Hey, you've got a deadline to meet, but I'd like to pick your brain. Reporters see things regular folk don't." I take a break to let him absorb what I just said. "All off the record, of course."

"When and where?"

"How about next Wednesday morning?"

"Sure. How about that greasy spoon next to the Bugle's office? Meet you there at ten."

"Go make your deadline. I'll look for your story online."

Mike Waters is next on my list, but the call goes directly to voice mail. I leave a vague message in hopes he calls back. His wimp brother, the Floozy's description, not mine, is not on the list, but I'm going to meet with him anyways.

Now I feel restless. I glance at the bookcases in my office

and don't see anything that would hold my attention. I feel like talking with somebody, touching somebody, and he touching me. Yeah, I'm thinking about Jack. I glance at my phone. The Rooster is closed Tuesdays. He's probably kicking back at home.

Get a grip, Isabel. You're not his good-hearted woman anymore.

Downstairs, I grab another beer from the fridge. I ask my mother, "Wanna watch a movie?"

"Go ahead," she says. "Find something good."

And then the lights go out.

What's Up with the Old Farts

It's Thursday morning. I spent most of yesterday trapped inside as we waited for that damn ice to melt. The only one who went outside was the dog, Maggie, because she had no choice. I was thankful I had enough firewood in the basement and the power came on sometime mid-morning. I went over my meager notes and found chores to do. Ma, of course, had her trashy novels.

I'm going to take a ride to the store and pester the Old Farts. I'm relieved when I arrive that only the regulars are here. I don't have to hold back or have them explain to any Visiting Old Farts what the heck we're talking about. And I don't want the visitors blabbing all over town what I'm doing.

Yes, it's become a routine with these guys that the Fattest Old Fart is the official greeter and the Serious Old Fart is the pourer. Of course, I smile at his stupid espresso joke.

"What brings you here, Isabel?" the Bald Old Fart asks.

"Do I need a reason? Maybe I just like to see your faces and drink bad coffee. Good way to start the day, I'd say."

My smarty-pants comment draws a round of chuckles.

"That's why we do it every day," the Skinniest Old Fart says.

"Even yesterday?"

The Skinniest Old Fart shrugged.

"You think an ice storm is going to stop us from meeting here and talking about what you've been up to?" he says.

I laugh.

"You mean me and everybody else in town." I reach into my jacket pocket. "I brought you all a small gift. Here are my business cards in case you ever need me. My daughter, Ruth, had them made."

I hand them out. Each man studies his card.

The Fattest Old Fart snorts.

"As if we didn't know how to reach you," he says as he pulls a wallet from his back pocket. "But thanks."

Now it's the Bald Old Fart's turn.

"Heard you were up at Sinclair's the other day."

The other Old Farts turn their heads toward their buddy. This is the second time he's come up with news about me.

I shake my head.

"I'm not gonna even ask how you know. But I will ask you all about Al Sinclair. What can you tell me about him?"

"Is he on your suspect list?" the Skinniest Old Fart asks.

"Sorry. That information is private."

The Skinniest Old Fart makes a high-pitched laugh. "I will take that as a yes."

"No comment," I say as I take a different tack. "So, none of you know a thing about him. Frankly, I'm surprised. You sure know a lot about me."

"Isabel, we just like getting a rise out of you," the Skinniest Old Fart says. "Al's an okay guy, loves his sons."

"He told me they lost big to Chet Waters one night in a poker game," I say. "He seemed unhappy about it."

The Silent Old Fart nods.

"I was at Al's the day after it happened."

This is indeed an historic occasion. Other than a grunt or a chuckle the Silent Old Fart indeed lives up to his name. He even surprises his compatriots, who stare at him.

"Tell me more," I say.

"You're right. The boys lost big. There was something about a gold watch that belonged to Al's father, Eben. Al was livid about it. There has always been bad blood between Chet and Al, but this only added fuel to the fire."

"Bad blood? More than a rival junkyard and cheating at cards?"

The Silent Old Fart nods at his buddies. He's done talking. I look from one man to the other. It's the Serious Old Fart who speaks next.

"Long before you got here, when we were all just kids,

there was a bad car crash. Chet was at the wheel. Al's kid sister, Amanda, was in the front passenger seat. Chet was going a bit fast and lost control when his car hit ice. It was New Year's Eve. The poor girl died at the scene. A couple in the backseat got hurt." His head shakes a bit. "We didn't have an ambulance in those days. No seatbelts."

"Who was in the backseat?"

"Al and his girlfriend. She's now his wife. Kate's her name," the Serious Old Fart says.

"Wow. Chet and Al used to be friends?"

"Back then they were."

"Was Chet drunk?"

"They probably all were," the Serious Old Fart says. "But something like that never leaves you."

A pall has dropped over the backroom. I don't know what else to say, except, "I bet."

A Meet Up with Pete

Pete Woodrell is finishing a transaction with the man who owns the pickup parked next to the Pit Stop's gas pumps. I recognize the guy, who has come into Rooster, not a regular, but then again he has a memorable scar running along the side of his face. We exchange hellos, and then he is gone with a jingle of the bell above the front door.

"Hey, Isabel, let me get you a chair from out back," Pete says.

"Barbie here? I was hoping to catch her before her bus route."

"Nah, she left already," he shouts from the backroom, and then he wheels a chair behind the counter. There's just enough room for two chairs if I don't mind having my back to the front door. "Take a load off."

Pete seems in an easy-going mood, but I still plan to use my usual reporter's trick of tossing a few softball questions first.

"Did you grow up in Caulfield?" I ask.

"No, ma'am, I'm from New Hampshire, a small town like this one you probably never heard of unless you lived there," he answers. "How did I get here? That's a long story."

I smile and plan to be my friendly reporter self.

"That's okay. I've got time for a long story. I like getting to know the people I'm interviewing. So, how did you get to Caulfield?"

His chair creaks a bit as he leans back.

"After I got out of the Air Force, I drove truck for a big outfit, but I got tired of that, 'specially after I married Barbie. I thought we were gonna have kids, but that didn't happen." He pauses. "Anyways we were home visitin' my folks when a buddy told me the Pit Stop was for sale. He'd been thinkin' of buyin' it, but changed his mind. We took a look and liked what we saw. Lucky for us Barbie's folks helped out. That was about fifteen years ago. And here we still are."

"Being the only store in town, you must know everybody in Caulfield."

"Yup, just about, and the towns around it. We're open seven to seven, so we get people goin' to and comin' from work."

"Coffee in the morning and beer at night?"

"You got it. Plus gas. It's a little more expensive than what the city gas stations charge. And people ain't gonna shop here for their week's groceries. We're more of a convenience store."

"You mentioned before Chet was a regular."

"He sure was. He stopped in every day for smokes or booze and usually both. He liked putting away the hard stuff. I recall he really liked Barbie's muffins and complained if we ran out before he showed up. Most times he took his sweet time, talking about what was going on in town or something he read in the paper. He liked making Barbie laugh with his corny jokes."

"He read the newspaper? Well, bless his heart."

"Heart?" Pete chuckles. "I don't know if he had one."

"What'd you mean?"

"I won't be the first to tell you probably he cheated at cards. He sure didn't mind rippin' people off."

"But some people told me he was a fair businessman when it came to fixing or selling cars."

He mulls my words.

"Yeah, I heard that, too, although his daughter is a better mechanic."

"When was the last time you saw Chet?"

"The day before we heard about the fire actually. He came in for a bottle of Jim Beam. I'm guessin' he must've been pretty loaded when his place caught fire."

"You said Chet liked to talk. Do you remember your conversation that day?"

97

He bites his lip as he thinks.

"To tell you the truth, I was too damn busy that day to pay much attention to Chet. The beer truck had just arrived and I was busy dealing with that. We go through an awful lot of beer here in a week." He flashes a gold tooth when he grins. "But back to Chet. We exchanged a few words. He complained some newcomer who didn't like junkyards was tryin' to close his down. He brought it up before." He makes that grin again. "We store owners are a little like bartenders and shrinks. We listen to people's problems all the time. He sure liked havin' Barbie's ear."

"Do you remember the newcomer's name?"

"Oh, yeah, Anthony Steward."

I smile. That name is on Annette's list of suspects.

"I read a newspaper story about the fire. The reporter quoted you."

He nods.

"Yeah, me and a lot of folks went to Rough Waters when we heard about the fire. I closed the store to see what was happenin' then came back. That's when the reporter asked me about Chet."

Pete's not giving me a whole lot of new info, except that tidbit about the newcomer, Anthony Steward. Too bad Pete was too busy to talk with Chet. I wonder if Barbie did.

"To back up a little, was Barbie here when Chet came that day?"

"Hmm, she was. He tended to show up after she was done her morning bus route at ten. I could set my watch by him. I used to kid her about that."

I can visualize old Chet chatting it up with the missus. She's sweet and attentive. Plus she bakes. I'm gonna have to interview her separately someday after ten, it seems.

"You said you believe the fire was accidental. Let's pretend it wasn't." I wait for a nod from Pete. "Who do you think would be likely suspects?"

He fingers his chin.

"Pretend, eh? Well, I believe it could've been one of his poker victims if the stakes were high enough."

"You ever play with him?"

He snorts a laugh.

"Only if I was okay losin' that night. I just liked watchin' the man in action, makin' jokes and tellin' stories. He was a real character. He put on a good show. The town sure ain't the same without him."

"Anybody else?"

"Well, there was the newcomer I mentioned. Chet did complain about the Beaumont brothers, Gary and Larry. He didn't like their line of work, if you get what I mean. Somethin' else happened there, but I don't know what."

If Ma were here, she'd get that pocketbook clicking. It's time to leave.

"I'm not gonna take up any more of your time, but if you think of anything more, here's my card."

Pete takes the card from my hand.

"Will do, Isabel. Come again real soon."

Dirty Work

It's Friday, and I'm parked on a city street to spy on a man who claims to have hurt his back so badly in an accident he should get a ton of money from the insurance company of the driver who hit him. The alleged victim, Wilson Barry, was a pedestrian in a crosswalk. According to Lin Pierce, Barry was indeed injured, but the insurance company doubts it's permanent or as bad as he claims.

"See if you can catch him doing something a person with a disabling injury couldn't do," Lin told me over the phone yesterday.

I'm not crazy about this line of work. My mother calls it dirty work although she comes along anyway for moral support. My job is to take photos. It's kind of tricky. I can't enter Wilson Barry's property or tip him off about what I'm doing. But Lin has a hunch the guy is faking it.

"You do take good photos, right?" he asked.

"Yeah, I learned that on the job. I have a nice Nikon with the right lens."

We've been outside Wilson Barry's address for forty-five minutes. Luckily, there are a number of parked cars on this city street, so mine doesn't stand out. I'm getting a bit cold sitting here, but I don't want to run the engine too often. At least, it's warm enough to have melted the ice from that storm the other day.

My mother taps my arm.

"That him?"

I check the photo Lin emailed me.

"If it's not him, it's got to be his twin brother. Hey, he's getting in his car. It's about time."

Barry uses a cane as he walks around his car. He's maybe

in his early thirties or younger. He's dark-haired, and although it's hard to say from the heavy jacket he's wearing, I believe he's on the thin side. I snap a shot as he throws his cane and gets in the front seat. I wait until he's driven halfway down the block before I follow. My mother is the navigator.

"He taking a right," she warns me before I do the same. "Slow down, Isabel. He's stopping at the convenience store."

I pull over and wait. Minutes later, Wilson Barry has a lit cigarette between his lips, likely his reason for stopping. He doesn't use a cane. Snap.

Then he's back in his car. I do my best to keep up without being obvious, letting a vehicle or two get between us. I've seen enough cop shows and movies to figure out this part. We are at a city park, and I trail his car to a basketball court. He's shed his jacket and is wearing a sweatshirt. He calls to the guys already on the court. One guy shoots the ball toward Wilson Barry, and I'm shooting as he dribbles and does a nice floater off the rim. Snap some more.

"Got you, you bastard," I say.

I keep shooting from the car until I believe I've got enough for Lin to present as evidence.

"Are we done?" my mother says.

"Yes, ma'am. Let's go buy some groceries."

Baxter's

Marsha picks me up in her beater of a car around nine on Saturday night. The way that car rattles it wouldn't take much for it to find a final resting place at her cousin's junkyard. She smokes with the window down, doesn't even ask if I mind.

"Where were ya last night?" she asks.

"You mean at the Rooster?"

She blows smoke out the window.

"Where else?"

I try not to sigh.

"I wasn't up for it. Why, did something happen?"

Her eyes dart toward my side of the car.

"People were askin' for you."

"Oh, yeah? I had something else to do."

I'm lying. Ma and I came home in the afternoon after a trip to Whole Foods, where my mother went "tsk, tsk" over the prices, and a quick visit with Lin Pierce, where he downloaded the photos I shot, praising me for the fast work. I told him I felt a little slimy helping out an insurance company, in my opinion one of the bottom feeders in this world, but he brushed me off with one of those it's strictly business lectures.

After supper, I mostly stayed in my office, sorting the papers Annette gave me. The medical examiner wrote in his report Chet Waters probably died from smoke inhalation rather than the burns that covered his body. He appeared to have hit his temple hard because there was a crack in his skull, likely made when he fell to the floor or it could have been a piece of the house that fell on him. That would have been a contributing factor to his death.

The fire chief wrote there was no evidence an accelerant was used. According to the state police report, the garage wasn't broken into, so nothing valuable was taken. Annette confirmed for them the safe was intact.

I did go through the envelope of records from Rough Waters. It seems Chet did a lot of business with a used car lot in Springville, but nothing stood out, no big debts or anything like that. The '78 Corolla appeared to have a clear title.

When I came downstairs I pestered my mother, who told me she wanted to finish the book she was reading. I ended up half-watching a nature show on PBS and sulking.

Now Marsha snorts on the other side of her car.

"Too bad. It was a good band. A new one. The Country Plowboys. I guess they all work on highway crews or plow driveways during the winter. They weren't half bad. People were dancin' their brains out. Even Jack." She chuckles something low and dirty. "Don't ya worry none. It was Carole, the new cook. She's married." More laughter. "Gotcha goin' there for a second, didn't I?"

Yes, she did, but I won't admit it.

"You're hilarious, Marsha."

The parking lot at Baxter's is full of the usual winter assortment of snowmobiles, pickups, and cars. This bar's big night is Saturday, the Floozy told me on the way over, and the owner usually books a band.

As we head toward the front entrance, I hear music, something by the group Alabama, bouncing through the walls. Beer signs flash through the windows. Ahead of me, Marsha marches inside as if she owns the damn place. She stops short of the dance floor, nods, and then points toward the far end. Annette already has a table. Some guy is talking in her ear while he stares at the cleavage rising about her low-cut sweater. She paws at him as she laughs.

Marsha turns toward me.

"My cousin's a slut, what can I tell ya?"

"She looks like she's just having a good time."

"Same difference." Marsha slaps my arm and points at the band. "Well, well, look who's playin'. It's the Country Plowboys. You didn't miss 'em after all."

When the song ends, Marsha and I make our way across

the thinning dance floor. Annette, aka the Tough Cookie, gives the guy she's with a friendly push and says, "You gotta get lost now. Maybe later."

The guy, in the usual country attire of flannel, canvas, and denim, checks us out, but he clearly isn't interested. We take our seats. Marsha whistles sharply through her teeth to get the waitress's attention.

I lean forward.

"I'll get this round," I say.

"All right," the Floozy says.

I glance around the barroom. It's three times the size of the Rooster, with a long bar on one side and an actual stage. Tables border the dance floor on three sides. It's dark inside except for the wide-screen TVs lit over the three shelves of booze behind the bar. The clientele is on the rustic side, which I expect and enjoy. Frankly, as a reporter and a denizen of the hilltowns, I found the natives often more interesting than the white-collar folks who commuted to the city.

That's when I notice the beer cans. Everybody who doesn't have a mixed drink has a can of Bud or whatever. The woman who took our order is carrying a tray of them.

"No beer in bottles here?" I ask my companions.

"Nah, it's safer with cans," the Floozy says. "Even the glasses are plastic. I'd say that was being real smart with this crowd."

I hand the bills to the waitress.

"Keep the change," I say, remembering the buck-a-round-rule at the Rooster.

The cousins are gabbing about the men, which ones are decent looking and who's available for a roll in the sack. They appear to like men with hair and a steady job, which is a sound idea, or as Annette puts it, "I don't want some guy spongin' off of me. Did that. Won't do it again." They also don't like guys with big beer bellies or steady girlfriends and wives. No sloppy seconds, the Tough Cookie says.

"What about you?" Annette asks with a grin. "See anybody here you might be interested in?"

"Me? I really haven't checked out the men," I say.

She snickers.

"Well, that guy over there is sure givin' you the eye. See him over there next to the juke? He's one of those silver foxes."

I turn as casually as possible. The aforementioned guy is an older man with indeed silver hair, actually on the handsome side. He is definitely staring in our direction, but when I glance around, I notice plenty of women of all shapes and sizes are sitting at the tables behind us.

"I don't think so," I say. "Are the Beaumont brothers here?"

Both women shake their heads.

The Floozy leans toward me.

"Not yet. We'll let you know when they come."

I raise my chin.

"Hey, isn't that Pete Woodrell from the Pit Stop over there? See the back table?"

"Yeah, that's the dick," Annette says.

"What's the matter with him?"

Annette gulps down the last of her beer and smacks the table with the empty can.

"Let's say I don't think he's very nice to his wife. Sometimes she's got bruises I know she didn't get from bumpin' into things." She raises her hand to get the waitress's attention. "Too bad it's the only place around I can buy gas and beer."

"You ever say anything to her?"

"Hard to. The dick's always there." She nods toward Pete's direction. "See her hidin' there in the corner? He's got her under his thumb."

Barbie sits tucked beside her husband, who yaks it up with a couple of guys at his table. She's off in a zone somewhere as she sips her drink with a straw. So it turns out Mr. Friendly Storekeeper might not be so friendly after all, at least to his wife. What's that saying? The bigger the front, the bigger the back.

"Yeah, I do. You ever see him lose his temper?"

"Not me, but I've heard stories. You'll see what I mean if

105

you keep comin' to the Pit Stop." Annette sniffs. "Maybe you can do somethin' about it. I hate to see anythin' bad happen to her. Even my Pop liked her."

I'm thinking about Pete, Barbie, and crappy marriages when the Country Plowboys strike up the Allman Brothers' "Ramblin' Man." Wouldn't you guess the silver-haired guy makes his way through the dancers to our table?

"Care to dance, ma'am?" he asks me.

The Floozy elbows me. Oh, why not. I get to my feet and hold out my hand. "Ramblin' Man" is not one of my favorite dance songs, but it'll work.

I let my dancing partner take the lead while we make steps around the floor. If I were to rank him, I'd say he was on par with Jack but not as good as Sam. Actually, it's fun dancing with a perfect stranger.

The song ends, but before the next one begins and I can escape, he leans in to say, "Name's Dave. What's yours?"

"Isabel."

"Never seen you in here before."

"It's my first time," and before he or I can say more, the Country Plowboys are working up Elvis' "Jailhouse Rock." Now if there was ever a heart-pumper of a song, this is it. Heck, I'm not gonna turn this one down. Dave grabs my hand without asking. He knows what he's doing, so I just go along, moving back and forth, a twirl here and there. I wouldn't have been surprised if he'd spun me over his back, but thankfully, he doesn't.

At the end, the County Plowboys call it quits for a short break. I thank Dave and before I can leave him behind, he says, "Maybe we can dance some more later."

I nod and smile. Isabel, what the hell are you up to? I suppose having fun with another man.

Naturally, the cousins laugh their heads off when I join them.

"See? We told ya," Marsha says. "Hee, hee, check her out, Annette. She's as red as a beet."

"No, I'm not."

Annette laughs so hard, beer spurts from her mouth.

106

"Yeah, you are."

Marsha jabs my arm with her elbow. She's stopped laughing.

"Look who just walked through the door. The Beaumont bastards," she says. "They're already stinkin' up the place."

"They're so much alike," I say.

"Hard to tell 'em apart, eh?" Annette says. "Well, the ugly son of a bitch with the mustache is Gary. The other ugly son of a bitch with the scar down the side of his face is Larry. It's from a car crash, not a knife fight although he's been in a couple of those."

I study the brothers as they order beer and bark with their drinking buddies. They're wearing the usual aforementioned male country attire and, yes, they have mullets.

Marsha grabs my wrist when I stand.

"Where in the hell are you goin'?"

"To talk with Gary and Larry."

"Are you fuckin' nuts?"

"I wanna go before I lose my nerve." I nod at Marsha and Annette. "Wish me luck."

The band is on break still, so Baxter's is relatively quiet, except for the loud voices of its customers, likely louder now because of the booze. I make my way across the empty dance floor toward Gary and Larry's table. It takes them a moment to realize I'm standing in front of them.

Gary, the mustached brother, gives me a hard squint.

"What'd ya want, old lady?" he says.

Beside him, Larry, his brother with the scar, snickers.

"First off, I'm not old. Second, I'm no lady," I say.

Gary gives me an appreciative nod.

"I like your attitude," he says. "What can we do for you?"

Larry's head swivels.

"Uh, we don't do business inside, if that's why you're here."

I shake my head.

"Not interested. May I sit?"

Larry uses his foot to push a chair forward.

"Take a load off," his brother says.

I fish two business cards from my wallet and place them on the table, one for each brother.

"My name is Isabel Long. I'm a private investigator. I'd like to ask you a few questions about Chet Waters."

"Chet Waters? He's a crispy critter." Gary laughs into his raised beer can. "Why do you care about him?"

"His daughter, Annette, believes somebody killed him, and she wants me to find out if that's true. She's here with me tonight. See her over there?" I jab my thumb toward our table. "I live in Conwell, so I don't know these parts very well. I thought maybe you could give me some information that'd be helpful."

The brothers eye each other.

"Yeah, I see that bitch over there," Gary says. "What kinda information?"

"For starters, how well did you know Chet Waters?"

"He bought junks, fixed some of 'em up, and sold the rest for parts," Gary, who appears to be the spokesman, says.

"I already know that much. What was your relationship with him?"

"Relationship?" Gary sneers. "You fuckin' with me, lady? Chet was an asshole."

"Did you ever do business with him?" I ask.

"Sometimes. But it's not what you think."

"I heard you were at the junkyard a few days before the fire. Is that right?"

Gary nods.

"My brother's into truck pullin'. You know what's that?"

"Sure, I've been to a few truck pulls."

"Huh? Well, we walked around checkin' over his junks for a truck my brother could fix up. We found a couple, but the old bastard wanted too much for 'em. We tried talkin' him down, but he got so pissed, he threw us out. We ended up goin' to Sinclair's instead. Got a better deal there."

Behind me, the band returns to the stage. Soon the Beaumonts and I will be out of hearing range. I'm wondering if the drugs and money in the trunk of the Corolla could have belonged to the brothers. Maybe they weren't searching for a truck but to check whether the car with the drugs had arrived. This is getting trickier.

"You weren't interested in a Corolla he had?"

Gary sneers.

"Corolla? You couldn't pull a shoppin' cart with that piece of crap." He slaps the table. "Besides, we only buy American."

"Say, it's gonna get real noisy in here. Could we meet some other time? I'd like to ask you more questions."

"What for?"

"You got a long look at Chet's junkyard just before he died in that fire. Maybe you both saw something."

Gary raises an eyebrow.

"Maybe we can do that," he says.

"Okay, you have my number on that card. Could I have yours, please?"

"Please?" Gary's lips quiver. "Yeah, here it is."

I pull my phone from the back pocket of my jeans and type in the number he tells me.

"This a real number?" I half-joke. "You're not fuckin' with me, are you?"

The brothers laugh.

"Yeah, that's a real number," Gary says. "Why don't ya call me right now? Go ahead."

I push the call button on my phone and within seconds, Gary's is ringing.

"We're all set," I say. "How about later this week?"

"Yeah. Just don't call too early," Gary says.

"Fair enough. Thanks, guys."

Of course, when I get back to the table, the cousins pester me for information. They want to smoke, so they drag me outside to a deck with the other smokers. The moon shines onto the lake's black water.

Marsha bumps my arm. I swear it's going to be bruised tomorrow.

"What did those assholes say?" she says.

"Not too much. They or rather Gary the talker claimed he and his brother were at the junkyard to find a vehicle to fix up for truck pulling. But they couldn't work a deal with your father, Annette, so they went to Sinclair's instead. Actually, he said your father ordered them to leave. Do you remember that?"

She blows a long stream of smoke.

"Now that you mention it, they were walkin' all over the place with Pop. I wouldn't put it past Pop to kick 'em out. He had no patience for those assholes," she says. "Hey, maybe they were casin' the joint."

"Could be. When I asked if they were in the market for a Corolla, they acted like I was nuts."

Annette's eyes narrowed.

"That's all you got from 'em?"

"For now. I'd say it was more like an icebreaker than an interview. The band was about to start. Gary gave me his number. We're going to meet again in a few days."

"You sure he gave you his real number?"

"Uh-huh, I even called him at the table to make sure. It's the right one."

Annette grins.

"That's smart," she says. "I don't trust those guys."

Annette takes the last long drag of her cigarette. She and Marsha are ready to head inside.

"Hold on a sec, Annette," I say. "I heard about a fatal accident that happened when your father was a teenager. He was at the wheel when Al's sister died. You ever hear about that?"

She makes a grinding kind of hum.

"Shit, that happened when Pop was in high school. My mother told me the story after I asked her about it. Some kid at school mentioned it. Ma told me not to bring it up around Pop. He'd get upset."

"I was told your father and Al were good friends before that happened."

"That's what she said, too," Annette says.

Marsha squints.

"So, do you think Al did it?" she asks.

"You think he snapped after all these years? I guess that's my job to find out."

110

"Yup," Annette says.

The cousins drop what's left of their butts in a can left on the deck just for that purpose. Once we're back inside, we find fresh beers on the table none of us ordered. Moments later, Dave is back and sitting at the table's empty chair.

"I thought you ladies looked thirsty," he says above the noise.

"Thank you very much," I say. "That's mighty thoughtful of you, Dave."

He chuckles.

"Well, I have an ulterior motive," he tells me. "How about another dance, Isabel?"

The Country Plowboys are cranking up a Lynyrd Skynyrd tune, so I'm game. I end up dancing two more times with Dave, who now has the nickname Dancin' Dave.

After a break, he asks for one more fast one.

"Hope I see you here again, Isabel," he tells me.

The cousins and I stay put until last call. The Beaumont brothers stick around, too. I watch them. Sometimes I catch them watching me.

Annette hooks up again with lover boy before they take off together. I get totally buzzed from beer in a can and am grateful Marsha drives us home in one piece. For once, I'm back after my mother's gone to sleep.

News from the Old Farts

It's Monday morning, and I'm on a Sophie pickup outside the Conwell General Store. Yesterday was a wash for me. I was hung over in the morning. I can't recall the last time I drank so much beer. My mother, of course, wanted to hear all about it. I played down Dancin' Dave and played up the Beaumont brothers. I took a long walk along the road past the maple trees, strung up with tubing. The official name is a sugar bush. Winter's on the decline, mercifully. It's only a matter of time when that sap starts flowing.

I arrive a little later at the store than I planned, so I can't visit the Old Farts first. But as Ruth pulls away, I tell my granddaughter, "What do you say kiddo? Let's visit the… " but I stop mid-sentence. Ruth would string me up if Old Farts were the first words out of her baby's mouth.

The usual gang is inside. The Fattest Old Fart, who naturally sits alone, announces my entrance.

"And she's brought the baby with her," he says.

I sit with Sophie beside him.

"Nice to see you're all alive and kicking," I joke.

"Yeah, it's been a while," the Fattest Old Fart says.

"Like maybe a few days."

"That long?"

They gush a bit about the baby. The Skinniest Old Fart gives me a cup of coffee and the usual line about the espresso machine. But then the joking dies down, and everyone is as serious as the Serious Old Fart.

I glance from one man to another.

"What's going on?"

"You haven't heard," the Bald Old Fart says.

"Heard what?"

The Fattest Old Fart gives me a long look.

"Eleanor Smith passed away last night," he says.

"Eleanor? What happened?"

"What we heard is that when Jack came home from the Rooster, her part of the house was dark. The dogs were barking outside. He thought it was strange, so he went over to her place. That's when he found her on the floor. He called the ambulance, but Eleanor died on the way to the hospital. Seems she had a heart attack."

I say nothing. I let the others do the talking. They say Jack is broken up about his sister's death. He's keeping it quiet. He's not putting in an obit until after she's buried tomorrow at the family plot in the town cemetery, the same one where Sam's ashes are in the ground. Jack wants to get his sister buried as soon as possible, so there won't be a wake or service at the church. He doesn't want to draw any attention from the newspapers and TV stations that went nuts over the Adela Collins case. Snoopy reporters would be back in town pestering the locals. I can see the headlines now. How about: **Convicted killer dies months after confession**.

If Eleanor had died without my chasing the case, Adela's disappearance would have remained an unsolved hilltown mystery. Finding out helped the woman's family reach some resolution, albeit an uneasy one. I wonder if it contributed to Eleanor's death in some way. If so, that means I did, too.

Stop it, Isabel. Just stop it. Eleanor may have had limited mental capacities, but she was responsible after all. She's just lucky Adela's father, Andrew Snow, showed compassion and didn't press for a prison sentence.

"It's a private service," the Serious Old Fart says. "Jack's not even having anything at the church. He's meeting the minister at the cemetery."

"Isn't the ground too frozen?" I ask.

"Jack asked his cousin, Fred, to get a piece of equipment to dig the grave. He needs just enough space for an urn."

"When is it?"

"Eleven o'clock tomorrow morning," the Fattest Old Fart says quietly. "We thought you'd want to know."

I zip Sophie's snowsuit and pull on her mittens.

"Yes, I do. Thanks for telling me."

The Fattest Old Fart leans toward me.

"Are you all right, Isabel?"

"Yeah," I whisper.

I rush back to my car. I almost bump into Andrew Snow as he walks between two pickup trucks with his head down.

"Hey, Andrew, how've you been?" I greet him.

Andrew isn't smiling.

"You must've heard about Eleanor," he says.

"Just now." I tip my head toward the store. "In there."

"It's a tragic story all around," he says.

"I agree." I shift Sophie in my arms. I like Andrew a lot, but I'm not interested in deliberating about Eleanor with him or anybody else. "Sorry. I gotta get going. The baby."

"Yeah, I understand," he says.

In the car, Sophie is strapped into her seat. She plays with a silly, squeaky toy I gave her. I pull my phone from my purse and scroll through the contacts. I find Jack's number. My call goes directly to voice mail.

"Hey, Jack, this is Isabel. I'm sorry to hear about Eleanor, real sorry. Call me if you want. Bye."

Good-Bye Eleanor Smith

I arrive at the town cemetery as Jack takes a metal urn from the back of a hearse. He's talking with the driver from the funeral home. The minister of the Conwell Congregational Church and Jack's cousin, Fred, are the only other people here. Everybody is in black. Jack wears only a suit and tie but no coat despite the cold.

They all turn my way. Jack nods as I shut the Subaru's door and walk toward them. They wait for me.

"I hope you don't mind my coming," I tell Jack.

He hugs the urn of his sister's ashes.

"It's fine, Isabel, really," he says quietly, and then he tells Fred, "Why don't you get the dogs?"

As we walk uphill through the snow, Fred goes to Jack's pickup parked behind the hearse. It's a sweet gesture on Jack's part to bring the creatures that mattered the most to his sister to her burial.

Fred wrestles with the dogs in the pickup truck's cab as he gets them leashed, and then they're barking and tugging him toward us. They obey Jack when he orders them to sit and be quiet. He continues to hug the urn.

"Ready?" the minister asks.

The reverend talks about Eleanor in glowing terms. It's obvious he never met her, but he managed to glean some things from the people in town like how she enjoyed cooking for her brother at the Rooster and at home. She loved taking her dogs for walks in the woods and sitting with them in her sunroom. He, of course, leaves out the nasty stuff.

Jack steps forward, and taking a knee in the grave's cleared spot, he places the urn inside the hole. His head is down a few minutes before he walks behind a stone, where he picks up two shovels.

Fred hands me the dogs' leashes.

"You mind taking 'em?"

"Not at all."

I hold the dogs in place, clucking to keep them calm, while Jack and Fred cover the urn with dirt and set the shovels on the ground when they're done.

Jack stands beside me. His cousin, who takes the dogs' leashes from my hand, is on my other side.

No one says a word. The only sounds come from the crows perched high in the trees and a cough from the minister.

Then Jack takes my bare hand. I give his a gentle squeeze.

"I loved my sister," he says. "She loved me. I was a very lucky man to have her. Good-bye, Sis."

Jack sobs beside me. His shoulders shake. I pull him close and wrap my arms around him.

"Oh, Jack," I whisper.

I just let him cry. I cry for him.

Fred gives Jack a pat on the shoulder. The minister does the same before he leaves.

"It's okay, buddy," Fred says kindly.

Jack nods, and I let him go as he reaches for a handkerchief in his pants pocket. I am about to leave as well when he touches my arm.

"Isabel, we're having some food at the house. The Rooster's new cook, Carole, made it for us. Why don't you join Fred and me?"

"You sure?"

He gives me an honest grin.

"Yeah, I'm sure, Isabel."

"Let me call my mother, and I'll meet you there."

The Scene of the Crime

Ma, of course, gives her whole-hearted approval when I call her. After I learned about Eleanor's death yesterday, we had a lengthy discussion about whether I should show up at the cemetery even though I wasn't invited. Jack never returned my phone call, but I wasn't going to let that stop me.

"I want to be there for Jack," I told her.

"Then you should go," she said.

I pull my car beside Jack's pickup that's parked in his driveway. I heave a big sigh when I get out. The last time I was here, I discovered Eleanor was the person who killed Adela Collins, and then she tried to do the same to me, or at least knock me out, when I chased her into the woods. Jack found me and carried me to his bed. Then everything fell apart.

Could it all have happened only a few months ago?

The mutts are on Jack's porch, hollering their heads off, and he comes through the door to calm them down. He's still wearing a white shirt and black pants, but the tie is gone. The top buttons of his shirt are undone. He grins as I walk toward him.

"They'll get used to you comin' around," he tells me.

I try not to read too much into his statement.

Fred is at the kitchen table with an open bottle of beer. The table is set, even with a vase filled with red and white carnations.

"Did you do this?" I ask Jack.

"Nah, that's Carole for ya. I just added an extra place. I hope you like venison stew. It's from the deer Fred shot last year." He chuckles. "I heard you were one of those natural food nuts."

117

"You can't get any more natural than venison."

"Good point." Jack takes my coat. "Have a seat, Isabel. We were gonna make a toast while the stew's heatin' up."

I glance at the clock on the stove. It's not quite noon. Jack pours three shots from a top-shelf whiskey. I'm not into the hard stuff, but what the heck, it's a toast to his dead sister.

Jack lowers the flame beneath the stew pot before he sits beside me. His cousin is on the other side of the table, an arrangement that amuses me.

"Ah, the good stuff," Fred says.

We hold up our glasses while Jack says, "To my sister, Eleanor. I'll miss the hell outta that funny little gal."

I take a sip from my shot while the guys down theirs. Top shelf or not, this stuff burns.

"Uh, Isabel, ya gotta drink it all," Jack says. "That's how a toast works."

"Yeah, don't be such a lightweight," his cousin says.

As soon as I put down my empty glass, Jack pours again. Shoot, all I had this morning was coffee and a piece of toast. That was hours ago. I'm going to get looped if we keep this up much longer.

"Not all the way to the top, please. Yeah, I am a lightweight when it comes to the hard stuff."

Jack gives me a sideways glance as he fills my shot glass halfway.

"Here you go, weakling," he says.

It's Fred's turn.

"To Eleanor, one woman who laughed at all my jokes and never broke my heart. God bless her," he says. "Down the hatch, Isabel."

"Okay."

Jack pours another round. He obliges me with half a glass.

"Your turn, Isabel."

I think as I roll the shot glass between my fingers. The booze is already working. Yes, I am definitely a weakling as Jack called me.

What can I say about Eleanor? We both loved one man, her brother? She was willing to kill for him? That I'm glad she didn't hit me harder? Oh, be nice, Isabel. You're not that drunk.

Jack and Fred wait.

I raise my glass.

"To Eleanor, a damn good cook, a dedicated dog owner, and a loving sister."

I down the whiskey and place my hand over the top when Jack shakes the bottle. He has a playful grin on his face.

"More, Isabel?"

"No way I could keep up with you guys," I say. "Are you both trying to get me drunk?"

Jack hasn't dropped that grin.

"Maybe."

"Oh, yeah?" I glance toward the stove. "That stew's gotta be hot enough. Let me serve it before the bottom gets burned."

I get to my feet, feeling a bit wobbly. But I manage to bring full bowls to Jack and Fred. I take a half bowl for myself. There's already bread on the table.

My first spoonful is awfully good. The second is, too. Carole made a flour base and added lots of chunky potatoes, carrots, and onions.

"This is really tasty," I say out loud.

Across the table, Fred nods.

"You should have Carole make stuff like this instead of that swill she's servin' at the Rooster."

"You got a point," Jack says. "Maybe beef instead of venison unless you're planning to donate what's in your freezer."

Fred snorts.

"Fat chance, cuz."

I keep eating, so I can get something inside my stomach beside whiskey. I reach for a piece of bread.

Jack and Fred tell stories about Eleanor, what she was like as a kid and how she worked the farm. School was hard. Her teachers didn't understand her. She used to have a pet goose named Ingrid that followed her around like a dog.

Jack gets out an old album to show us photos. He laughs about the time she got a blue ribbon for a hog at the county fair, and it took a whole lot of convincing her that it was supposed to be slaughtered.

"She sure loved Elvis Presley," he says. "She complained the bands at the Rooster hardly played his songs."

I don't have any stories to offer, but I enjoy listening to theirs.

Jack opens bottles of beer for his cousin and him. I turn him down.

"I'm gonna tell you both somethin', but you gotta keep it a secret." He pauses for our okays. "Eleanor got off easy thanks to Andrew Snow. She didn't have to go to prison. But it drove her nuts she couldn't leave our property. But once in a while I'd take her for a ride around town late at night. I stuck to the back roads, so some nosy son of a bitch wouldn't rat us out."

Jack talks about the time he sneaked Eleanor in the back door of the Rooster on one of the nights it was closed. She walked through the kitchen, opening the fridge and turning on the stove's burners. She touched the tools she once used. He could see how much she missed working there.

"That was just before Carole started," he says. "Not that long ago. I'm happy I did it for her."

I'm touched by Jack's brotherly devotion. Eleanor did wrong, but nobody could put together the pieces of that night she killed Adela. Even Eleanor couldn't.

The stories continue. The guys drink beer. I stick with water, and by the time Fred leaves, I'm sober again. He assures us he can drive home just fine. I've decided I like him a whole lot better than I did a few months ago.

"Glad you came." Fred winks at me. "You make my cousin one happy man."

Of course, I am red-faced and red-necked, the closest I will ever get to being called that. I check on Jack, who chuckles as his cousin shuts the door behind him. He sits back in his chair. He studies me.

"He's right, you know." He pauses. "You made today a whole lot easier. Thanks for comin' like that. I did get your message by the way. I appreciated it."

"I wasn't sure how you'd take it if I just showed up. If you had kicked me out, I would've understood. I mean after what happened… "

He waves his hand.

"You don't have to finish. I take some of the blame. I should've known somethin' was up. Lookin' back, I see the signs. And I really did love Adela. I was gonna ask her to marry me."

"You know what they say: hindsight's twenty-twenty," I tell him. "Are you ready for what's gonna happen when word gets out about Eleanor? The Old Farts told me you weren't putting in her obit until after the memorial."

"The Old Farts, eh? Those guys in the backroom know everybody's goddamned business. They probably know you're here alone with me." He chuckles. "I expect to get phone calls at home and the Rooster tomorrow. Maybe a reporter will show up. Some might call you."

"I don't plan on talking with them."

"Me neither."

Jack takes a long swig from his beer bottle. I've lost count how much he drank today.

I stand.

"You leavin', too?"

"Not yet. I'm gonna clear the table and wash the dishes."

I stack the bowls and grab the silverware to bring to the sink. If there were dirty dishes before, I bet Carole washed them. I plug the drain, find the soap, and let the hot water fill the sink halfway.

Jack is on his feet and behind me. He's got his hands on my hips.

"Aw, just leave 'em, Isabel."

He turns off the water and spins me around. From the expression on his face, I know what's next. I've been in this spot before with him. We kiss, and then we do it again. My back is pressed against the edge of the sink. Jack's got his hands all over me. It's just so damn easy with him, but then I have my doubts.

"What's going on, Jack?"

"Well, earlier I was kinda hopin' to get you good and

drunk, then have sex with you."

"Uh."

"Yeah, yeah, I'm being bad. Today, I buried my sister's ashes, and here I'm flirtin' with you."

"I'd say this was more than flirting, Jack. I believe you're the one who got good and drunk."

"I guess I am. Maybe a little." He chuckles. "The God's honest truth? You drive me crazy, Isabel."

I close my eyes momentarily.

I drive him crazy? He's playing with my hair and driving me that way, too. Shoot, I miss you, Jack, but I could go to hell for this. There has to be a law somewhere you don't have sex after a family member's funeral.

"Jack."

"Yeah, Isabel?"

We keep kissing, and then he's guiding me from the kitchen into a hall toward his bedroom. We fall onto his unmade bed. There's no turning back.

Pillow Talk

Jack is stretched beside me. The guy is spent. Here was a man who wanted comfort in a big way, and I gave it to him. And, yeah, I'm feeling pretty comforted myself.

He rolls to his side after I get up to use the bathroom and return. I face him.

"How's the P.I. business?" he asks.

"Fred probably told you about the case I'm working on. Annette Waters, Marsha's cousin, wants me to find out who killed her father, Chet. Most people think it was just an accident. The story is he drank too much and died in a fire. She doesn't believe it."

"Heard those Beaumont brothers are high on the suspect list."

"How do you know? Let me guess. Fred. Or was it Marsha?"

"Both. That's why you make a good investigator. You figure things out. Marsha did tell me you two went to Baxter's and met her cousin there. Baxter's, now that's really slummin' it. All the people who get kicked out of the Rooster go there."

"Yeah, I had a chance to speak with Gary and Larry Beaumont."

"How was that?"

"All right. They gave me a hard time, but I pitched it back to them."

He chuckles.

"I can see that."

"I'm planning to meet with them again this week, but I'm gonna bring my mother. That should throw them off."

Jack's fingers play on my shoulder, and then they're sliding toward a breast.

"Heard you danced up a storm."

Aha, he's talking about Dancin' Dave. Did Marsha tell him to make Jack jealous? Thank you, Floozy, for that. This is getting interesting.

"Yeah, he asked real nicely and bought us a round. Besides, I didn't want to get rusty. I hadn't danced in a while. Dave was a pretty good dancer."

"Better than me?"

"I can't remember. It's been a while."

He playfully pinches a nipple.

"Naughty girl."

I glance over his shoulder at his alarm clock. Crap, it's almost five.

"I gotta get going. My mother must be wondering what happened to me."

"Maybe she figured it out." He's got one of those mischievous Jack grins. "Before you go, I gotta ask somethin'. Why'd you skip out the other night without sayin' bye? I went lookin' for you."

He's, of course, talking about when I left after the band started playing "Good Hearted Woman."

"You're gonna think I'm really silly. I heard that song, you know which one, and I was hoping it'd be like it was before, when you rang that bell, and we danced. Suddenly, I was disappointed that wasn't going to happen and embarrassed I felt that way. I just had to leave."

"Aw, Isabel." His voice is a drawl. "Yeah, I heard it, too, but I was in the middle of somethin' with a customer. It was easier when you and I worked together behind the bar. Then after, I couldn't find you. I asked around, but you'd disappeared."

"I guess I was confused."

He kisses me.

"Are you confused now?"

"No. But I still gotta go. We can do this again soon."

"You can count on it."

Back at Home

Ma has a curious expression on her face when I finally get home. The cat's on her lap and the dog's at her feet as she watches TV.

"That must have been some funeral dinner," she says.

"Sure was."

As I build a fire in the woodstove, I tell my mother about the ceremony and the dinner afterward, how we made toasts to Eleanor and ate venison stew. Jack and his cousin told stories. Naturally, I leave out the sexy stuff.

"They must've told a lot of stories. You were there for a real long time."

"We found other things to talk about," I say. "By the way, I brought us back some venison stew. Jack insisted."

"That was nice of him."

"I did invite him to dinner tomorrow night. I hope you don't mind. The Rooster's normally open, but he thought he'd keep it closed because Eleanor's obit will be in the morning paper. He figures nosy people would come to make a big deal about it."

"More than the nosy people in this town?"

"Uh-huh, I'm talking about the ones who do it for a living."

"Like you."

I smile. The fire picks up behind the woodstove's glass.

"That's right."

Later that night, I get three phone calls. I answer one from a number I recognize, Mike Waters. I keep a list of contacts from this case near the phone in the kitchen and my office. The other two, as the callers tell me in their messages, are from reporters. Eleanor's obit went online and some sharp-eyed person in the newsroom spotted it. One call is from the Daily Star, my old paper, and the other, a TV station in Springville. I don't feel I owe either a comment. I bet they bugged Jack, too.

I'm pleased gruff-voiced Mike Waters returned my call.

I call him back.

"Did my sister tell you to call me?" he asks.

"Yes, she did."

"She still hung up about Pop and that bullshit story of hers?"

"I'm not sure if I'd use those exact words. She's hired me to investigate your father's death. She has questions. I do, too."

He snickers.

"I bet she thinks I'd be capable of doing it. Right?"

"She says you might have some info that'd be helpful," I lie.

"That so? Like what?"

"It'd be better if we met in person."

"I'm kinda busy."

"I'd only take fifteen minutes tops."

There's silence on the other line.

"You know Baxter's?"

"Yes, I do."

"Meet me there Thursday at five. And you owe me a beer."

"Sounds good."

Ma asks who I was talking with when I get off the phone. Man, that woman missed her calling. She would have made a great reporter or a P.I. instead of working as a cafeteria lady at the junior high school in our town.

"Mike Waters, Annette's brother." I smile. "How'd you like to come with me Thursday to Baxter's to meet him? It's not such a bad place and it's beside a lake. They serve food, too."

She gestures toward the dog and cat.

"What? And miss all this excitement?"

"I knew you'd see it my way."

126

At the Greasy Spoon

Sean Mooney beats me to that greasy spoon near the Berkshire Bugle office. It's a nothing-fancy place in the heart of a dying downtown. Once this city, named Mayfield for its founder, Louis May, was a lively place of commerce due to manufacturing. Even people from Conwell commuted to work there. That ended a couple of decades ago.

Sean already found a cup of coffee and a table. I haven't seen him in a while. He's put on a bit of weight, an occupational hazard of having a mostly desk job. I recall he was an eager beaver intern although I was cautious about giving him or any intern, for that matter, a controversial assignment. Still, he showed the instincts and skills necessary for the profession. I wish I could have hired him, but at least I helped him find a job at the Bugle. In my new position as a P.I., I will take all the connections I can get.

We exchange the usual pleasantries before a waitress pounces.

"Tea with milk for me." I give Sean a nod. "You want anything else? My treat."

"No, coffee's just fine. I ate already."

I wait until the waitress is out of earshot. I'm not being paranoid. It's better to be on the safe side. For all I know, she could be a second or third cousin to Gary and Larry Beaumont.

"You weren't working for the Bugle very long when they sent you to the scene of that fire in Caulfield," I say.

"A month in but they were shorthanded that day. The regional editor said to give it a shot."

"Like I said over the phone, Chet's daughter doesn't think it was an accident. Did you have any suspicions yourself?"

127

He leans back in his chair.

"Interesting you should ask. When I was walking around, I saw blood on the snow. Not a lot mind you. It wasn't close to the burned house, so I don't think it could have been from Chet Waters' body if he died in the fire like they said he did. I think I only found it because I happened to be wandering around."

Whoa, nobody mentioned blood at the scene.

"Blood? How much?"

I recognize his gotcha smile.

"Not a lot but enough." He pulls out his phone. "I even took a picture. Wanna see?"

Is he kidding me? Of course, I do.

"That was really smart."

Sean and I wait as the waitress sets my cup of tea and a small pitcher of milk on the table. He hands me his phone.

"What'd you think? Human or animal?" he asks.

Like Sean says, there isn't a lot of blood, so it would be easy for people other than a sharp-eyed reporter to miss it, and of course, I don't know how deep. But it's blood all right. The snow around it is crushed by boot prints.

"Well, his daughter found Chet's dog dead a couple of days later in another part of the junkyard. But the dog's neck was broken. And from this photo, I don't see a long trail of blood. Maybe something happened here before the fire." I study the screen. "Did you tell anybody about it?"

"I tried, but no one paid attention. His daughter was pretty distraught. Everybody was focusing on the burned house and Chet's body. Wait a sec, I take that back. One of the town cops was interested. I think she's the chief now. But she wasn't part of the investigation."

"Nancy Dutton. Yes, she's the Caulfield Police Chief now."

"Yeah, that's the name. I showed her the photos on my phone, but by time she was able to break away, people had walked all over it. It was just a muddy mess."

"I spoke with Chief Dutton. She thought something was amiss, but that's about it. Just cop instincts. I'm guessing that's similar to reporter instincts. I think you're born with it."

128

Sean chuckles.

"Definitely."

"Can you think of anything else?" I ask.

"I tried to find my old notebooks but couldn't. They're somewhere in one of the desk drawers. Sorry. Don't know if I could read them anyways. But I'll keep looking."

I smile about the illegible handwriting. Yup, journalism ruined mine, too.

"Would you mind texting me the photo?"

"Glad to," he says, working on his phone. "Done."

"Thanks. Here's my info."

He studies my card after I hand it to him.

"What's it like being a P.I.?"

"I'm not an official one yet. I'm an associate of a guy in Jefferson. I have to do that for three years before I can earn my wings."

"I saw the wire story about that woman in your town."

"Eleanor Smith?"

"That's the one. Seems like nobody wanted to talk with the reporters who called."

"Yeah, me included. Sounds like I'm getting soft, but it was a tough case. I'm glad I solved the mystery. Too bad it was Eleanor Smith."

"That was an odd twist to that story."

It's time to change the topic. I'm tired of talking about Adela and Eleanor these days.

"How are they treating you at the Bugle?" I ask.

"Better than they did you at the Star."

I laugh.

"So you heard. It's okay. It's probably a blessing. By the way, if I solve this case, I'll give you first dibs on the story."

He smiles.

"I'd like that."

"What are you working on these days?"

We talk about the news biz for the next twenty minutes or so. He's moved up from the rookie schools beat to cops and courts. There's nothing like news that comes with a siren. He tells me about his personal life, how he's got a steady guy in his life, and I tell him a little bit about mine, mostly about the family. There really isn't that much else to talk about these days.

Sean almost makes me wish I worked for a newspaper. It's been weird stepping away from the news. But then I think about working holidays and trying to break away for a vacation. Of course, there were the internal politics with those on the ad side whining about the editorial side being unfair to their clients. The hardest part was managing people, luring them to work for low pay at the paper, turning them into solid reporters, and then watching them move onto something bigger and better after I got attached to them. Yeah, I don't miss that at all.

Stopping at Rough Waters

I head east to Caulfield, so I can show Annette the photo on my phone. It's the sort of thing I'd want to do in person. Yes, this is the long way home, but it'll also give me a view of the town from another direction.

Crap, it starts snowing as the car begins to climb in elevation, and it's small flakes, too. Ma, the weather watcher in our household, didn't warn me. Then again, maybe she thought I was coming straight home from my meeting with Sean Mooney. Or maybe this storm just sneaked in. Sometimes the weather can fool all of the experts. It happens on occasion. I just keep hitting the wipers.

When I pull into Rough Waters Junkyard, I'm relieved the dogs are in their pen although I've smartened up and brought a box of dog biscuits. It was my mother's idea, of course. I throw a couple of Milk-Bones over their fence before I head to the garage.

Once inside, I call for Annette, who slides on a dolly from beneath an El Camino, one of those half-cars, half-trucks that's totally a Mrs. Redneck vehicle. She waves a wrench.

"Hey, there, what brings you here?"

"I got something I want you to see." Annette is on her feet and wiping her hands on a rag as I work the phone. "Here you go."

Her head is down then up.

"That's blood. Where's that from?"

"Your junkyard."

"Huh?"

"I just met with the reporter who covered your father's death. When people were too busy to talk with him, he wandered around the yard and found some blood at the scene.

It's not a lot, but it sure looks like blood. You can see boot prints near it."

"Shit, why didn't I see that?"

"Sean, that's the reporter's name, said you were upset. Everybody else was too busy to pay attention to him, well except for Chief Dutton, but she was only an officer then. When she finally got around to looking, that spot was a muddy mess. Besides, by then people had made up their mind about how your father died."

Her head rocks as she agrees with me.

"You're right about that."

"Where do you think the blood came from?" I ask.

"Damned if I know."

"What's curious is that it's not near the fire. He even drew me a little map. Wanna see where it was?"

"Yeah, let's go."

Annette grabs a jacket from a hook near the door and curses when we go outside.

"Snow again? Jesus."

We go to the spot Sean marked on his map. It's between the two rows of snowbound junkers to the right toward the end facing the road. I point downward.

"I'm guessing it was here."

Annette studies the map.

"Yeah, you're right. I can't believe I missed it."

"Everybody but Sean did." I nod. "If my mother were here, she would offer two theories. One would be the blood belonged to your father before he went inside his house, or it came from somebody else. Maybe your father's dog attacked whoever was in the junkyard and drew blood. You did find the dog dead later." I pause. "At this point it's a mystery. But something violent happened in this spot. I'm sure of it."

Annette nods.

"Me, too."

The snow keeps up, but I decide to visit the Pit Stop on the way home. I don't need gas. I filled the tank in Mayfield, where it's cheaper, but I could find something to buy here among the cans of chewing tobacco and beer. When I was a reporter, I called it checking the traps. I kept tabs on what was happening in the hilltowns I was covering by calling or visiting people like shopkeepers, school secretaries, and certain town officials to see if they had heard about anything newsworthy. I got some good stories that way. When I became an editor, I told my reporters to do the same. I also reminded them that checking the traps has another meaning. Make sure somebody isn't feeding you fake shit to throw you off.

But back to the first meaning, the Pit Stop would qualify as a trap worth checking. Barbie is alone today. She's got her back to the door as she works behind the counter, but she does a quick flip around when she hears the bell.

"Howdy," she says brightly. "Isabel, right?"

I respond in kind, but I'm trying not to be obvious that I see she's got a shiner. It looks a couple of days old because the colors around her right eye have melted a bit. But she notices I've noticed. I'm certain I can't be the only one.

"You okay?" I ask.

She squeezes a giggle.

"Oh, this?" She points to her shiner. "I was trying to get something off a closet shelf and the whole thing came down on my head. Hurt like a you-know-what, but I'm okay. I put ice on it right away."

"Yeah, that helps."

Her story sounds suspicious. Did hubby, Pete, knock her around? I recall what Annette said about him. Yeah, I bet he did.

"Hon, what are you doing out in this snow?" she asks.

"I had some business in Mayfield, and then I met with Annette. I needed to show her something."

Barbie plays with her pretty necklace. Frankly, it's the only pretty thing about her. The rest of her is flannel and denim.

"How's your case going?"

I smile.

"Not bad. I've been talking with people, and today I got a solid lead."

"A lead? What's that?"

"That's like a big clue."

"What is it?"

"Sorry. I can only share things like that with Annette. It's confidential."

She nods as she absorbs what I'm telling her. It's my intention to let the people who come in here, which is likely most of the town and some from the ones around it, understand I'm taking this investigation seriously.

"Confidential," she repeats.

"Where's Pete?"

"Oh, he had to run a few errands in the city. Somethin' I can help you with?"

Bingo. Yes, Barbie, there is.

"Tell me. You knew Chet Waters pretty well since he was a regular here at the store. What was he like?"

Barbie slides her pendant back and forth.

"Oh, a lot of people didn't like Chet. He could be kinda grumpy. But he was really, really nice to me. He came by every morning for coffee and one of my muffins. I always tried to save him one if we were runnin' low." She nods as if she's agreeing with herself. "Chet was a real talker. You name it. He had somethin' to say about it."

"When's the last time you saw Chet?"

She scrunches her lips.

"The day before he died. He came in that mornin' as usual."

"You said he was a real talker. What did he talk about that day?"

She glances at the window.

"Not much. Small stuff like the weather."

"Do you remember what kind of a mood he was?"

She thinks.

"I'd say friendly enough," she says. "I'm sorry I'm not being more helpful. Pete could probably tell you more."

Uh, no, he didn't.

"Can you think of anything else?"

She bites her lip.

"I was real sorry when I heard what happened to Chet," she says. "He didn't deserve to die like that."

"No one does."

I feel my conversation with Barbie has neared its conclusion not long after it started. My problem now is to find something worth buying in this store. I settle on water.

Barbie takes my money.

"Have a safe trip back, hon," she says.

"Sure. Keep the change."

Our Dinner Guest

Jack makes a nervous twitter of a hello when I answer the door. He's happy to be invited, he told me so, but he's a little apprehensive about my mother. He shouldn't feel that way. Ma is one of his biggest fans. She's been rooting for us to get back together. I understand though. I'm feeling a little shy myself. Actually, it's like I'm in high school, and I'm bringing my new boyfriend over to eat, although the God's honest truth, I was a social outcast then and never had one until I went to college. Jack isn't spending the night, not because of my mother, but because he can't exactly leave his sister's mutts either inside or outside for that long.

"Sorry, Isabel," he told me yesterday. "I gotta figure out somethin' to do with those dogs when I'm not around."

I patted his cheek.

"You'll make it up to me, I'm sure," I said, which got him grinning like a lunatic.

I kiss him at the door, which is easy because Ma is in the kitchen working on the mashed potatoes that will go with her roasted chicken. He brings a bottle of red wine that's better than the stuff he serves at the Rooster. Behind him, the snow comes down still, adding a fresh, white layer to the stuff still frozen on the ground.

"How much are we supposed to get?" I ask as I take his coat.

"Last I heard, a dustin'. Those are the ones you gotta watch out for." He makes an appreciative hum. "It sure smells good in here."

"Well, my mother doesn't want you to starve."

He pats his gut beneath his red wool shirt.

"No danger of that."

136

I let him open the bottle of wine after he greets my mother and compliments the spread on the table.

My mother wipes her hands with a dishtowel.

"I was sorry to hear about your sister," she tells Jack. "I know you two were close."

Jack's head bobs.

"Thanks, ma'am," he says. "Appreciate it."

As we eat dinner, Jack asks my mother a bunch of questions about her life before she moved to the sticks, as she calls it here. Ma talks easily about living beside the ocean and about my father, who was a real character. Everybody in my hometown knew my Dad. I believe the stories relax Jack a bit.

I try not to laugh out loud when I hear her say, "What's it like growing up in the middle of nowhere?"

Naturally, the conversation swings to the investigation.

"Did you know Chet Waters well?" I ask him.

He holds his fork mid-air.

"That old coot? He was a classic."

I glance toward Ma.

"I heard from a couple of people he cheated at cards," I say. "You ever play with him?"

He snorts.

"Only once. That was enough. I learned my lesson. Too bad others didn't." He frowns. "Chet had the quickest fingers I've ever seen. He should've gone to Vegas and made big money. But he preferred livin' in the country and fleecin' the locals. Chet came to the Rooster when I used to have poker night on Wednesdays. There wasn't supposed to be any money involved, but I let it slide. He was a regular."

"Why did you stop card nights?"

"It was obvious Chet was more than a lucky card player. Course, sometimes he'd lose just to throw people off. But he made a bit of money." He chuckles. "One night, things got really ugly when he cleaned out a couple of kids. I swear they were gonna lose it. One of them even had a gun."

"Was their last name Sinclair? Junior and Roy, right?"

"Hey, how'd you know?"

I smile.

"I heard about it when Ma and I interviewed their father."

"I forget who I'm talkin' with sometimes," Jack says. "Anyways, Chet wouldn't give 'em back their money. I believe one of them even put up his grandfather's gold watch. I don't think he ever got it back. One of the boys, Junior, ran out to his truck for a gun."

Ma leans forward. She's been hanging on every word coming from Jack.

"Did you call the cops?" she asks.

"Nah, if I did that, it would've taken them an hour to arrive. Besides, I didn't want the cops to shut down the place for illegal gamblin'. I asked the Sinclair kid to put his gun away. He listened to reason. Chet slipped out. I gave the boys some money out of the cash drawer cause I felt a little responsible. That was the end of card nights. I heard the incident didn't sit right with their father."

Al didn't mention anything about a gun, but maybe he didn't have the whole story. Besides, a bullet didn't kill Chet. The medical examiner would have figured that out.

"Did Chet still come to the Rooster?"

"Oh, yeah, the guy had no shame. He liked to drink a bit. Besides, he used to be good pals with my Pop."

"What about the Sinclair brothers?"

"Junior and Roy? They still do. Next time they show up, I'll point them out. You'll recognize 'em."

I pour Jack and myself more wine. Ma waves her hand. She only drinks a tad. If Jack and his cousin think I'm a lightweight, my mother is a featherweight.

"Did they ever have a run-in with Chet after that cheating incident?"

"Sure, they had words. I kept an eye on them and never let it get too far."

"What about just before Chet died?"

"Gosh, that was three years ago, wasn't it?" He thinks for a moment. "Come to think of it, they did. It had somethin' to do with business. I recall my cousin callin' it junkyard wars. It got pretty hot and heavy. I told the boys they had to calm down or I'd have to ban them for six months. They left a while later, but I don't think they ever calmed down."

I glance toward my mother.

"Looks like we've got another set of brothers to visit."

"I hope they're not as scary as the other ones," she says.

"You talkin' about the Beaumonts?"

"Uh-huh, Ma's my secret weapon."

Jack looks at my mother.

"You don't mind her using you like that?"

Ma laughs.

"It's better than being cooped up inside."

I mutter "oh, brother" under my breath.

"They call that cabin fever in these parts," Jack tells her.

"Cabin fever?"

"Uh-huh, it can drive people nuts."

Ma makes a motherly chortle.

"Oh, I'm not planning to do anything like that."

I believe Jack's hesitancy about spending time with my mother is now long gone. The two of them are yakking it up. He's telling her stories about the mid-winter breakups and hookups he's witnessed at the Rooster, where else, and Ma, a big romance novel reader, is enjoying herself.

Finally, there's a break in the conversation. I jump in before Jack and my mother find another topic.

"Uh, what can you tell us about the Beaumonts?" I ask Jack.

Jack makes a sound deep in the back of his throat.

"I never liked them comin' to the Rooster, but I put up with it. I even warned them once about dealin' drugs or even doin' drugs. To the best of my knowledge, they were on good behavior for a couple of years. I still didn't like them though." He takes a sip of wine. "Then I got word they were doing business outside. The last thing I need is to have the cops come or to lose my business. I didn't even put them on the six-month list. They were out for good."

"How did they take it?"

"Not well. I waited for the next time they showed up. I had them step outside and told them what's what. At first, they denied the whole thing, the little liars, but they wised up after I said I wanted to leave the cops out of it. Besides, I had Fred back me up."

"I'm liking your cousin more and more."

"I hope not too much," he says with a chuckle.

"You don't have to worry about that," I say. "Did the Beaumonts ever come back?"

"Nah, they knew better. Besides, the guy who owns Baxter's doesn't seem to mind what goes on in his parking lot. I hear the brothers do a good home business, too."

I glance at Ma.

"You sure you wanna come?"

She smiles.

"Now more than ever."

The three of us finish eating. Ma went all out and even made dessert, pumpkin pie. What did I say about her being a big fan of Jack?

I start collecting dirty dishes.

"We have a rule in our home," I say to Jack. "Whoever cooks doesn't have to do the dishes. It looks like it's my turn tonight."

My mother's mouth drops open.

"What do you mean it's your turn?" she says. "You do the dishes every night."

I tip my head toward Jack.

"Shh, I was trying to trick him into helping me."

Now Jack's laughing.

"I'd be glad to help you, Isabel." He stands. "Just hand me an apron, and we'll get to it."

We excuse Ma and indeed get to it. I find a country station on the radio while we clear the table. I load the washer and put the food away. Jack scrubs the pots. Nah, he was only kidding about the apron.

I give him a playful hip check.

"You're doing a real good job there."

"Yup, I've scrubbed a few pots in my life."

It's all teasing and playful talk between us. Lots of giggling on my part. As I wipe the pots dry, I can't stop my silly smile. Boy, I sure missed this.

140

"Isabel, I was wonderin' if you'd like to come back to work one night. Fridays. The crowds are too big for me to handle alone. Carole's got enough to do in the kitchen."

I dry my hands and toss Jack the towel. I don't have to think this over.

"I'll come back but only under one condition," I say.

"Condition? What is it?"

"Don't look so nervous. I'm not asking for a raise. I want you to promise we'll dance one song that night."

Jack makes a fun-loving guffaw as he slaps my behind with the towel.

"It's a deal."

Baxter's Again

It's five o'clock at Baxter's. While I look for Mike Waters, my mother checks out the place. This is the second genuine bar she's been inside ever, and the first was the Rooster. The place has that yeasty smell of beer and a whiff of smoke, tobacco and pot, when the door onto the deck opens. Drinkers, all male, sit on the stools at the bar. They're a matched set with wallets bulging the back pockets of their jeans, plus the usual flannel, canvas, and denim ensemble. They give us a backward glance, but they are definitely not interested. We're too damn old for them.

Ma clutches her purse.

"This is another interesting place you've brought me to, Isabel."

"And just for Valentine's Day."

"Valentine's Day. I forgot about that."

"Me, too. I just saw the sign behind the bar." I lower my voice. "See that guy in the corner table, the one wearing the blue shirt. I think that's him."

"Oh, my, he looks mad at the world."

"Good description. I see the family resemblance."

Mike Waters sets down his beer when we reach his table. I hold out my hand. He gives it an uneasy grab.

"Mike? I'm Isabel Long. This is my mother, Maria Ferreira."

He snorts.

"You need a bodyguard or something'?"

"Ha. My mother is my partner on these cases." I pull out a chair for Ma to sit, and then take one beside Mike. "Thanks for meeting with us today. Let me get us a round." I turn toward my mother. "The usual?"

142

The waitress hustles right over to take our order: another Bud for Mike, a Bud Light for me since I'm driving, and a Diet Coke for Ma.

Chet Waters may have been a son of a bitch, but this guy's a son of a son of a bitch. That's my first impression of the man. I bet the same goes for Ma. He's got a scowl permanently plastered to his face. His hair has thinned to a few strands on top but hangs thick and long around the bottom. From the photos I've seen, he unfortunately got his father's looks.

"What the hell did you wanna ask me you couldn't say over the phone?" Mike growls.

"As I explained, I'm investigating your father's death. I live in Conwell and didn't know him. Anything you could tell me about him would help."

"My sister put you up to this?"

"Annette? She gave me a list of possible sources," I lie. "Your name was on it."

"Did she tell you I wanted nothin' to do with that asshole?" he says without an ounce of regret that he uses the word in front of my mother.

The waitress sets down our drinks. I glance toward Ma. We rehearsed this line of questioning on the ride over from Conwell.

"Annette said you had a difficult childhood."

"Difficult childhood?" He slams the empty to the tabletop, and then reaches for the fresh can of beer. "Those her words or yours?"

"Mine. She said your father was real hard on you and your brother."

"Yeah, he was real hard on us all right. He liked to beat the shit outta me. I could never do nothin' right for that bastard. Same goes for my brother." He glances toward my mother. "When I was old enough to make it on my own, I split. Ma was okay to me, but she couldn't do much to stop him."

"Was it the same for your sister?"

He makes a loud snort of a laugh.

"She was his little princess." He shakes a finger. "I'll give

143

him this though. A year before Pop died, he met up with me. He said he was real sorry for the way he treated me. I almost crapped my pants. He said that's the way his Pop raised him. It was the only way he knew how to raise a boy. He saw it was wrong."

"You believe him?"

I swear the man is tearing up.

"Yeah, I did. It doesn't take away what he did to me and Chester. But I understood him a little better. I remember his father. We kids were scared shitless of him."

"Did he talk with your brother?"

"Yeah, I heard he did. Dunno what got him goin' on that."

"Did you and your father get together after that?"

"Sometimes. Nothing like Christmas or his birthday. We'd meet up at Baxter's for a couple of drinks, or I'd go over to the yard just to shoot the shit." He lowers his voice. "I am sorry he went that way in a fire."

As I listen to Mike, I wonder why the other brother, Chester Junior, isn't on her list. I decide he's at least worth a phone call, and if he's working at a school nearby, maybe a visit.

"Annette thinks someone could've killed your father."

"I heard that."

"You don't believe it?"

He shrugs.

"Anything's possible."

"When we talked over the phone, you thought it was a bullshit story. What changed your mind?"

Mike sucks snot up his nose.

"My old man sure pissed off enough people in his lifetime. Maybe he crossed the wrong person. But it wasn't me."

"Where were you that night?"

"Stuck in a fuckin' huge snowstorm in a Pennsylvania truck stop. I was workin' for a moving company then. They closed down the interstate. If you don't believe me, you can call my old boss, Luke, at Big Movers in Mayfield. We parted on good terms."

I nod. I can call Big Movers and check online to see if

144

there was indeed a fuckin' huge snowstorm in Pennsylvania then.

"You're the only one other than your sister so far to say it might be possible somebody killed your father. Do you have any suspects?"

"Probably the same as her. The Beaumonts. You meet 'em yet?"

"Yes, I have. I'm going to their house tomorrow."

"You've got brass balls, lady."

"I've heard that before," I say. "Besides, my mother is coming as my bodyguard."

Mike downs the rest of his beer and belches.

"Thanks for the beer," he says, and then he's gone.

Ma and I watch him stroll to the bar.

"What's your opinion?"

"That was an awfully sad story Mike told about his father. He seems to have an alibi you can check, so it wasn't a total waste. It's down to a process of elimination." My mother reaches for the menu. "Besides, I'm hungry. Could you get the waitress?"

"Sure, but I'm paying this time."

"You pay all the time."

"You can do the next one."

"That's what you always say."

The waitress recommends the lasagna, which we both order even though it's loaded with meat. Everything else on the menu has meat. At least, the lasagna comes with a house salad.

"When are we going to meet those boys tomorrow?"

"Around one. I think that's when they get up." I giggle. "Just kidding. The older one, Gary, said over the phone they'll be waiting for us. I took down the directions. It'll be easy to find them."

"Did you tell them I'm coming?"

"Nah, we'll just throw them off guard."

"Who's that guy over there that keeps giving you the eye?" Ma asks.

"Me?"

145

"Yeah, you."

I casually turn in that direction. Dancin' Dave is indeed giving me the eye, and now that I've made an ever-so-slight contact, he's up and heading our way.

"That's the guy who asked me to dance here the other night."

Ma smirks.

"Another gentleman caller, I see."

"Shh, here he comes." I glance up. "Hey, Dave, I didn't expect to see you here today."

"I'd say the same. Who's your dining companion?"

I make the intros, and then Dave sits. He tells my mother what a great dancer I am.

"So I've heard," Ma says.

"You coming this Saturday?" he asks me.

"I wasn't planning on it," I answer.

Ma nods.

"She's back working at the Rooster on Fridays."

If my mother weren't ninety-two, I would've kicked her leg.

"The Rooster? I haven't been in there in a long time. Now I have a reason to go."

Dave gets to his feet when our food arrives. He's got good country manners, I'll give him that. And then when he's on the other side of the room, I ask my mother, "Why'd you tell him that?"

She chuckles as she cuts her lasagna.

"It wouldn't hurt none for Jack to have a little competition."

"Ma!"

A Check from Lin

The next day, Friday, I find a check and a note from Lin Pierce in the mailbox when I take the dog, Maggie, for a walk.

Here's what he wrote.

Isabel, enclosed is a check for your "dirty work" the other day. You helped nail that guy. I've included your regular pay. Give me a call soon about your case in Caulfield. I'd like to hear about your progress. Lin

Lin dutifully pays me a buck a day. He even includes the weekend, which is generous. He pays me a hundred bucks for that surveillance job.

I cluck to Maggie.

"Maybe it's time I bought me some new dancing shoes," I tell her.

The Beaumont Boys

The Beaumont brothers live in one shit box of a house. It probably was a decent ranch maybe in the fifties or sixties, but it has to have been years since it had a new coat of paint, if ever. The roof is shot. I bet the snow covers a pile of junk in the front yard. I can only imagine what it looks like inside. Well, I'm about to find out all by myself. Ma backed out last minute. She woke up with a cold, and frankly, I'm relieved. She is my secret weapon, but one I want to use judicially. Exposing her to two redneck brothers who are up to no good most of the time might just be too much to expect of an elderly mother, even one as spunky as mine.

Instead, I promised her a full report.

As to be expected, Gary and Larry have brand new, juiced-up pickup trucks in the drive. I pull my Subaru behind one, and then navigate the narrow space between a pickup and a blackened bank of snow. I'm grateful no dogs race out to meet me although I hear a couple barking in the backyard. They're likely chained or penned although I do have some security dog bones in my pocket in case they aren't.

I ring the doorbell on what appears to be the kitchen side of the ranch. Minutes later, Gary answers. He makes a goofball laugh when he recognizes me. He's stoned already, but then it is afternoon.

"Just in time," he jokes. "Come in. Larry's in the toilet. He'll be right out."

The kitchen is a pigsty. I'm not surprised. Dirty dishes are stacked in the sink and counter. The Linoleum floor doesn't look like it's ever been washed. The same goes for the appliances. Funky wallpaper, likely from when this ranch was built, is peeling from the wall. The air smells like bacon grease

148

and pot smoke.

I follow Gary's lead and sit at the Formica table, which holds an ashtray the size of a hubcap that's filled with butts and roaches.

"Thanks for seeing me," I say.

I already decided I would not record this conversation. I'm not going to take notes either. I figure it would spook these two guys. I plan instead to record everything I remember as I'm driving home.

Gary's got a shit-eating grin on his face as he reaches for his pack of cigarettes. He doesn't ask if I mind, so much for good country manners. I don't like smoking, but this is his home, and I want him to relax. I believe I can stand it for a while.

"I'm kinda curious," he says as he lights the butt. "You asked us about a Corolla at Chet's junkyard. What's that all about?"

"I'm gonna be upfront with you. Anything you tell me about your, er, business activity will not be shared with anyone, including the cops. My goal is to solve this case. Nothing more. I'm not a stool pigeon."

His eyes close halfway as he exhales the first puff.

"Good to know. Appreciate it."

"Likewise, I'm asking that you and your brother not repeat what we talk about to others. This conversation is between you two and me."

"Gotcha."

Larry Beaumont walks into the kitchen, stinking like he's just had a smelly dump and didn't wipe himself well. I won't be shaking his hand. Mercifully, he sits next to his brother on the other side. Even Gary wrinkles his nose and mutters something beneath his breath.

Gary gives his brother a Reader's Digest version of what we just went over.

"Okay," he says.

I begin now that I have both brothers' attention.

"You mentioned the Corolla. A few weeks before Chet was killed, he found some drugs and money stashed in the spare

149

tire in the trunk. Annette says when she looked a month or so after the fire, the stuff was gone."

Gary and Larry eye each other.

"You straight about not callin' the cops?" Gary says.

"I give you my word."

He taps his butt on the edge of the ashtray.

"Yeah, it was ours."

Crap, I wasn't expecting a confession like this.

"Go ahead. Please tell me more."

Gary waves his lit cigarette.

"The stupid guy from Springville delivered the Corolla to the wrong junkyard. It was supposed to go to Sinclair's. We had a sort of business arrangement there."

"With Al?"

"Nah, his boys. Well, that business arrangement ended when old man Sinclair found out. Lucky he didn't call the cops on us, but then again we'd have taken his boys down with us. He knew that." He makes a low chuckle. "Me and Larry went to Rough Waters to search for the Corolla. We told Chet we were lookin' for a truck to fix up for pullin'. A winter project. He let us look around. While I talked with Chet, Larry here scoped the place out and found the car. Then we got into a fight with Chet about somethin' stupid and he kicked us out."

"Did you come back for the stuff?"

"Yeah, we went one night when we knew Chet'd be gone. It was card night at the VFW in Fulton. The old guy liked to screw those vets outta their money." He smirks. "Larry climbed the fence, and I was the lookout."

"What about his dog?"

Gary chuckles.

"It's amazin' how easy a piece of raw meat will buy off a dog, especially if it has a little somethin' extra in it, if you know what I mean." He stabs his butt into the ashtray. "Larry found our stuff, and we got the hell outta there. It was a couple of nights before the fire."

"Here's my next question. Where were you two the night Chet Waters died?" I ask.

Gary snorts.

"How in the hell should we know? For us, it was just a regular night. We were likely home watchin' dirty movies and smokin' weed. Or we could've been at Baxter's. Or gettin' laid with a couple of the skanks that hang out there."

I roll my eyes.

Larry speaks for the first time.

"Would you remember what you were doin' three years ago?"

"You've got a point. But it's not every day someone dies in a fire up here. Something's gotta jog your memory."

"Nope," Gary says.

Larry purses his lips as his head jerks side to side.

"If I'm hearing correctly, you two don't have alibis for that night," I say. "Right?"

I believe I just stepped into it big time because Gary and Larry's foreheads clamp so hard their brows hang heavy over their bloodshot eyes. Their lips curl.

Larry slaps his brother's arm.

"What's she mean?" he asks.

"It means she's callin' us liars," Gary answers.

I speak up.

"I didn't call you liars." I try to make my voice as warm as I can muster given how nervous I am. "What I said is that you can't account for your whereabouts the night Chet Waters was killed."

Gary's fist hits the table.

"You bitch, what makes you think we'd have anythin' to do with that?"

My heart pounds. I must be nuts confronting them like this. I can think of a few moments when I was a reporter that I got myself into a foolish situation but never a dangerous one. People warned me, but I clearly underestimated these two. I feel like I've just approached two rabid dogs.

"Hear me out, please, while I lay out the facts. A valuable shipment ends up at Chet's junkyard. He finds out about it and shows it to his daughter. Maybe he figures out who it belongs to before the night of the fire. Maybe you didn't break into the place a few days before the fire but that night. Do you get

151

where I'm going with this?"

The two brothers give me death-ray stares. My heart continues to pump hard.

"If you can recall where you were that night and who you were with, it'd be easy to eliminate you. I'd just look somewhere else. Other people I questioned have told me exactly what they were doing."

Gary's lip is glued in a sneer.

"I can see it was a big mistake talkin' with ya. Now you're gonna blab your mouth about us."

I raise my hands with the palms facing out.

"Nope, I promise."

"Sure. A big, fuckin' mistake."

The mood in the room has slipped fast and deep to the ugly side. Gary and Larry mutter beneath their breath to each other. I bet they have guns in their house. This is great, Isabel. Annette is only paying you with free maintenance on your vehicles until you die, which could be any minute now. And you thought journalism paid poorly. Think fast.

"I should inform you that my boyfriend, Jack Smith, knows I'm here. I believe there's no love lost between you and him." I pause. "I'm supposed to call him at two o'clock. If he doesn't hear from me, he's sending the state cops here. I told him it wasn't necessary, but he doesn't trust you guys one bit."

Gary pounds the tabletop with his fist.

"Get the hell outta here," he yells. "And if I hear one word about us comin' from the likes of you, we're gonna find you. I know you live in Conwell. It'd be easy."

I raise my chin. I focus my eyes on them.

"Gary, Larry," I say in the most confidant voice I can muster. "If you do recall anything more, especially about the night, you have my number."

"Fuck you, bitch," Gary says.

Inside the car, I take a deep breath and let it out. The part about Jack was a big, fat lie, but frankly after that confrontation, I wish I had thought of it before I came here. But the bluff works, and I'm sure they'll never call Jack to confirm it. As I back the car out of the driveway, I decide unless Gary and Larry can come up with alibis, they remain high on the list of suspects.

I drive about a mile down the road, checking the rearview mirror to see if they follow me. No, that's not happening, so I stop the car. I dig in my purse for my phone, set up the recording app, and as I pull away, I begin.

"Today I interviewed Gary and Larry Beaumont about Chet Waters. I'm relieved to say I got outta there alive."

Reporting for Duty

I show up for work twenty minutes early to get myself situated with the new cook, Carole, and her routine. Jack's head swings up from the cash register, where he's loading bills into the drawer.

Wiseass that I am, I salute and joke, "Isabel Long reporting for duty."

He reaches beneath the counter and tosses me an apron.

"Here's your uniform," he says with that happy-to-see-you grin of his. "How are you, Isabel? Keepin' out of trouble?"

"I had a close call today."

"With the Beaumonts? You okay?" He tips his head toward the kitchen and mouths that Carole is a second cousin to the brothers. "Tell me all about it later."

I nod.

"Who's playing tonight?" I ask.

"The Lone Sums."

"I thought they stunk up the place the last time they played."

"One of the guys told me they're a lot better. They've been practicin' and playin' a whole lot more."

"I'll believe it when I hear it."

"Me, too."

I go over Carole's expectations. I know her from the Rooster and from casual run-ins at the general store, and when I was a reporter, at such events as truck pulls and the annual pig roast at the Conwell Rod and Gun Club. She's country through and through with high hair, which she tames beneath a hairnet for the kitchen work, and a hard expression on her face. But she's got a quick smile, and once I get her going, a

154

pleasant laugh. She used to be my kids' bus driver. I recall she held command on the bus without being a you-know-what about it.

"Just write your order so I can read it. I'll ring the bell when the food is ready. You can set the dirty dishes on the counter next to the sink. If you can, scrape the plates into that bucket on the floor, but I'll understand if you're too busy."

The system doesn't appear too different from when Eleanor was here, except Carole actually speaks and doesn't grunt or shoot me daggers with her eyes. And she didn't kill anybody or try to do me in.

"Good to know."

"We've got some new stuff on the menu. Check it out."

The True Blue Regulars start showing up as soon as the Rooster opens. As expected, they comment about my return.

"It's about time Jack smartened up," one of the True Blues says loud enough for him to hear.

Jack gives me a wink.

Things get busy fast. Jack waits on tables. I man the cooler and tap. We take turns making the sweep for dirty dishes and empties. Of course, people offer their condolences about Eleanor to Jack, who accepts their kindness with fond comments about his sister. Of course, they all know his sister was a killer, but it's more for Jack's sake than any love for Eleanor. It's just good country manners all around.

During a break in the action, Jack offers me a bit of news, "Fred's movin' in."

"With you?"

"Nah, on Eleanor's side as soon as I can clear her stuff outta there," he says.

"Need any help?"

"I'd appreciate it. There's an awful lot of stuff, and I'm not sure what to keep or give away." His eyebrows make a playful rise. "There might be somethin' in it for ya."

"I don't think your sister and I take the same size," I say, and then I give him a playful pinch on the cheek. "Gotcha."

"Yeah, you did for a second."

The side door opens, sending a cold wind through the

155

Rooster as the Lone Sums haul equipment through the door. Damn, this winter's hanging tough.

Jack's cousin, Fred, walks in between the musicians and right to the bar.

"I let those mutts out like you asked," he says. "Where's my pay?"

"Comin' right up," Jack says as he opens a Bud and pours Fred a shot of some rotgut whiskey.

"And I thought I worked cheap," I say.

But Fred is happy for the free booze. He glances around to appraise the crowd and search for women who might be interested. He makes a beeline for a table near the dance floor for some floozies in training.

Speaking of floozies, Marsha shouts my name as she approaches the bar with Annette aka the Tough Cookie.

"How ya been?" the Floozy asks.

It appears Marsha and Annette have already imbibed. They're joking and slapping each other's arms. They're waving and chatting up anybody who comes close.

Annette leans in.

"How'd it go? You know… " She raises her eyebrows, expecting I will fill in the blank.

I lower my voice so only she can hear me.

"Awfully scary there for a moment. But I found out some interesting stuff. And, yeah, they don't have alibis."

Annette slaps the bar top.

"Those little bastards," she said.

I glance around to make sure Carole the cook is out of earshot.

"Yeah, but that's not proof enough. I'll talk with you later," I say, and then in my best bartender's voice I ask, "What can I get you two ladies?"

They both make snorting laughs.

"Ladies, eh?" Marsha says. "Make it the usual."

I reach inside the cooler for two Buds when I notice Dancin' Dave enter the side door. He appears to know most everybody because there are howdies and handshakes all around. Then he makes a beeline for the bar, and just my luck, there's an empty stool.

"Hey, Jack, nice place you've got," he says, and then he raises a finger. "Ma'am, could I trouble you for a Bud?"

"One Bud coming up," I say.

Jack goes over to shake Dave's hand. It's the usual small talk and chuckles between guys.

"Hey, Dave, what brings you here tonight?" Jack asks.

"Why, I was hopin' to see Isabel. She told me she works here Friday nights," Dave says.

Jack purses his lips as he nods. He hums.

"She sure does."

I try not to laugh as I place Dave's bottle of Bud in front of him.

"Here you go. We don't mind glass bottles here at the Rooster."

Dave chuckles.

"Thank you, ma'am. I heard Jack likes to keep his clientele in line."

Jack speaks for me.

"Sure do," he says.

The band takes a break, and I'm grateful for the rush in orders for beer. I haven't a chance to talk with Dancin' Dave, who is big into staring, or Jack, who brings those empties back faster than I recall. He doesn't make much chitchat at the tables. He's all business tonight.

On one of his runs, he says, "Isabel, did I tell you I like your hair that way? It looks pretty up like that."

Uh, no.

I'm about to answer one of Dave's questions, when Jack clangs that cowbell and announces the bar is closed for the next song. I had lost track of Jack for a few minutes, but now I'm supposing he went to the Lone Sums to make a request because he's got a shit-eating grin when the band plays the opening chords to "Good Hearted Woman." He holds out his hand.

"Isabel? Here you go."

I giggle, yes, giggle, as he grabs my hand. He leads me onto the floor. It's been a while, but I catch onto his moves

157

fast. He's smiling. I'm smiling. Yeah, Jack's back.

But about halfway through the song, Dancin' Dave comes beside Jack and taps his shoulder.

"I'd like to cut in, if you don't mind, buddy," he says.

Jack, who's been intent on twirling me around the floor, stares at the man as if he doesn't believe what he's hearing. His face is blank, but then, being the country gentleman he is, he grins and nods as he passes my hand to Dancin' Dave. He steps back a few feet out of the way of the other dancers as Dave gets me going. It takes me a few moves to catch onto his style, which is a bit more aggressive than Jack's. I try not to smile too hard, for Jack's sake, and I follow every step, for Dave's. I aim to have a good time, but not too good a time, if you get what I mean. This is a bit awkward, but what choice do I have?

And just when I think things will roll along with Dancin' Dave, Jack steps forward and taps the man's shoulder.

"Okay, I'll have her back," he says.

Dancin' Dave tips his head and hands me off just in time for the end of the song. As we walk back to the bar, people stare. I smile at Dave and say, "Thanks for the spin," before Jack cranks up the cowbell and yells the bar is back open. Dave returns to his stool. He shakes what's left in his bottle of beer.

"Ma'am, I'll have another and a shot of tequila. Make it top shelf please."

Behind me, Jack says, "I'll get it, Isabel. Why don't you shag empties? Watch out for Joe though. It looks like he's losing control of his feet on the dance floor."

I smile at his joke.

"Sure enough, boss."

I wander through the Rooster picking up empties and gabbing with the drinkers. Of course, I know most of them since most of them live here in Conwell, but there are outsiders, too, who by their gear came here by snowmobile, including I discover at my next table, Pete and Barbie Woodrell.

"Didn't know you worked here at the Rooster," Pete greets

me.

"Just Fridays. Jack gets swamped when there's a band." I eye their drinks. Pete's drinking something hard. Barbie's got something pink. I remember the order Jack gave me: cranberry and vodka. "Looks like you're still working on those."

Behind me, the band strikes up something lively by Buddy Holly. This is the first time I can remember any band's played "That'll Be the Day" at the Rooster. The Lone Sums and the dancers are getting into this old rockabilly tune when a guy bumps me from behind. After a quick apology, one of the True Blue Regulars leans across the table and asks Barbie to dance.

Barbie checks in with her stone-faced hubby.

"No, no, I can't," she says.

"Sure, you can. You don't mind, Pete, do ya?"

The True Blue Regular doesn't wait for Pete's response. He takes Barbie's hand and pulls her onto the dance floor.

But from the way Pete's mouth is set, I believe he does mind. His brow forms a hard ridge. Barbie makes a tinkling little laugh as she dances. I think about Annette calling Pete a dick and about Barbie's black eye, now almost gone. I shake my head before I move on. I've got empties to clear.

The tray is half full when I come to Marsha and Annette's table. Bobby Collins, Marsha's beau, and another guy I don't know sit beside them. Marsha grabs my arm. She makes a full-bodied laugh.

"That was some show on the dance floor, Isabel." The Floozy doesn't hold back on the volume. "Two guys fightin' over you like that."

"You're making that up," I say. "Hey, Bobby, how've you been?"

But Marsha isn't going to let Bobby talk. She's over full with mischief.

"You're shittin' me, Isabel. Dave Baxter came all this way to another guy's bar? He can drink for free at his own. He wanted to see ya."

I set the tray on the table. Whoa, what did the Floozy just say?

"Dave owns Baxter's? That biker bar?"

"I thought you knew that," Marsha says.

"No, I didn't have a clue." I glance back toward the bar where Jack and Dancin' Dave are talking. I reach for the empties on their table. "I'll take these for you."

Annette laughs. She slaps the arm of lover boy beside her. These gals like grabbing and slapping people.

"Isabel, you crack me up." Her head tips back. "You ready to bring your Subaru in for that oil change? I noticed it's gettin' close the last time you were at my place."

"How'd you know?"

"I saw the sticker on your windshield, and then I checked the mileage. I'm no charity case." Her head swivels around. "Besides, we need to talk. Come around noon tomorrow." She gives the guy she's with a shove. "I need my beauty sleep."

"Sure enough."

I return to the bar with the tray of empties, but Dancin' Dave is gone. I think about teasing Jack that he scared him off. He's making change for a customer although I catch him peeking at me out of the corner of his eye.

I reach for the empty and shot glass from Dave's spot. Beneath the bottle, he left a folded five-dollar bill, which is an excessively large tip for the Rooster. A torn piece of a matchbook tucked inside the bill falls onto the counter. The handwriting says: **Call me soon. Chet Waters.** There's a phone number.

Shoot, I casually stuff the paper in the front pocket of my jeans as I throw the five into the tip jar behind the bar.

"That's a mighty generous tip," Jack says. "You must've given him great service."

I study Jack's face to test his mood. I never thought he would be the jealous type, but I guess I'm wrong.

"No more than any other customer. Guess he's just a generous guy." I slide over beside Jack and give him a playful hip-bump. "But he's not as good a dancer as you."

He laughs.

"All right then."

Last Call and Then Some

I stay until the end because so many people do. Jack has to practically kick out the stragglers.

"Don't you all have a home to go to?" he asks one True Blue Regular.

"Yeah, but it's more fun here," he answers.

Carole left after she cleaned the kitchen and had her official drink, a Long Island Iced Tea, which has a heckuva a lot of booze. Jack won't let just anybody order that drink, but Carole's hubby was here to give her a ride home. Plus, Jack's pleased the new menu items, which includes a beef stew, sold out fast.

Jack shuts off the neon beer signs. The Rooster is as clean as we can make it tonight. I already called my mother, who's watching a good movie. She told me not to rush home, but then again, she wants to hear everything about tonight. I bet she will be amused about Dancin' Dave's appearance. She's feeling a lot better.

"Glad to hear it," I told her.

Jack and I sit side by side at the counter with our beers. Right off, he asks about the Beaumonts and not Dancin' Dave, which I find amusing.

"I'll bet a hundred bucks your visit to the Beaumonts wasn't a lot of fun," Jack says.

"You'd win that wager."

Jack listens closely as I give him a blow by blow about my meeting with the brothers. I skip the parts about the drugs found in the Corolla or their former business arrangement with the Sinclair boys. It's not that I don't trust Jack, but a promise is a promise even to a couple of bums like the Beaumonts.

"That was a foolhardy thing you did, Isabel. Be careful."

161

"Foolhardy. That's a good word." I reach for the bottle. "I was glad my mother didn't come. It might've been too much for her."

Jack shakes his head and clicks his tongue.

"Why are you doin' this, Isabel? How much is Annette payin' you anyways?"

"Uh, free service on my and my mother's cars, and actually Lin Pierce's cars, for a long, long time." I laugh into the bottle. "Yeah, yeah, I don't wanna hear it."

"What about? You having a soft spot in your heart for rednecks?"

My shoulders shake as I laugh.

"I thought you were gonna say I work cheap."

He chuckles.

"That, too."

And so it goes back and forth, the teasing and the laughter.

Jack eyes my bottle.

"You're gettin' low there. Want another beer? It's on the house."

"Thanks, but no thanks. I'll stick with my one and only tonight. I should get home."

Jack's stopped talking. He peels the label from his beer. I give him a close read.

"Something you wanna tell me?" I ask him. "Go ahead. Spit it out."

He shakes his head.

"It's nothin'."

"Nah, I can tell it's something."

"Dave Baxter is quite taken with you."

"That so?"

"But I told him I had dibs on you first."

"What!"

He gives my cheek a gentle pinch.

"Ah, gotcha!"

Report

Of course, Ma is awake when I get home. She's got her feet up on a stool with the cat on her lap and the dog beside her on the floor. The TV is on but likely only for background noise. She sets aside her book, one of those sleazy romance novels that have a bodice-ripper illustration on the front cover. She borrowed it from the library. I believe the librarian, Mira, gets a kick out of the fact my mother reads that stuff.

"How'd it go?" she asks as I hang my jacket in the hall closet.

"Just fine. And you won't believe who showed up. Dancin' Dave."

My mother's head tips back as she laughs.

"Ha. Jack's got some competition," she says with a merry note to her voice.

"Yeah, Dave cut in when Jack and I were dancing."

"How did Jack take that?"

"He was cool about it, but I could tell he wasn't thrilled." I laugh. "Then I found out from the Floozy and Tough Cookie that Dave owns Baxter's, that biker bar where we met Mike Waters."

My mother laughs with me.

"Hmm, so my daughter has two bar owners fighting over her."

"I don't think they're fighting, Ma. Maybe more like interested."

She sets her book on the side table.

"You trying to tell me a man visits another man's bar just because he's interested. Come on, Isabel, I may be old, but I'm not dumb. You're an attractive woman. Face it."

"He did leave me a five-dollar tip for two beers and a shot

163

of tequila," I say with a giggle.

"Is that a big tip?"

"At the Rooster, yeah." I reach into the front pocket of my jeans for the paper. "He also tucked this inside of the bill. Take a look."

She reads what Dave wrote then hands the paper back to me.

"Hmm, interesting. You going to call him?"

"Sure. Adding Chet Waters' name might be a trick, but it's worth a call." I finger the paper. "Hey, I'm taking the Subaru to Annette's garage tomorrow for an oil change. She insisted. Besides, we couldn't talk about the Beaumonts at the bar. Turns out the Rooster's cook is related to them."

"Is there somebody not related to somebody here?"

"Yeah, the newcomers. Do you wanna come with me tomorrow? Or maybe you're tired of hearing about the Beaumonts."

"Not yet."

"Hey, you won't believe who was also there tonight. Pete and Barbie Woodrell, the owners of the Pit Stop. Guess they came on their snowmobiles."

"That's nice." She picks up her book. "I'm thinking about making a trip to your brother's. The last time I was there was Thanksgiving."

I nod. She's experiencing what it's like to have a long winter. Back home, as she calls it, there are already signs of spring. At least the snow, if it got any, is long gone. We still have quite a bit although I detect it's beginning to shrink. I kept hearing comments at the Rooster that the sap in the maple trees has started running. The sugarhouses have begun boiling.

"Sure. Give Danny a call. I can do any day that works for him."

I let the dog out before I check what's on the tube and decide the movie playing on the TV isn't interesting enough. I head upstairs to my office to survey my crime scene wall. At the center is the photo of Annette and her Pop. I recently tacked a road map beside it that I've marked up with the locations important to this case such as both junkyards,

Baxter's, and, of course, the Beaumont brothers' shit box of a house. Annette gave me the address of her brother, Mike, and just because it's a hotbed of activity, the Pit Stop. They form a sloppy triangle if I connect the dots.

A recent addition is the bloody photo Sean Mooney, the reporter from the Bugle, took on his phone. I also created a map of Rough Waters showing the rows of junks, including the Corolla, plus the fence, garage, and house. I mark where Chet's body was found, and now where Sean shot the bloody spot, plus where Annette thinks she found the dog's body.

I have Annette's list of suspects on the wall. The Beaumonts are still at the top. Al Sinclair hasn't been eliminated. I grab a pen and add his sons' names, Junior and Roy.

I ponder a dilemma about the Beaumonts. Should I tell Annette about the brothers' connection to the dope found in the Corolla? She is my client after all, but I worry she'd blab it to her cousin, Marsha, and then word would get around to the brothers, who surely would keep their promise of looking me up. Crap, Isabel, what are you going to do now?

I move closer. There are still two people on Annette's list I haven't contacted: Anthony Steward, a newcomer who wanted to shut down Chet Waters' junkyard, and JoJo Tidewater, one of Annette's loser ex-boyfriends. Of course, I should look up her brother, Chester, and the Sinclair boys. Curious, nobody ever says much about Annette's kid, Abe.

I tack up Dancin' Dave's note beside the newspaper clippings. I'll give the guy the benefit of the doubt and call him tomorrow. Maybe he does have something useful for me.

A Call to Dancin' Dave

I ring the number Dancin' Dave gave me before Ma and I leave for Annette's garage in Caulfield. I believe I might have woken him up, or maybe he's just not a morning person, but he revives quickly when I tell him who I am.

"Glad you called, Isabel," he tells me. "You found my note. I was hopin' you would."

"Uh-huh, that was a rather generous tip."

"Eh, you deserve it. You're good behind the bar. You could work for me anytime."

I ignore his offer.

"You wanted to talk about Chet Waters?"

He laughs.

"I see you're the kind of woman who gets right to the point," he says. "I like that."

"Good. What did you want to tell me about him?"

Another laugh.

"Ah, not so fast, Isabel. I wanna talk with you in person."

Uh-oh, I knew there was a catch.

"I see. When would you like to meet?"

"How about tonight at my place, say around seven-thirty? The band doesn't start playin' until nine, so it'll be a little quieter. Besides, I'd like to treat you to dinner."

"Your place. You mean Baxter's? By the way, I didn't know you owned it until last night."

"You didn't, huh? What kind of a private investigator are you?"

"A rookie private investigator," I say. "Dave, it's really not necessary to treat me to dinner."

"But I want to. You're comin' all that way to talk with me. You've gotta eat. I've gotta eat. We might as well do it together. We might even make it onto the dance floor," he says with a chuckle. "Uh, it won't be necessary to bring those bodyguards with you tonight."

"Bodyguards?"

"You know, those two women you were with last Saturday, Annette and her cousin. I'd like to talk with you in private."

I'm getting a bit suspicious of Dancin' Dave's motives. But maybe he has something I can use to solve this case and wants to keep it between us. I get it. Anyway, we are meeting early in the evening, and I can always bow out before it gets too late. I'll ask Ma to give me a call at ten to see how I'm doing and whether I need an excuse to split.

"I'll see you tonight at seven-thirty," I tell him.

"Looking forward to it."

Oil Change

Ma and I talk over my dilemma about the Beaumont brothers on the way to Rough Waters. Her advice? Gauge Annette's trustworthiness. It's not like the woman is paying me big bucks to risk my neck, a fact Lin Pierce reminded me. I reminded him back to take his vehicles up there. I've been keeping track of my hours. In the future, I'm going to figure out this business part. Yeah, the house is paid off and I have money in the bank from Sam's life insurance but still.

Now, as we meet Annette inside her garage I'm doing exactly as my mother suggested. Annette wears coveralls and her hair is wrapped in an oil-stained bandana. She rolls a chair across the floor.

"Here you go, Mrs. Ferreira," she says, but then her attention is on me. "Tell me about the Beaumonts. I'm dyin' to hear what those assholes said."

"Like I told you, neither of them had an alibi for that night," I tell her.

She pounds a fist into the palm of her hand.

"Those little bastards. What else you got on them?"

"There's more, and this is where it gets tricky." I pause. "They told me some things, and I promised not to tell anybody. But it's key to this case you hired me to solve. Things got really ugly when I was at their house. They threatened me if what they said gets out. Not about they're not having alibis. Something else." I pause again. "If I tell you this information and you blab it to somebody else, like your cousin, Marsha, it could put me in danger. I'm not kidding."

Annette nods as she listens.

"Yeah, they'd do somethin' like that. I'm sure of it. There was a guy in the next town over who squealed on 'em to the cops. It wasn't even that big a deal. They put him in the hospital."

I glance at my mother.

"Great."

"Let me guess. It has somethin' to do with what Pop found in the Corolla. Am I right?" She waves her hand. "Yeah, yeah, I can tell. You don't have to say nothin'. When you solve this case, you can tell me every damn thing."

"Thanks, Annette. I've been struggling with this."

She snorts.

"It's not like I'm payin' you big money to find out who killed Pop. Speakin' of which, I better get on with this oil change. There's another chair in the office if you want, Isabel."

"That's okay. I think I'll take a walk around the yard. I see your dogs are in their pen."

"Yup, they're not gonna bother you."

"Oh, I forgot to tell you I met your brother, Mike."

"What'd he have to say?"

"He claims he has an alibi, but I'm gonna check on it for sure. Says he was driving truck in the Midwest when a big snowstorm hit."

Annette frowns.

"That sounds about right. He had a tough time gettin' back for the funeral. But glad you're checkin' his story. The only thing he cared about was gettin' his share of the land."

"He did tell me an interesting story."

Annette smirks.

"What was it?"

"He said your father apologized for the way he treated him and your other brother. They sort of made up after that."

"When was that?"

"About a year before he died."

Annette is silent for a moment. She nods.

"Yeah, I suspected somethin' like that. Pop never mentioned anythin' like that to me. I did notice him gettin' together with Mike at least. Dunno about Chester."

"Interesting. I wonder what inspired him?"

169

She shrugged.

"Somebody must've, I suppose. I can tell you it wasn't me."

Outside, I avoid the mud and stick to the slushy snow as I pass the dogs' pen. I toss the barking mutts a few biscuits before I stroll to the yard's backside. This would be a good opportunity to check the Corolla again without Annette hovering over me.

The snow around the vehicles has shrunk a bit due to the gaining sunlight. Still, I have to yank open the Corolla's front passenger door through the frozen stuff to get inside. I search the glove box and beneath the seats. Nothing. I even pop the hood and the trunk. All that's left is the torn spare tire. Nothing else.

I walk the grounds. My reporter's instincts tell me there is a clue somewhere here. A big clue in fact. I stand near the spot where Sean found the blood. Damn, there's still so much snow. But something's here. I can sense it. I'll just have to come back.

Inside the garage, Ma and Annette are talking a blue streak. Annette lets the hood fall into place.

"Car's just fine. I told your mother you should bring in her Ford next week. And she shouldn't leave it sittin' so much."

"You're right." I turn toward Ma. "Maybe you should drive it. It's not good for you to be sitting so much, too. Gotta keep you on the road."

"As long as you're not a backseat driver," Ma says.

"What'd you mean? I hardly say anything about your driving, well, except when you go too fast."

"I see you hitting the brake on your side of the car."

I laugh and raise my hands in surrender.

"Guilty as charged." Now I speak with Annette. "How about Wednesday? Same time?"

"Works for me," Annette says. "Will I see you tonight at Baxter's?"

"You might if you're there early enough. Dave wants to talk with me about your father."

Annette snickers.

"Oh, really? Ha. Now that's a come on," she says. "Mrs. Ferreira, you should've seen him dancin' with your daughter. He was slobberin' all over her."

"No, he wasn't," I say.

"Sure, sure." She hands my mother her purse. "You have a funny daughter."

"Yes, I do."

"Hey!"

On the way back home, I decide to get gas at the Pit Stop. So far, I haven't gotten much of anything here.

"I'll be right back," I say before I head inside to pre-pay.

Barbie's at the counter, straightening up stuff, but she calls hubby, Pete, when she recognizes me. I tell her I want ten bucks worth of gas before Pete hustles behind her.

"Hey, Isabel, how's it hangin'?"

I don't believe I've got anything hanging, but it's Pete's way to be friendly.

"It's hanging just fine. Nice to see you both at the Rooster last night."

Barbie smiles for me.

"We haven't been in years… "

Pete cuts her off.

"I like Baxter's better. More my crowd." He grunts. "But with the full moon it was a nice night for a ride. Don't know how many of those we've got left."

"That's what the guys were saying last night. The snow's shrinking." I turn toward Barbie. "You're a good dancer."

Barbie doesn't reply. Instead her white face turns red. She watches Pete from the corner of her eyes. I reach into my wallet for a ten. Barbie takes the bill, and that's when I notice a ring of bruises on her wrist as if somebody yanked her hard, and I don't believe it was from dancing last night. I bet Annette is right about Pete. Crap, I don't like this situation at all. I'm beginning to not like Pete either.

"How's the case going?" he asks.

"Slow but sure," I answer. "Got any tips for me?"

"No, ma'am."

Barbie's head bobs like a puppet.

"Hon, I did hear Sunderland's sugar shack had its first boiling yesterday," she says.

"Now that's something," I say. "Spring's on its way for sure."

Dinner and Dancin'

I ask the bartender at Baxter's if he's seen his boss.

"Isabel, right? He says to sit tight. He's straightening out some business in the backroom. Can I get you anything?"

I take a stool.

"I'm fine for now."

"Just holler if you do." He winks. "I was told to give you the royal treatment."

I smile when I ponder what the royal treatment means in a biker bar. Do I get a black leather cape and chrome tiara? Yeah, yeah, I'm only being a wiseass. I spin around to take in the place, which is full of drinkers, diners, and I suppose, dancers. I don't recognize a soul, but I'm not surprised since I'm in another county and maybe, world. After all, anyone who isn't civilized enough to drink at the Rooster has to come here.

But that scenario changes fast when the Beaumont brothers, Gary and Larry, arrive. Larry elbows Gary, who nods when he notices me standing near the bar. They're talking it over, and when that's done, they march my way.

"What the hell you doin' here, Isabel?" Gary says.

"Nice to see you, too," I give him back.

Gary takes a step forward.

"You're kinda outta your league hangin' out at Baxter's, don't you think?"

"Why? Cause I haven't been kicked out of the Rooster like you two?"

They're silent for a moment. I've caught them off guard. Maybe they thought I'd be scared after getting kicked out of their rat's nest of a house. I was but I'm sure as hell not going to let them know. I remember my parents telling me when I was a kid not to show a mean dog you're scared. I believe that advice applies with the Beaumont brothers.

"Maybe she's spyin' on us."

But before I can come up with something snappy, Dancin' Dave says behind them, "Isabel is my guest here tonight. If you two have a problem with that, then I suggest you find someplace else to drink."

The Beaumonts step back. The threat to be banned from Baxter's is a real one. I wonder how many other drinking establishments have kicked them out forever. Maybe this is the only bar that will take them in. If so, I wonder what kind of a deal they made with Dave, who strikes me as a no-nonsense kind of guy.

"Nah, we were just jokin' with her," Gary says. "You knew that, right, Isabel?"

Dave doesn't wait for my smart-ass answer. He grabs each brother's shoulder as if they're going into a huddle.

"Why don't you two fellows get yourselves somethin' cold to drink and stay outta trouble. All right?"

Dave lets the Beaumonts go after they mutter something in agreement I can't hear. I wait until the brothers shuffle off to a table across the room before I speak.

"Thanks for rescuing me from those thugs."

"Thugs. That's a good word," he says. "Hey, you don't have a drink. What'll it be? Some fancy schmancy cocktail? Nah, you strike me as a beer and wine kinda gal."

"You're right. I'll take a light beer, if you don't mind. I have a ways to drive home."

Dave signals to the bartender and relays our order. Then he holds out his arm when I lower myself from the stool. I giggle, yeah, a bit. This guy thinks he's some gentleman cowboy. But I play along and let him lead me to a corner table. He even pulls out my chair. Ma is going to get a kick out of this when I tell her.

"How long have you owned this place?" I ask Dave.

"Almost twenty years. I'm third generation. I grew up in this place. When my grandfather owned the joint, it was nothin' more than a fishin' shack. My parents built it up a bit

174

and ran a mom-and-pop kind of place after that. When I took over, I doubled the size and made lots of upgrades. That's when Sue and I were together."

"Is Sue your wife?"

"Late wife. She died a few years ago. Cancer. It's an awful way to go. Sue was a real sweetheart. We knew each other since we were kids."

"I lost my husband about eighteen months ago. Sam was a great guy."

"I believe I met him. Carpenter, right? Kinda quiet? Yeah, I did."

The waitress brings our drinks. We both get Buds although mine is the light version. I forgot beer comes in cans and hard drinks in plastic glasses here at Baxter's. I skip the offer of a plastic glass.

I get the immediate feeling I won't be rushing Dancin' Dave. At least I have Ma lined up to give me that phone call at ten. Just before I left, she asked whether Jack knew what I was up to tonight. I told her no, but I was sure word would get back to him.

I put a bit of thought into this meetup with Dave. I decided not to wear a skirt or anything too feminine. It's not that I don't want to look good, but it might be too suggestive, like I was dressing up for him. I settle on jeans, not too tight, and a v-necked sweater, not too low. Of course, it's black. Seventy-five percent of my wardrobe is black, not because I'm a widow, but it's my favorite color. I'm wearing earrings, something dangly. I always have them. It's the only jewelry I wear since I removed my wedding ring months after Sam died.

Dave hands me the menu.

"Whatever you want, Isabel."

His voice is so smooth, it makes me feel we're on a first date, which isn't my intention, but maybe his, if the Chet Waters' thing is only a lure. But I'm going to go along and not pester him, at least not yet.

He raises his beer can.

"Thanks for comin'," he says.

This guy is really smooth. I tap my can against his.

"Thanks for inviting me."

He orders a steak. I ask if I can have a salad and a baked potato. The waitress seems a little perplexed until Dave nods.

"Give the lady what she wants," he says. "I heard you're one of those vegetarian types."

"You heard right although I've loosened up since my mother came to live with me."

We talk while we wait for our food. Dave wants to learn more about me. I find it hard to share. I'm usually the one asking the questions. I give him a quick rundown about growing up beside the ocean, that my family is Portuguese, what that was like. I talk about Sam and the kids, and working for the newspaper. I mention my mother. I'm not that interesting, if you really want to know, but Dave sits back in his chair, nodding at the parts he likes, laughing at my snide remarks and stories. He's a handsome older guy, with good lines on his face that make him appear both wise and humorous.

"How serious are you and Jack Smith?" he asks.

I don't answer right away. That's a real good question. We were hot and heavy until his sister got caught, thanks to me, and then he dropped me until she died. But I like being with Jack. He's sweet, but not too sweet, and he makes me laugh, appreciative qualities in my book.

"I believe we're figuring that out," I say. "We took a little break after... you probably heard all about that."

He chuckles.

"Uh-huh, at least I don't have a sister who was a killer. Sorry, that was a bad joke."

"That's okay. I kinda have a gallows humor myself," I say.

"Gallows humor. I like that. Oh, here's our food."

As we eat, I turn the questioning toward him. Of course, the good reporter I am, I lob him a couple of softball questions first. Eventually, I'll get around to Chet Waters, but right now I'm having a whole lot of fun grilling Dancin' Dave about his life.

"Why do you take in the Rooster's rejects like the Beaumont boys?" I ask.

He holds his fork mid-air.

"It's strictly business. I don't care much for those little punks, but they know better than to conduct any business in the parking lot. That was plain stupid what they did at the Rooster. Maybe they learned their lesson. Dunno. But I keep a real close eye on them and a few of the others. It's easier for me than Jack. I'm not working behind the bar or shagging empties. I pay people to do that."

"You must see a lot in here."

"I could write a book or have one of those reality TV shows."

"Okay, you've got me real curious. What did you want to tell me about Chet Waters?"

He laughs.

"I was wonderin' how long it would take you to ask that. You sure know how to play a man."

I make that stupid giggle again.

"Dave, I wouldn't say I'm playing."

We're interrupted when the waitress comes to clear our table. She asks about dessert.

"The lady says no. How about another round?" He eyes me. "The lady says yes."

"To get back to my question about Chet… "

"You must've been a real good reporter."

"I was relentless. Back to my question, please."

Dave chuckles.

"We used to have after-hours poker games here. Bettin' and all that. Actually still do, but regular hours only on Tuesdays, which is kind of a dead night. But now that Chet's gone, it's a lot friendlier. The stakes are much lower."

"Friendlier?"

"Don't get me wrong. Chet could be a blast to be around if he wasn't being a pain in the ass. Told stories. Made jokes. Course, it was all a ruse to distract his fellow players. Well, a couple of weeks before he died, he was in a big game here. I had already exceeded my limit of losin' that night, so I just watched. Chet was goin' head to head with another guy, who ended up givin' him quite a load of money. It turned really

177

ugly. I managed to break it up without anyone gettin' hurt. But it was damn close. There was blood in their eyes."

"Who was the sore loser?"

Dave leans over the table. He's got a shit-eating grin on his lips. "Al Sinclair."

"The guy who owns the junkyard?"

"The very one."

"When I talked with him, he was mighty P.O.'d his boys lost big to Chet," I say. "He didn't say anything about losing his shirt to the man."

"Interesting he left that out."

"Thanks for the tip." I think about what I want to ask next, and give myself the okay. "Somebody told me about a fatal accident many years ago involving Chet and Al's sister. Do you remember that?"

"Sure do. I went to school with Amanda. She was a little doll. I forgot about it but I bet Al hasn't. It was a tragedy. I can see why he used every opportunity to speak ill of the man. He still does even though Chet's dead."

Dave sits back. He appears to be weighing what he will say next. I'm wondering if he has more to say about Chet and Al when he hits me with this: "Heard you're workin' with Lin Pierce."

"Yes, I am. I need to be employed by a P.I. for three years before... wait, you have something on him you wanna tell me?"

"It might help if you know who you're dealin' with. The story happened a while back, but it still applies. Nobody else told you about him?"

Of course, I'm curious. I can't help it. It's part of my genetic makeup.

"No. What's Lin's deep, dark secret?"

Dave does a quick look around.

"It was probably before you moved here." He sits forward. "Lin was supposed to give evidence for a personal injury case. Guy fell at a construction site. He was a subcontractor. The contractor wouldn't pay him a dime even though his crew messed up. Anyway, Lin blew it and the man lost the case."

"How did Lin blow it?"

"He was drinkin' heavy then, and when he came drunk to court, he was in no shape to testify. Poor guy lost his case and ended up killin' himself cause he couldn't support his family."

"That's awful."

"Let's say it scared Lin sober, but his reputation was a bit tainted." He lowers his voice. "He did try to make good with his widow and kids. I'll give him that. Most don't."

"That's a really sad story."

"Sure is."

Dave glances toward the side door. The band and their helpers haul their equipment to the stage. I recognize the Lone Sums, which played last night at the Rooster. Baxter's must be part of the redneck circuit. Dave sits back with a beer can in his hand. He is studying me.

"Now that we've got that business outta the way, we can have a little fun on the dance floor. The night's still young."

By the wall clock, it's getting onto eight-forty. I figure I'll split around ten after I get that call from Ma.

"Yes, it is," I tell him.

I glance up when I realize someone is crowding our table. Pete Woodrell hovers above me as if he's my bodyguard. Dave gives him a nod. The two of them exchange the usual country guy pleasantries, and then Pete pats my shoulder.

"Isabel, nice to see you in my neck of the woods," he tells me.

Dave sits back.

"Isabel is my special guest tonight," he says.

"Special guest, eh? Saw you two dancin' up a storm at Jack's place last night."

"Yeah, I expect we'll be doin' more tonight," Dave says.

This conversation is making me a bit uneasy. I like Dave, but I don't want Pete getting the wrong idea about us.

"Is Barbie here?" I ask.

Pete shakes his head.

"Nah, she stayed home. Not feeling up to it. Female problems." He slaps the table. "Hey, I'll leave you two alone."

Dave nods, and after Pete has moved far enough away, he

179

says, "Like I said, we could do one of those reality TV shows in here."

"Yeah, you could."

The Lone Sums are into their first song, something Southern rock I don't recognize right away, but Dave does and he grins.

"Wanna dance?" he asks me.

Oh, why not?

Dutifully, my mother calls, but I tell her everything is fine. I almost joke that so far I haven't been molested, but that would be over the top for Ma.

Dancin' Dave keeps me moving on the floor, and when the Lone Sums take a break, he locks me in a conversation about this and that, about him and me. He has two daughters and a few grandkids. He likes to fish but not hunt. He takes his RV to Maine, and the only time he's flown was to Florida with his late wife for vacations and once to California for a wedding. He'd like to see more of the country. Course, he has a motorcycle, a Harley. No rice burners, as he put it. Maybe I'd like to go for a ride when the weather is warm enough. Or maybe I'd like one on his snowmobile although the snow is starting to get thin in spots on the trails.

Uh, this guy wants us to make plans.

"Dave, I need to head home soon. I've got a ways to go," I tell him.

"You could just head out in the morning."

I laugh when he says that. Yeah, I'm having a swell time, but I'm not about to go to bed with the guy. Besides, I'm a bit unsure right now. Dave hit it when he asked about Jack. What is going on between us two anyways? Are we co-workers with benefits? Or is there something more? Jack has no hold on me, but it would definitely complicate things if I hooked up with Dave. Take it slow, Isabel.

"You're a fast worker," I tell Dave.

He made a low rumble of a laugh.

"I am when I want something."

I let him walk me to my car, a sound idea given the Beaumont brothers kept a watch on me all night. Ditto for me

180

on them when Dave wasn't on my radar. Dave and I talk a bit in the parking lot until I insist on leaving, and, yes, he clinches me in a kiss that gives me no doubts about his intentions.

About all I can say is a breathy "Well," which comes off sexier than I intend. Dave doesn't stop smiling. He waits until my car leaves the lot.

Driving is fine. I can handle three light beers over three hours, no problem. I pass the Rooster, still lit up, ponder stopping but think better of it. I'm not about to test Jack's feelings for me. I'll see him Monday anyway.

Old Farts

It's time to pay a visit to the Old Farts. This morning, I'm going solo without sweet little Sophie because her parents are on vacation at someplace warm and sunny this week. I'm a bit surprised the Old Farts didn't tell me Lin Pierce's backstory. My conclusion is there has to be some connection to one of them, hence, the silence. Plus, I have a few other questions for them. Of course, I'll see what they have on me.

As expected by the cars parked outside the store, the regulars are in full attendance with a couple of Visiting Old Farts who have yet to earn a name, so I'll call them Visiting Old Fart One and Visiting Old Fart Two. Naturally, the Fattest Old Fart announces my arrival. He pats the bench.

"I've been saving this spot just for you, Isabel," he says.

Across from him, the Serious Old Fart quips, "Face it. Isabel is the only one who could fit in that space."

His comment draws chuckles from his colleagues and a sputter of lips from the Fattest Old Fart. Then we go through the usual routine of a cup of coffee by one of the group and that lame joke about the espresso machine. I don't mind although it confuses the two visitors until one of the regulars brings them up to speed.

Across the way, the Bald Old Fart clears his throat.

"Heard a certain woman was hired back at the Rooster," he says.

Beside him, the Old Fart with Glasses nods like there's a spring in his neck. "Yeah, my sources say only Friday nights though."

I roll my eyes. "I see you guys have your spies reporting back to you."

More chuckles from the whole gang.

The Fattest Old Fart clears his throat. I'm expecting another revelation, and I'm not disappointed but a little embarrassed when he announces, "Now I heard there was an interesting scene when Jack and his recent hire were on the dance floor. Seems he had a bit of competition when somebody cut in."

Everybody including the two visitors swing their heads my way.

"I heard that, too," I say.

Across the way, the Serious Old Fart mouths, "Who?"

"I'm not one to gossip, but he owns a bar in West Caulfield," the Fattest Old Fart announces.

Not one to gossip. Who's he kidding?

I can see I'm not going to get far with these guys today. Besides, I don't know how trustworthy the visitors are. I down the rest of my coffee, crush the cup, and toss it into the open trashcan about four feet away.

"As usual, thank you for the coffee and conversation." I get to my feet. "I'm gonna head out."

The group makes a collective groan. I came here expressly to ask about Al Sinclair and Lin Pierce, but that's not going to happen. I bid my farewells and turn for the door. I'm barely outside when I hear my name. The Fattest Old Fart stands near the doorway.

"Isabel, what brought you here today?"

I smile because he's also my Favorite Old Fart.

"I was gonna ask about Al Sinclair. Is the guy on the level? I just found out a couple of things about him that are troubling."

The Fattest Old Fart sets a hand on my shoulder.

"Mind telling me what it's about?"

"I heard from a trustworthy source that he lost a bundle to Chet Waters in a poker game just before Chet died. My source says things got ugly."

The Fattest Old Fart listens intently.

"That may be true, but between you and me, I don't see Al killing anybody, even a sworn enemy like Chet."

"That's what my mother said last night. She's betting on

183

the Beaumonts."

"Your mother? How's she doing?"

"She's just fine," I say. "Hey, I have a question. What's with Lin Pierce? The same source told me an interesting story about him. When I asked about him before you guys clammed up."

The Fattest Old Fart checks behind him.

"I'm glad you didn't bring him up inside." He mentions the real name of the Silent Old Fart. "His son was the client. I heard Lin tried to help out the family, but definitely all was not forgiven."

"So it's true?"

"I'm afraid so."

Packing up Eleanor

Jack is drinking coffee at his kitchen table when I arrive to help him pack his sister's things. He raises his mug.

"Want some?" he asks.

"No, thanks. I had a really bad cup of coffee at the store a few hours ago. It's still giving me the jitters."

"You visited those old guys again? What do you call them? The Old Farts?"

"Uh-huh, but please don't go spreading that around. They don't know. And I don't want to lose them as a good source." I laugh. "I see you built those dogs a pen."

"Yup, Fred and I got it done this weekend. Neither of us wants to have to come home to let them out."

"They still bark their heads off when they see me."

"It might take those dumb mutts a while." He downs the rest of his coffee. He's up and dumping the mug in the kitchen sink. "We might as well get down to it. I appreciate you helping me with this." Then he surprises me by leaning in for a quick kiss on the lips. "I really, really appreciate it. Maybe later I can show you."

There I go giggling again. Damn it. That Jack can get me going like some silly girl.

"You might be tuckered out from all this packing."

"I'll make sure I'm not," he says grinning like the happy man he is right now.

Eleanor's side of the house is neat but filled with things that belong to a child, such as the immense collection of stuffed animals and tiny figurines that cover every available space in her living room. Except for a comfy-looking couch covered by a blanket with Disney characters, the furniture, with its ornate carvings, must have belonged to Jack and

Eleanor's parents or rather grandparents. They are definitely antiques.

Jack shakes his head.

"I dunno what to do with all of this stuff," he says. "Fred's not gonna want 'em when he moves in."

I pick up a stuffed dog that resembles one of Eleanor's mutts.

"Do you have space in your attic?" I ask. "The antiques are worth putting in storage. Or you could sell them although I imagine they've been in the family for a while." I point toward the couch. "I'd pack up the stuffed animals and the clothes. The figurines are interesting. Some of them look old. They could be worth money. Maybe you should save them until you figure something out."

Jack nods.

"Yup, that's what I'm gonna do. But let's do her bedroom first. Fred wants to start sleeping here."

I smile at the Holly Hobby print on Eleanor's bedspread. My daughter, Ruth, wanted one so badly when she was a kid.

"I guess it all goes," he says.

For the next couple of hours, Jack and I just do that, filling garbage bags with clothes, an extraordinary amount of overalls and sweatshirts, and stuffed animals. We move into the bathroom, which doesn't have much except for soap and shampoo, and then the living room, where we box up the figurines. Jack says he and Fred will haul the furniture up to the attic.

Of course, we talk most of the time. Jack tells me stories about his sister, like the one where she begged him to take her to the beach for her fortieth birthday. She wore their mother's old bathing suit that was a little big on her. She couldn't swim, so Jack walked out with her until they were neck-high in the water. He says she held on for dear life whenever a big wave swept over them.

"It was a lot of fun. I kept asking her if she wanted to go again, but she told me once was enough."

"You were a good brother."

"I suppose I was." We move back into the bedroom. He

ties up a black garbage bag of clothes we missed. "Hey, where were you last night? I thought for sure you'd show up."

I was wondering if our conversation would drift in this direction, and here it is. I don't plan to lie, of course.

I take a breath. "I got the Subaru's oil changed at Annette's place. Last night, I went to Baxter's."

Jack squints a bit as if he didn't hear me right, but he did because he says, "Baxter's? How come?"

"Dave Baxter had some info he wanted to give me for that case, but he insisted I meet him at his place."

Jack grunts.

"That's awfully clever of him."

"Huh, that's what I thought, too, but he actually gave me some useful tips." I'm trying to interpret the expression on Jack's face. Jealous? Maybe. Curious? Oh, more than that. "For your information, I was out of there by eleven."

"You two dance?"

"We did."

He's quiet for a moment.

"What's going on between you and Dave?"

I smile but not too hard.

"Ha, he asked the same question about you and me."

"What'd you say?"

"That we're figuring things out."

Jack nods.

"Fair enough. Now what about you and Dave?"

I shrug.

"I honestly don't know. He's a lot of fun and very attentive. But I kinda had my heart set on another guy."

Jack's got that happy as a pig-in-you-know-what grin. His fingertips graze my chin before he moves in for a kiss, a big kiss, and then another, and another. We fall together onto the mattress, and I'm thinking this is a bit crazy, doing it on his dead sister's bed. But I don't have to worry because Jack's cousin Fred hollers our names as he enters the front door. Jack and I disengage and sit up.

"We'll have to continue this some other day," he says.

"But maybe a different location," I say.

Jack chuckles.

"Oh, yeah, I see your point."

Fred steps through the doorway.

"Am I interrupting something?" he jokes.

Jack has his arm around me.

"As a matter of fact, yeah. What are you doin' here?"

"Nice to see you, too, cousin. Uh, look at the time."

I check the alarm clock beside Eleanor's bed. Shoot, I've been here for hours.

"We've been doing this most of the day," I say.

"Doin' what?" Fred jokes.

"Never mind." I stand. "Everything is packed up and ready to go, except for the furniture."

"You really gotta leave?" Jack asks.

"My mother's going back home for a couple of weeks, and I'm meeting my brother halfway tomorrow morning. I want to spend some time with her tonight." I muss Jack's hair. "I'll see you soon."

"Hmm, your mother's gonna be gone?"

Fred groans.

"I dunno if I can stand being around you two."

I spin toward Fred.

"Hey, I have a question for you, Fred," I say. "What can you tell me about Annette's boy, Abe?"

His eyebrows flick upward.

"Abe? Good question. He was only a boy when I was married to Annette. She got knocked up when she was in high school. Ended up dropping out. I think it was her senior year." He pauses. "He wasn't a bad kid, just a kid, let me put it this way, who couldn't sit still. Drove me nuts his hollering and running around. He probably had that AD-whatever they talk about now."

"Attention-Deficit Disorder?"

"That's it."

He raises his hands palms out.

"I will admit I wasn't much of a father to the boy. He never warmed up to me either."

"Annette doesn't talk about him much."

188

"I'm not surprised. He hangs out with a crowd of local boys. I see them around. None of 'em seem the ambitious type. I think Abe pumps gas somewhere. His mother probably helps out."

"What was his relationship with his grandfather?"

"Chet? The old man didn't have a lot of patience for the boy. Then again, he didn't with his own sons, or me, for that matter. I suppose Annette filled you in there."

"Who's his father? Annette was kinda vague about it. All she told me was that it wasn't you. She said I wouldn't know the guy."

"That sounds like Annette." He makes a soft noise deep in his throat. "If I tell you, do you promise not lettin' her know I told you?"

I glance at Jack, who is attentive to this part of the conversation.

"I can keep a secret."

His eyes flick from me to Jack and back to me.

"She admitted it to me one night but then regretted ever sayin' it. She said she'd kill me if I ever told anybody, and I kinda believe her."

My hands are on my hips.

"Go ahead."

"Gary Beaumont."

"What!"

"You heard me."

"Shoot, she had a kid with that bum."

"He was hot stuff in high school. So was she. She still is if you're into that kind of woman. I sure was back then."

Wow, I am pondering this bombshell. It would have been helpful if Annette had told me the connection. All she did was finger Gary as a suspect for her father's death. She even told me I wouldn't know her son's father. Wrong.

"One last question. Does Gary know?"

Fred's head bobbles a bit.

"Haven't a clue. Good luck, Isabel, finding out. Promise you'll tell me if you do."

"I sure will."

189

Dropping Off Ma

Of course, I tell Ma that Gary Beaumont fathered Abe. It's part of our conversation that evening and the next morning when I drive her to our rendezvous with my brother, Danny, which sounds a lot fancier than the fast food restaurant off the Mass. Turnpike where we are meeting. Ma is excited about the trip. It's definitely more spring-like where she is going than it is here. Of course, we brought along the dog, Maggie, who's conked out in the backseat.

I go over my list of interviews tomorrow with her. I'm meeting Chester Waters at his school and the nosy newcomer, Anthony Steward, at his home. I want to look into this case involving Lin Pierce, just to satisfy my nosy self. And I need to check out Mike Waters' alibi. Of course, I plan to confront Al Sinclair about his run-in with Chet at the Rooster. If I'm brave enough, I will ask him about his sister. Was his last fight with Chet enough to send him over the edge? I have my doubts, but I'm not ready to rule him out just yet. Then there are his boys, Junior and Roy. Everybody keeps saying they're good guys.

"I still can't get over Gary Beaumont is the father of Annette's son," I tell Ma.

She nods.

"It seems an important detail to leave out," she says.

"Actually, she purposely misled me about that. Maybe she's embarrassed she had a kid by that loser."

"What are you going to do with the information?"

I decided as soon as Fred shared that piece of news I would tell Ma even though I swore to keep it a secret. After all, we are confidants. I need her input. And, frankly, who would she tell? My brother hasn't expressed any interest in my investigations. Neither have my sisters.

"I'll see Annette again soon to get your car's oil changed. I'll have to figure out my approach."

"Yes, the Tough Cookie needs special handling."

"You're right about that, Ma." I laugh. "I also want to check out how much snow has melted in that junkyard of hers. You might've noticed it's warmed up a bit. My reporter's instincts say there's something on the ground that will help solve this case."

"Like what?"

"I don't know, but it could be something Chet's killer left behind. We know there was blood on the ground away from the house. I've got the photo to prove it."

"Don't forget to call me when you find whatever it is."

"Ma, you'll be the first to know. Maybe the second if I have to call the cops."

She hugs her purse.

"Fine. Will you be going to Baxter's again? Those were very nice flowers Dancin' Dave sent to the house."

Ah, yes, the flowers. I came home from Jack's yesterday to find a big bouquet delivered from a florist in the city. It must've cost him a bundle. Of course, there was a note: **Isabel, I hope to see you very soon. Dave.**

Very soon, eh?

I called Dave to thank him for the flowers. It was the polite thing to do although I'm afraid my call only encouraged him.

"When can I see you again?" he asked over the phone. "I could come to the Rooster again, but you'll be working. I get the feeling Jack was a little put out when I asked you to dance. We wouldn't have to go to my joint. I prefer to make it a night out. Just you and me."

Just you and me, yikes. And what did I tell him? "You're so sweet, Dave."

Gee, Isabel, you can't do better than that?

"Well, if you hadn't noticed, I'm sweet on you," he said next.

I sighed. I have never, ever, ever had two boys or men interested in me at the same time.

191

"Can I get back to you on that?" I asked.

"I'll be waiting," he said. "I should warn you though. I'm not a man who gives up easily."

"I'll keep that in mind," I told him.

I hit the Subaru's directional to take the pike's exit.

I tell Ma, "I don't know what I should do about Dancin' Dave. You met him. What'd you think?"

"He's definitely a charmer."

"Charmer. That's a good way to put it." I slow the car for the tollbooth. "Who do you like better? Jack or Dave?"

She snorts.

"I was a fan of Jack from the start. But Dave confuses me."

"That's exactly how I feel." I hand the ticket and the correct amount to the woman in the booth. "I guess I'll see how this plays out. And, yes, you'll be the first person I call."

"Good girl." She glances over her shoulder at Maggie in the backseat. "And please take care of my dog and cat."

"You bet, Ma."

192

Jack

"How about I come over?" Jack asks.

"Sure, the coast is clear," I joke over the phone. "I dropped my mother off this morning."

"I thought she liked me."

"She does. I guess I'm a bit shy about having a man over with her here."

He chuckles.

"I hope you get over that."

Jack arrives around seven with a bottle of a good red and a big smooch at the door. We're laughing as I shut the door behind him.

"Hello to you, too," I say.

"Just happy to see you, Isabel."

"I can see that."

"I hope the feeling is mutual."

I playfully pinch his cheek.

"Of course, it is. Here, let me take your jacket."

Jack wears a button-down shirt and black pants. I smell aftershave. He's combed his hair back. All for me, I suppose.

"You look real nice," I say.

He glances down.

"Oh, this old thing," he jokes.

I giggle, yes, giggle, as I grab his hand.

"Come on. I made us something to eat."

Actually, my mother made the chicken soup. I doctored it up with a little bit of red chile powder and sliced some bread. I even light candles and dim the lights. I let Jack open the wine and fill our glasses. He tells me about his day, about dropping off bags of his sister's things at the Goodwill store.

"After you left yesterday, Fred and I hauled most of the

furniture up to the attic. He's sleeping at the place, but he expects to fully move in this weekend." He lifts his wine glass. "Am I wrong, or do you like him better?"

"Sort of. I think we've reached an understanding. He seems to have accepted the fact I'm not interested, so he's stopped being a dick around me."

"Yeah, I set him straight about that."

"You did, huh?"

"Now I have to do the same with Dave Baxter."

Ah, I was wondering if we would get around to Dancin' Dave.

"Dave's just being friendly since this case is in his neck of the woods."

"Friendly? That's what you call it? He shows up at my place, and then he lures you to his."

"Lures me? He gave me some useful information."

"You admitted dancin' with him."

Wow, Jack is jealous. He's not being a jerk about it, but he's definitely on the offense.

"Yeah, we danced a bit."

He nods toward the bouquet of flowers on the kitchen counter. I wish I had stashed it upstairs in my office because I'm guessing what Jack's going to ask next.

"Did he send you those flowers?"

Bingo.

"As a matter of fact, he did."

Jack sets down his glass. His lips form a straight line.

"Seems like he was grateful for somethin'."

I sit back. I like Jack, a lot, but the man has no claim over me and vice versa. I could get pissed, really pissed at him for jumping to conclusions, but I laugh instead.

"Yeah, it's a bit over the top for dinner and a few turns on the dance floor. The note said he wants to see me again soon. When I called to thank him for the flowers, I told him I'd think about it."

Jack makes a stuttering laugh.

"Think about it? I believe I'd better step up my game."

I cross my arms.

"How are you planning to do that?"

He pushes back his chair and slaps his thigh.

"Why don't you come on over here for starters?"

When I come on over here, he grabs my hand and pulls me onto his lap. His arms are around me as he starts in on those deep kisses. He's feeling me up. I feel him back. I know where this is going fast, upstairs and into bed. We ignore the ring of his cell phone. Twice. He reaches into his pocket and places the phone on the table.

The cell rings again, and then minutes later my landline. Fred's voice comes next over the phone's speaker.

"Isabel, real sorry to bother you, but I need to talk with Jack."

I get to my feet and grab the phone.

"What's up?"

"The dogs got out and I can't find 'em."

"Here he is."

Jack groans as takes the phone.

"Those stupid mutts," he tells his cousin before he hangs up.

"You need to go?" I ask.

"Yeah, I'm sorry. Real sorry. Those dogs won't come to anyone but me."

"I understand."

Jack shakes his head. He apologizes again.

"I owe it to her," he says.

"Sure. Sure. Let me get your jacket."

He glances at the kitchen clock. It's nine-forty.

"Want me to come back after I find 'em?"

"I'll stay up until eleven for you. If it takes longer than that, we'll have to do this another time."

Jack nods slowly.

"Fair enough."

Outside, he gives me one glance back as he walks toward his pickup. I wave and watch him drive away. I sigh. Once again, Eleanor Smith gets in the way of things.

Chester

It's February school vacation, but Chester A. Waters Jr. is meeting me at his office. He calls himself Chester, not Chet like his father. He's also a school principal, an educated man, not a junkyard owner. I am betting he has distanced himself in other ways as his sister and brother already hinted.

As I drive north, I notice the snow has shrunk a bit although we could still get one of those heart-breaking late-season storms. I concentrate on my route.

I bet you're wondering what happened last night after Jack left. Nothing. Absolutely nothing. Eleven o'clock came and went. No Jack. No phone call. Not even this morning. I suspect it took a while to find those three mutts. He didn't want to wake me to tell me the news. So be it. I can't worry about Jack. I have a busy day ahead. After Chester, I'm meeting Anthony Steward at his home in Caulfield. I might swing by Rough Waters to check in with Annette although I'm due there tomorrow for work on my mother's car. Will I stop by the Rooster? Probably. It's not normally open Tuesdays, but Jack wants to see if it'd be worth opening for six days instead of five.

I arrive at Clark Elementary School in Manley, where kids from that town and Caulfield attend. Conwell is lucky to still have an elementary school within its borders. It robs something from a small town when it loses its school. Long, long ago, these hilltowns had a slew of one-room schoolhouses, which were eventually reduced to one, and in some instances, none, as the population couldn't support one. It's called regionalization.

The side door is open as Chester said it would be. I follow the signs down a hallway to his office, where he sits behind a desk.

"Isabel?" he greets me.

I reach across the desk for a handshake. Chester looks a bit like his father, but he appears to have overcome that with better grooming and a healthier lifestyle.

"Thanks for meeting with me today."

"I was intrigued by our phone call. So, my sister has convinced you our dear old dad was murdered, eh?" He chuckles. "Am I on her suspect list?"

"No, you're not. But it makes sense for me to interview everyone who was close to him."

Chester snorts.

"Close? The only time I was close to my father was when he caught me with his backhand."

I cringe when I hear those words.

"Annette did say your father was unkind to you and your brother."

"Unkind? That's putting it mildly." He eyes his coffee mug. "Where are my manners? Can I offer you some coffee?"

I hold up my hand.

"I'm just fine. I would like you to continue that line of conversation. What did you mean by putting it mildly?"

His eyes shrink a bit.

"Some people have kids who definitely shouldn't. They make kids, but don't take care of them. I see it here. When I was a kid, I found a refuge in school. My father wouldn't pay a dime for me to go to college. I figured it out myself. He didn't like it when he found out I was gay, but by then I rarely saw the man."

"What about your mother?"

"She loved us kids, but truthfully, she was useless when it came to protecting my brother and me."

I nod.

"I talked with your brother, Mike. He said about a year before your father died, he actually apologized for being such a lousy father."

"Yeah, he apologized to me, too." Chester sniffs. "He said an odd thing, 'I guess I made you this way.' I believe that was

197

as close as he could get to accepting who I am."

"Did you hang out together after that?"

"Not a whole lot. He wasn't exactly comfortable being around my partner and me. We had him over for dinner one night." He shakes his head. "Pop was definitely out of his comfort zone that night. He didn't know what to make of my partner, Chris." He pauses. "Let's just say I understood him better."

Whoa, Isabel, you haven't lost your touch after all. You manage to squeeze information from Chester without trying too hard. He seems a pleasant enough man, but so far he hasn't said anything that would clear himself.

"Where were you the night your father died?"

"At home."

"At home. Is there anyone who can vouch for you?"

"Sure, Chris. I can give you his cell if you want."

I give him a close study. Definitely, I should call his partner, but instead I use my reporter's x-ray vision to see right through him. Am I getting soft? Nah, I think Chester is being truthful, so that's what I tell him.

"Yeah, I believe you."

He smiles.

"When was the last time you saw your father?"

"Oh, a few weeks before he died. We had dinner one night at Baxter's. Just him and I. He seemed to have a lot of regrets that night, mostly about the way he treated my brother and me. I told him I forgave him. I don't know how he came to that realization, but years of therapy helped me. Pop relaxed a bit after that, and then we just had a good time, like a father and son chatting and eating."

"Not everybody will admit when they're wrong like that."

"Yeah, I'm glad we had that last moment together."

I dig into my purse for a card.

"Give me a call if you can think of anything that might help me."

Chester reaches for a pad and pen.

"Will do. And here's my cell number."

198

The Newcomer

After leaving Chester Waters, I head to Caulfield, following the directions Anthony Steward gave me over the phone. On the main drag I pass the Caulfield police cruiser in the opposite lane. Yes, Chief Nancy Dutton is at the wheel. She makes a U-turn and hits the flashing lights. I'm driving under the speed limit, but I dutifully pull to the side of the road and wait.

The chief is smiling, so I'm not in trouble. I roll down the window.

"How's the case going?" she asks me.

"Nothing solid to report yet. Seems Chet liked to cheat at cards. But whether that's enough to get himself killed, I don't know."

"I heard that about him."

I reach over from my purse. I hand the chief a card.

"Here you go. My daughter had these made for me."

"Nice." She snaps my card between her fingers. "Sorry. I don't have anything solid either. See you around."

Minutes later, I find that nosy newcomer's house. Anthony Steward lives in a sweet old colonial that he and the woman, who answers the door, must have spent a fortune upgrading. The slate roof is intact. The clapboards, no vinyl or aluminum siding here, have a good coat of paint. The windows are high-end replacements. Yes, I learned all about this from Sam.

"Anthony is in the study," the woman who answers the door tells me.

"Are you his wife?"

She giggles.

"No, I'm his live-in housekeeper. Follow me."

Who in the heck has a live-in housekeeper? I guess

Anthony Steward does. I stand corrected.

"Thanks."

Anthony watches television, CNN from the sounds of it, in the study, but he flicks off the set with the remote when he spots me. The floor-to-ceiling shelves are lined with books. The furniture is quality, lots of it Mission-style. It's obvious the man's loaded. I am guessing he is in his seventies or eighties. He has a good head of white hair he wears combed back. Nothing grows on his face. The man is dressed in L.L. Bean country. I catch a whiff of cologne when he gestures at the chair beside his.

"I was a bit surprised when you called to set up this interview," he says. "Actually, I was amused to be linked to Chet Waters. You said over the phone you are investigating his death. I thought it was an accident."

"That's the official story anyway. His daughter, Annette, feels differently."

"Ah, Annette, the junkyard proprietor."

Proprietor? This guy has his head stuck up his you know what.

"I was told you were on the zoning board."

His head tips back.

"Yes, I am. I thought they could use my experience. I owned an architectural firm in Boston."

"And how has that worked out?"

He chortles. I bet he's one of those newcomers who want to show the old-timers how it's done. No more trailers. Keep the new houses far apart.

"Let's say, I am usually the minority vote on the board."

Right-o.

"What was your relationship with Chet Waters?"

He jerks his pointer finger.

"Plain and simple, I wanted to shut down his junkyard."

"How come?"

"It was a health hazard and a blight on the landscape of Caulfield."

A blight on the landscape? Rough Waters is on a back road, for Pete's sake. Nobody goes by there unless they want to have

200

their vehicle fixed or they need a part from one of the junks.

"I take it you weren't successful because his daughter is running it."

"Yes, but at least I tried. I called the state to determine whether the junkyard could be contaminating groundwater. That didn't get very far."

"Did you ever talk face to face with Chet?"

He snorts.

"Oh, yes, on numerous occasions. The man even had the nerve to show up here one day. I called the police, but no one came until after he was gone. Law enforcement is virtually useless here."

"Most small towns only have part-time officers," I say. "Did you ever go to his junkyard?"

"Once."

"When was that?"

He smiles.

"Actually, a week or two before the fire."

"For what reason?"

"One night, somebody did donuts on my front lawn with their snowmobile in the middle of the night. The next day, I did a little asking around and found out it was probably Chet. I went to confront him."

"How did that go?"

"As you can imagine, not very well. He did have the nerve to admit it was him. I was incensed. His daughter came from the garage to break us up."

"Break you up?"

"We didn't take a swing at each other, if that's what you're thinking, but it's the closest I've ever come to hitting somebody." He waves his hand. "But that was the end of that exchange. Setting a house on fire to kill a man, even one as despicable as Chet Waters?" He leans forward. "No, ma'am, I don't have it in me."

I'm afraid the man is right. I don't like Anthony one bit, but he's more of the suing kind of guy than the slaying kind. That would be his ultimate form of revenge. This interview has been a complete waste. I nod.

"I apologize for taking up your time," I say.

He smiles.

"Not at all. It's not every day that a person is a suspect in a supposed murder."

I'm bummed as I return home. Ma will be disappointed by my lack of progress. I'm a few weeks into this case, and all I've gotten out of it is another bar owner slobbering all over me and an oil change for the Subaru. The only ones on my list of suspects are two drug-dealing brothers who are complete assholes, a rival junkyard owner, and his sons. I still have to meet up with JoJo Tidewater, but being an ex of Annette doesn't make him a killer.

I pass the road for Rough Waters but keep driving. I'm going there tomorrow anyway, and now I'm ticked off enough to ask Annette about her relationship with Gary Beaumont. What does she mean I wouldn't know him? I'm about ready to tell her I'm off the case. We're even. Of course, I need to talk with Lin Pierce. He'll probably be relieved. Maybe, he'll fire me. It would serve me right for being so naïve.

The Pit Stop is on my right. What the heck, I pull into the lot and park. I check my phone now that I have some kind of service. Yes, there's a call from Jack. I play the message.

"Isabel, it's me, Jack. Sorry about last night. Those damn mutts. I didn't find them until two in the morning. I promise to make it up to you."

I'll accept that. It's only one or so, too soon for Jack to be at the Rooster. I might stop by his house if his truck's there. Right now, I'm walking through the front door of the Pit Stop. Barbie comes from the back after the bell announces my arrival.

"Hey, Isabel," she says. "How's it going, hon?"

"So-so."

I head for the cooler for a bottle of water.

"Only so-so?"

"Yeah, I don't seem to be making much progress on my case."

"Really, hon?" Barbie plays with that pendant around her neck. "Last time you were in here, you said you were."

That's when I spot Pete standing behind the open doorway, but to the side as if he thinks I won't see him. He sure is underestimating my observational skills. I pretend not to notice.

"You alone today?"

"No, no, Pete's back there somewhere," Barbie says with a cheery voice. "Here he is. Hi, darlin'."

"Hey, Isabel," Pete greets me.

Barbie grins at her hubby.

"Isabel says she's not making progress on that case."

He shakes his head.

"What did I tell ya, Isabel? Annette just can't accept the fact that her father was a drunk who died when he set his place on fire."

I set the bottle on the counter and reach into my purse.

"Yes, that's the official word."

Trouble with the Beaumonts

I'm about a half-mile from the Pit Stop when I notice in my rear-view mirror a pickup truck is driving too close to the Subaru's back bumper. Huh? I may be spacing out thinking about this stupid case, but I'm driving the speed limit. I can't be holding up this guy.

We are in a section of the road where the pickup could pass me easily, but it stays put. I speed up a little. The truck does, too. What the hell's going on?

That's when I notice who's behind the wheel. Gary Beaumont. His idiot brother, Larry, is beside him. The truck's front end is only a few feet from the Subaru's back bumper. I'm wondering when these f'ing idiots started following me. Did they see my car at the Pit Stop and wait until I left?

I am definitely not feeling good about this. Clearly, they're trying to scare me. It's working. About all I can do is keep my head and my eyes on this winding road. I'm not going to speed up and risk an accident. Maybe that's what those Beaumonts want.

When I glance in the rear-view mirror, the brothers are laughing. Gary gives the pickup truck's horn a few unfriendly blasts.

Hands on the wheel, Isabel. Keep your eyes on the road. Don't let them get to you.

This goes on for a couple of miles. My gut is in knots. Gary has not eased up at all. Are they planning to follow me all the way home? Then what? It would be a great moment for Police Chief Nancy Dutton to pass this way, but luck isn't on my side right now.

Finally, I see my chance. I close in on a delivery truck tooling down this country road. There's a passing lane. I don't bother signaling as I press the gas pedal. The driver is probably cursing me out big time, and I don't blame him, but now he's between the Beaumont brothers and me. I feel safe for a little while because at some point Gary is going to do the same thing.

Then I see the sign ahead for Baxter's. I hit the directional for a right-hand turn and bullet into the parking lot as close to the door as possible. I kill the engine and rush from the car. I check behind me. The Beaumonts aren't there.

But maybe they're parked alongside the road. Shoot, why did I even take this case?

I'm almost crying when I enter Baxter's.

"Isabel, you all right?" Dancin' Dave calls as he comes from behind the bar.

I shake my head.

"No, I'm not."

He puts his arm around me.

"What happened, Isabel? Did you have an accident?"

"Almost. The Beaumonts were tailgating me for miles. They were trying to scare me."

"What the fuck?"

Dave guides me to a table. I glance around. The place is empty, except for a couple of old boozehounds sitting at the bar, so I keep my voice down as I tell Dave the details. He sits beside me. I have his full attention.

"I'm sure glad you're open," I say.

"Me, too. But I'm concerned about you getting home safely. I don't trust those guys."

I sigh.

"Yeah."

"Say, how about my following you home?"

"That's sweet of you, but you don't have to… "

Dave doesn't let me finish.

"But I want to. When do you need to head back? Could you stick around for a little while?"

"Soon, I'm afraid. I've got a dog I need to let outside."

"Just a sec."

Dave walks toward the bar. He talks with the bartender. His

205

voice is loud enough for me to hear across the room.

"If those damn Beaumonts show up, tell 'em they're not welcome in here until I have a talk with 'em," he says with authority in his voice. "If they give you a lick of trouble, call the cops."

"Yeah, boss," the bartender says.

"I'm gonna see Isabel home. I'll be back later." Then Dancin' Dave, all friendly-like is back at my table. "Let's go, sweetheart. I'll follow your car. "

Safe and Sound

There's no sign of the Beaumonts on the rest of my ride home. The only person tailing me is Dancin' Dave, and he's doing it at a respectable distance in his pickup. I make it safely to Conwell, noting Jack's pickup is already parked at the Rooster, but I'm not stopping for anything or anybody until I get to my driveway. I give Dave plenty of notice I'm turning. He parks beside my car, and then he's bounding outside to walk beside me.

"Let me go in first," he tells me.

I smile. Even though the Beaumonts scared me on the road, I doubt if they'd have enough nerve to break into my home. But I let Dancin' Dave, who is being Chivalrous Dave, lead the way. Maggie barks on the other side of the door as I stick my key in the lock.

"You might want to get out of her way," I tell Dave. "She might knock you over."

The dog rushes outside, greets me briefly, then goes about her business as Dave and I make our way inside. Dave does a cursory look around.

"This is a very nice house," he says finally.

"Yeah, Sam was a great carpenter," I say. "Can I get you something to eat or drink?"

He grins.

"I wish I could stay, but I can't." He lightly touches my face with his fingertips. "By the way, you still haven't accepted that invitation of mine."

I sigh. I'm in a tough spot. Dancin' Dave is a nice guy, a lot like that other nice guy I know. It's clear to me what he wants: a close relationship, or at the very least, a romp in the sack, but I'm betting more. I'm no fool. A dinner out is like waving a flag at the starting line. But this guy just went out of his way to make sure I got home safely. Would Jack have done it? Yeah, I have no doubt about that.

Dave touches my face still. He waits for my answer.

"I'm gonna be honest with you," I say.

His brows rise.

"Oh?"

"You know I've been seeing Jack. I like him a lot. We've done things together." Okay, Isabel, let him read between the lines. "But you confuse the heck outta me."

His mouth twists into an amused smile.

"Confuse you?"

"Uh-huh, I've never been in this position before even when I was a girl. Two guys. But I do like you, and you were awfully sweet to help me today… "

"That's an awfully long answer, Isabel." He pauses. "I'm not gonna rush you. I just want us to have dinner and a good time together. We can take it fast or slow, whatever comes natural."

I nod.

"All right. I can't do Friday because I'll be working at the Rooster. What day is good for you?"

His grin has grown into a full-blown smile.

"Saturday is tough for me cause we have a band that night. The crowd gets kinda large, and I like to be there to keep things under control. You are most welcome to hang out. But for our night out, I say either Thursday or Sunday. What's your preference?"

Oh, dear, he said "our night out," but there's no way I'm getting out of this without being an ungrateful person.

"Sunday would be better."

"Sunday it is. I'll pick you up here around six. That okay?"

"Where are we going?"

"How about I surprise you?"

And then his hands are on my arms as he pulls me closer and plants a kiss on my mouth. It's a good kiss with enough passion behind it to show me he cares without being a slob about it. I go along, and we are into it for a while until we

208

break away. I think of nothing else, not Jack, the Beaumonts or the dog whining outside.

"Surprise me? I believe you just did," I say with a breathy voice.

At the Rooster

I head to the Rooster to visit Jack after I end my call to Ma. Naturally, she was horrified when I told her about the Beaumonts and their stupid stunt. She summed it up by saying, "Somebody sure didn't bring those boys up right." She was amused Dancin' Dave came to my rescue and that I actually drove fast, which is not a problem for her. I filled her in on the case and my discouragement. Her motherly advice? Give it a little more time. All right, Ma.

"Has the snow melted at the junkyard?" she asked.

"I'll find out tomorrow when I take your car up there," I told her.

"Remember how you had a hunch about the place?"

"Yeah, yeah, you're right."

My mother chuckled. She likes it when I tell her she's right, and frankly, she usually is.

The Rooster's lot only has a few pickups and clunkers from the True Blue Regulars, who all turn when I walk through the door. I get lots of nods and grins, and the same from Jack, who's behind the bar, and a cordial, "Here's my girl."

I give Jack a big smile.

"Nice to see you, too."

He pours my beer of choice even before I take off my jacket and choose a stool at the bar.

"Here, you go, Isabel." Then he leans in. "Did you get my message? What've you been up to today?"

Mentally, I answer his questions. The first is easy enough, but the second not so much.

"Course, I got your message. That's why I'm here. Have you and Fred locked those mutts up for good?"

"I believe so. Those damn buggers. You wouldn't believe where I ended up findin' 'em." He shakes his head. "I think they miss my sister and keep huntin' for her. I understand. But they're being a royal pain in the ass. If this don't work, I'm gonna put in one of those electric fences. It'd cost me some, but it might be worth it." He gives me a wink. "I don't like my nights getting interrupted."

I smile as I figure a way to answer Jack's second question. But then I hear, "Hey, Isabel," and Fred has taken the stool beside mine. He raises a finger to signal his cousin for a beer. Then he's focused on me again.

"Heard the Beaumonts were givin' you a hard time today," he says.

Crap, Fred knows, and now Jack knows. Let me guess. He stopped at Baxter's first.

Jack places a bottle of Bud on the counter.

"What are you talkin' about, Fred?" he asks.

Fred glances at me. His lips are curled in a know-it-all smile.

"You didn't tell him yet?" he asks me.

"I just got here," I answer.

Jack's hands are on the counter as he leans in toward us.

"Tell me what?"

Fred's head dips.

"Go ahead."

"Yeah, go ahead," Jack says.

I blow out some air.

"I was coming home from doing a couple of interviews. After I left the Pit Stop, I noticed a pickup was tailgating me. Gary Beaumont was at the wheel. His stupid brother was with him. It went on for miles. They were trying to spook me. It worked. Luckily, I was able to duck into Baxter's."

Fred sets down his beer.

"I was at Baxter's when those dumb asses had the nerve to show up. You should've heard Dave lay into them. He pulled them into the backroom, but he was yellin' so loud I could hear him from where I was sittin' at the bar. He told those Beaumonts if they ever go near you again, he was gonna ban

211

them for life from his place. He might even get the cops involved. You should've seen their faces when he was done with 'em."

Jack's eyes are on me.

"Isabel, you don't wanna go messin' with those guys."

My mouth is open. I'm about to agree. But Fred speaks first.

"Good thing Dave followed you home after that."

Crap again. Thanks a lot, big mouth Fred.

"Yeah, it was real thoughtful of him, especially since he only stayed a few minutes," I say as casually as I can make it.

Jack snorts.

"Yeah, mighty thoughtful," he says.

I hear a bit of something in Jack's voice. Of course, I'm not going to tell him about date night. This situation is getting a bit awkward. How much do I owe Jack? I honestly don't know.

Fred chuckles.

"I detect a bit of jealousy in that answer," he says for me.

Jack squints at Fred.

"Shut up, will ya?" He turns toward me. "Isabel, you know I would've done the same for you."

I smile sweetly for Jack and mean it.

"I have no doubt you would," I say. "Anyway, I'm thinking of quitting this case. All my leads are drying up. And I sure don't want to get chased off the road by a couple of local yokels who have it in for me, so I can get my car tuned up for free."

Jack reaches for my hand.

"Isabel, that's the most sensible thing I've heard you say in a while."

"Besides agreeing to work here again?" I joke.

He's back to grinning. He's got a twinkle in his eye.

"Yeah, that counts." He draws close, real close to whisper in my ear. "How about I come by later."

I giggle.

"I'd like that."

Fred slaps the counter.

"Shit, you two make me sick." He gulps the rest of his

beer. "I'm outta here. I'll take care of the dogs."

Jack's head wags as he laughs.

"See ya, Fred."

We are silent for a moment. I'm feeling rather guilty about accepting Dancin' Dave's invitation. Isabel, for someone who's so smart, sometimes you can be real stupid about people. What did Ma say over the phone tonight?

"You think that's a good idea, Isabel?" she said.

I answered, "Ma, I was in a tight spot. The guy just came to my rescue. It would've been rude of me to turn him down, don't you think? You and Dad taught me good manners."

She made a warm motherly chuckle.

"Of course, it's up to you how far you want to take it."

"Ma, I think you've been reading too many of those steamy romance novels."

"I raised such a funny girl."

Now Jack wiggles his fingers in front of me.

"Isabel, you there?"

I laugh.

"Oops, you caught me daydreaming."

His head bends close to mine. "I'm just about ready to throw these bums out. Nobody's bought a beer in twenty minutes. This was a big mistake opening on a Tuesday. What the hell was I thinkin'? Besides, I'd much rather be somewhere else."

"Really, where?"

"Anyone ever say you're a funny girl?"

"My mother did tonight. I think you have a few times."

Jack eyes the cowbell behind the bar, but instead he sticks two fingers between his lips to let out a loud whistle that would've called the cows home to their barn. Everybody in the joint jerks their head around.

"Hey, guys, we're closin' up early tonight. 'Fraid you're all gonna have to go home," he shouts.

I hear a collective groan from the drinkers and then a snicker.

"Isabel, you in here to start trouble?" one of the Rooster True Blue Regulars jokes.

213

I laugh with the rest of them.

"Sorry, I didn't mean to, guys," I reply.

Catching Up

Despite the moans and groans, and I suppose the kidding after I split, Jack does indeed close up early. I'm ready for him. No food tonight. I give him a, "Howdy, handsome," at the door and then lead him in a mad dash upstairs.

"Comin' to get ya," Jack jokes as he gives chase.

We fool around a bit before we get into the real business of it. Jack's got a knack for play, and I am happy to go along. As you may recall, I'm a bit embarrassed to say, our last romp in bed was the day of his sister's funeral. His cousin and those damn dogs interrupted our other attempts.

Afterwards, a breathy Jack rolls to his side.

"Aw, Isabel, I missed you."

I laugh.

"I'm right here, Jack."

"Funny… "

"Yeah, I'm a funny girl all right. Can you stay the night?"

"Just try kickin' me out, lady."

Morning After

Jack and I are up early for all of the fooling around we did last night. We talk a bit in bed, fool around some more, and then I make him breakfast. He's not in a super rush as Fred is going to feed the dogs and let them out in their yard. I have stuff to do, but I have time. I'm meeting Lin Pierce at his office to talk about this case, and then I will swing over to Rough Waters to check in with Annette. Depending on what Lin says, I may just call it quits.

"I could get real used to this," he says over his coffee mug.

Across the table, I laugh. Is that a proposal of sorts?

"Glad you feel comfortable."

"When's your mother comin' back?"

"Monday. I'm meeting my brother. She was gonna stay longer, but she told me last night, she misses the animals and me, in that order. She's got a great sense of humor."

His eyebrows flicker.

"We'd better make the most of her absence until then."

"She told me she didn't mind you staying over. After all these years, she's finally accepted I'm an adult and can be with a man."

He grins that big Jack Smith grin as he sets down his mug.

"As long as it's this man."

Shoot, I'm coming down with a good case of the guilts. Should I tell him about Dave's invitation? I would hate for him to find out via his cousin or some other guy who stops by Baxter's and hears about it. Hilltown men can be such little gossips. Besides, what kind of relationship would I have with Jack if I weren't honest?

I clear my throat.

"I've got something to tell you, Jack."

"Huh? Suddenly, you look serious. What's up?"

I press my lips together. Just spit it out, Isabel.

"I wanna be up front about something. I'm having dinner with Dave Baxter on Sunday."

"Dinner?"

"Just dinner. I didn't give him an answer when he asked me out before. Then, when he followed me home to make sure the Beaumonts didn't, he asked me again, and I felt I was in a tough spot." I watch Jack as he listens. His grin has shrunk to something a bit unsure. "I mean, I would've felt like a real wench if I told him no after he went out his way like that." I slide my hand across the table to touch his wrist. At least he doesn't pull back. "And I didn't want you to find out from somebody else like I was sneaking around or something."

Jack mulls over what I just told him. He's quiet, real quiet, and then, finally, he laughs.

"I'll give Dave credit for that maneuver," he says. "Isabel, I like bein' with you a lot. But I'm not gonna tell you who you should see or shouldn't see. I don't have that kind of power over you. I'm glad you told me. Just let me know if this thing with Dave goes somewhere else."

"I said only dinner."

"Uh-huh." He laughs again. "But I'm no fool. He wants a lot more than that. I sure did when I got to know you better last fall."

I feel myself go red from the neck up. "Is that why you hired me?"

He doesn't stop laughing. "You were the best one to apply."

"You told me a guy who wanted the job would've drunk you dry."

"Like I said, you were the best one to apply."

217

Lin's Advice

Lin Pierce is on the phone when I arrive. It sounds like business, so I hang out near the front of the office. As I suspected, his magazines are old and uninteresting since I'm not into hunting or fishing. Give me People magazine any day. I once told my dentist that I would quit him cold if he ever discontinued his subscription. Nothing takes my mind off somebody poking inside my mouth like reading about celebrities. The only thing better would be the National Enquirer.

Instead, I get up to read the newspaper pages framed on the walls. They're from decades ago, and all feature cases in which Lin was involved. Here's one of the headlines from my old paper, the Daily Star: **Man leads two lives with two wives.** I'd say the editor came up with a clever one there. According to the story, Lin worked for one of the wives after she suspected her husband was a bigamist. "It took a little legwork, but I got the job done," Lin told the reporter.

The next story was about a woman who felt she got cheated out of her inheritance when her ne'er-do-well nephew showed up a couple of weeks before her father died. Guess what? The nephew talked the failing man into leaving him everything. Lin was helpful on that one, too. The headline reads: Deathbed will killed in court. I give kudos again to the editor.

Another story involved a forgery — **Fake bills bring no thrills** — but I don't get too far because Lin is finished with his call.

"Ah, the good old days," he says as he stands beside me.

I point toward the forgery story.

"How did you get turned onto that case?" I ask.

"Another case of a jilted woman. She ratted her husband out." He chuckles. "I didn't make the arrest, of course. I just found out where he was doing it."

"Impressive."

He gestures toward his desk.

"Let's have that talk, Isabel."

Lin and I return to his desk. We sit opposite each other.

"Can I ask a nosy question first?" I say.

He snuffles.

"Nosy? Go ahead."

"What's with the cowboy getup?"

More snuffling.

"I do raise a small herd of cattle. Naturally, that doesn't make me a real cowboy, but I can fantasize a bit. This is Western Massachusetts after all."

"Fair enough."

He presses his fingertips together as if in prayer.

"But I believe that's not why you are here today, is it? Did you solve your case?"

"Uh, no. I feel like giving up instead."

"Give up? It hasn't been that long, Isabel."

I sigh.

"All the leads Annette's given me have been dead ends so far, well, except for maybe Al Sinclair and the Beaumont brothers. Al and Chet hated each other's guts. You probably knew that." I wait for an "uh-huh" from Lin before I proceed. "Then there are the Beaumont boys. Yesterday, they tried to run me off the road."

"What? Are you okay?"

"Yeah, yeah, I believe they only wanted to scare me. I'm fine. And then I think, I'm only getting free car maintenance for all of this trouble."

"That's what you agreed to. You'll learn."

"I'm learning all right."

He pauses again.

"You came for some advice, so here goes. How about giving it one week more?"

I mull what he says.

219

"One more week? Yeah, I hear you." I stare into space while I let that sink in. "I do have to confront Al Sinclair. I have yet to talk to his two sons or the last person on Annette's list. There might be something there." I smile. "Maybe I'll get lucky and find something on the Beaumonts."

"That's the spirit."

"There's also one thing I want to check at the junkyard. I'm going there next with my mother's car. You take yours in yet?"

"No, not yet." He chuckles. "You're frustrated, but in the end, you want to say you gave it your best shot even if things don't pan out like you hope."

If I were a callous person, now would be the moment to ask him about that case he blew, but I'm not and I won't. Lin is an okay person. I did look up that case in the Daily Star's online records. The Fattest Old Fart got the story awfully close. He told me Lin tried to make amends. That's a lot harder than doing it right from the beginning. That part wasn't in the story by the way.

"I'll give it one more week, just for you, Lin."

"No, no, do it for Chet Waters and his daughter. They deserve an honest answer. Remember what moved you to take this case. It certainly wasn't for the money."

He's absolutely right, and I tell him so.

Young Abe

Annette's not alone when I pull my mother's beast of a car into Rough Waters. She's outside, a rag in hand, talking with a young guy, in his late teens or early twenties, who I figure correctly is her son.

"Abe, this is Isabel. She's the one trying to find out who killed your grandfather."

Her son blinks and nods. He mumbles hello after I say the same.

Abe's a thin, tall guy with rounded shoulders and brown hair that hangs below his ears. I might have a hard time recalling his face, it is so unremarkable, except for the mustache that sprouts a sparse collection of rather long whiskers. He sniffs and wipes snot with the back of his hand until he finally reaches into the back pocket of his jeans for a raggedy bandana.

If my daughter Ruth had brought someone home like Abe as her boyfriend, we would've had a serious talk. But he's Annette's kid and a real country kid.

"Nice to meet you," I say, as I study him for any resemblance to his father, Gary Beaumont. He might have his father's beady, blue eyes.

"Abe's here to learn the business," his mother says. "Might as well. There's not a whole lot around here for work. Not much of a career pumping gas and cleaning toilets at the Flo 'n' Go."

"Flo 'n' Go," I say. "I don't believe I know that place."

"It's in Dayville, north of here. It's a lot like the Pit Stop but smaller." She points to my mother's car. "Abe, why don't you drive her car into the empty bay?"

"Key's in the ignition," I tell him.

Abe grunts and strolls toward my mother's car. There's nothing hurrying this boy. Annette watches him and doesn't speak. I can guess what happened. Abe got himself into trouble, lost his job, and now she's doing her best to turn him into a mechanic. It's tough being a single mom in the sticks.

As predicted, Annette speaks when Abe's out of earshot.

"I love my son, but he's so easily influenced by his buddies. Got himself fired from the only shitty job he could find. Now he's mine." She frowns as she shakes her head. "Takes after his father, I suppose."

"You mean Gary Beaumont?"

Annette's eyes get big, really big.

"How'd you find out?"

"Sorry. I can't say."

Her brow forms a hard roll.

"It was Fred, I betcha."

I wave both hands.

"I'm not saying."

"You tell anyone else?"

"No, no," I say, not counting my mother. "So, it's true."

Annette checks the garage for her kid.

"Please, keep that to yourself. I haven't even told Marsha." I hear a note of pleading instead of threat in her voice. "Abe just thinks it was some guy who was in the area for a short time. And that fucker Gary sure as hell doesn't know."

"I'm gonna be honest with you, Annette. I thought it odd you didn't tell me one of the suspects on your list is the father of your son, and one of our top suspects at that. That's an important detail to leave out, don't you think? Actually, you said I wouldn't know him."

Annette's shoulders rise in a half-shrug.

"I suppose. But sometimes I try to forget it happened. Gary and his brother turned out to be such assholes, I'm glad he wasn't a part of my son's life. When I see him now, I wonder why I ever went out with him." She spits on the ground. "He didn't force himself on me or anythin' like that. We were drinkin' and smokin' in his pickup, and you know what happened next. My father would've killed him if he ever found out."

Something clicks inside. It's one of those ah-ha moments I got as a reporter when things began to make sense.

"Any chance your father could've and he confronted Gary? Maybe things got outta hand?"

The toe of her boot taps into the mud.

"Never thought of that." We're both silent for a while as we let that possibility sink in. But then she shakes her head. "Nah, if that asshole found out he fathered my kid, don't you think he would've talked with me about it? He sure would've had somethin' over on me."

Oops, now I feel that fizzle a reporter gets when a hunch falls apart.

"Yeah, I can see that."

"So, how's the case goin'?"

I study her. She already knows.

"I don't seem to be making a whole lot of progress. I called your brother Mike's former boss, and he confirmed he was stuck in a snowstorm. That guy Anthony was a bust. Your ex, Fred, too. I haven't caught up with JoJo Tidewater yet. But be honest with me. Is he really a suspect or are you just trying to piss him off?"

She presses her lips hard.

"Piss him off. Sorry. He owes me money."

"So, that's the bum. Fine, I'll cross him off the list." I feel like slapping her, but I let it go. "The Beaumonts are still at the top of the list. I sure stirred something up in those guys."

"Yeah, I heard how they tailed ya."

"You did?"

"Everybody at Baxter's heard," she says. "What about Al?"

"I have some things to talk over with him and his boys. I'm working up to it."

Her hands are on her hips.

"Are you quittin' on me?"

"Not yet. I just met with my boss. He says to give it one more week. I agreed. I'm just gonna do my best for you."

"That's all I asked for from the start." She nods as her kid stands in the doorway of the garage and calls for her. "He's ready. Let's take care of your mother's car. By the way, I had to laugh when you pulled in with that Ford. Changes your whole look drivin' that old lady car."

I laugh.

"Maybe I'll use it to go under cover," I say. "While I'm here, I wanna take a look around. Looks like the snow's melted some."

"You really think somebody dropped somethin' on the ground that night?"

"That's what I'm hoping. Wish me luck."

Annette gives me a full-armed wave as she walks toward her son, whose head is down as if he's facing some sort of doom. Poor kid, lost kid, but Annette's a nice mom who wants to do her best.

I spin around and head to that spot where the reporter, Sean Mooney, got a picture of that patch of blood. Just like winter, it's taking a lot for the snow to leave around these rows of junkers. There's mud besides the snow, so I'm glad I'm wearing boots. I'll continue to do so until this damn season is over. I find a stick, likely the handle of some long-gone farm rake or hoe, and use the tip to poke around the mud, but I find nothing in the top wet layer. I give it a stir and a chop but still nothing.

To my left, snow is piled high against the nearest car, something old and American, yes, a Ford. How long has it been here? I jab at the snow, which thawed and froze into a sold block. I lean the pole against the car and march inside.

Annette and her son hang over the engine of my mother's car.

"Find anythin'?" she asks without looking up.

"How long has that blue Ford at the end of the first row been there?"

Her head tips to the right. She squints.

"We've had that one for a while, five years maybe. Nobody wants that hunk of junk." Her face brightens. "Hey, that's before Pop died. Why?"

"I just keep thinking there's something there, but that damn snow is in the way."

224

Annette turns toward her son.

"When we're done here today, I want you to take the pickaxe and shovel and clear the snow around that car. Just get it down, so the sun can do its job. Don't touch anythin'." Annette turns toward me. "I'll call you after he's done. Your' mother's car is ready by the way. Don't let it sit so much. Take that baby out on the road."

I smile as she drops the hood.

"Thanks for the advice."

Annette watches while I back the car from the garage. She bites her lip as if she wishes she had told me more. I'm ready to drive forward through Rough Waters' gate when I hear her shout. She waves hard with both arms.

"Wait! Wait! Isabel! Wait!"

I brake and roll down the window.

"What's up?"

"Be back in a sec."

Annette moves fast inside the garage and minutes later she is standing beside my car. Her hand is out. A gold watch lies in its palm.

"Is that what I think it is?" I ask.

"Yeah, it belongs to one of those Sinclair kids. I found it on Pop's workbench. Look on the back. There's writin'."

I turn over the watch, where I see the name Eben Sinclair etched into the surface. As I recall that's the grandfather's name.

"You want me to return it for you?"

"Uh-huh," she says with a flat voice. "I found the watch last year. I knew who it belonged to, but I held onto it. Give it to the kid. Maybe it'll make it easier when you meet Al and his boys."

"It just might. I'll talk with them tomorrow. It's getting late. I've got animals at home and my mother's away."

Annette's head bobs as if she agrees with every word I say.

"Sure, sure."

"I'll be waiting for your call when Abe is done." I smile to put her at ease. It must've taken a lot for her to give me that watch and admit her hand in it. "Okay, I believe I'm gonna drive this baby around town and fool a few people."

Annette and even Abe laugh when I grab a knit hat that belongs to my mother from the backseat and pull it low over my head. I take sunglasses from my purse. And then I gun my mother's car out of Rough Waters. In the rearview mirror, I see Annette slap her thighs as she whoops up a laugh.

I head for the Beaumont brothers' dump and park my mother's Ford along the side of the road. Nothing stirs in that den of iniquity. Their pickups are in the driveway, but there's no movement in the windows. Wait, I see a shadow move across a window on the left side of the house, the kitchen where we met, I believe. Instinctively, I lower myself in the seat.

Hold on, Isabel, what do you think you're doing parking in front of the Beaumonts' house? Do you honestly believe you will learn something that will solve this case? Or maybe you're just trying to spook them a little. They haven't seen your mother's car before. Maybe they'll think you're a narc. I laugh and shake my head. This ain't my style. Besides, I bet they're taking Dancin' Dave's threats seriously. They haven't even left any threatening messages on my phone.

I put the car in drive.

Another back way takes me past Baxter's, uh, no thanks, and then another loop brings me back on the main drag near the Pit Stop. Shoot, it's mid-afternoon already. Suddenly, I'm hungry. Maybe Barbie has some of those homemade muffins left.

I rush inside to the ring of the bell above the door and give a big, "Howdy, Barbie," but I stop when she steps from the backroom. Her arm is in a sling.

"Ouch, what happened to you?"

She makes a sheepish smile.

"I slipped on some ice. Nothing's broken. Just a bad sprain."

"Seems like you've had a run of bad luck with injuries lately."

She doesn't look me in the eye.

"Just a stupid fall. I'm a little clumsy. Just ask Pete."

I've heard that before from women in troubled relationships. I lean forward. I don't recall seeing Pete's pickup truck, but I'm not taking any chances. I lower my voice.

"Are you okay, really?" I ask. "Is there something you wanna tell me? Maybe I can help."

She shakes her head.

"I'm… " She stops then begins again. "I, uh… "

Barbie's head flips around. I hear boot heels in the backroom. Pete Woodrell makes a quick sweep into the store. I was concentrating on what Barbie was saying, so I didn't hear his pickup pull up.

"Isabel, how ya been?"

"Hey, Pete," I say, but nothing more since his greeting isn't a question but just an over-friendly hello.

He stands beside Barbie and gives her a half-hug.

I'm getting ill.

"Don't know what I'm gonna do with the clumsy little gal," he says. "Right, hon?"

"Uh-huh," she says without much conviction.

I'm not in the mood to buy anything here, and luckily, the muffins are gone. I'll be glad when I don't have to stop at this dump anymore.

"Gee, I came by for one of Barbie's muffins. But it looks like I'm too late. You got cleaned out."

Pete chuckles.

"Yeah, they go awfully fast. Right, hon?"

Barbie's head bobbles as if it's on string.

"Uh-huh."

I study Pete and Barbie. There's definitely something amiss here.

"I'll remember that the next time I swing through. See you both."

Family Intervention

Feeling a bit guilty, I take Maggie for a long walk when I get home. The dog is happy to run and sniff. Ma would approve. Upon our return, I find I have company. My kids are here.

"Hey, whose birthday is it?" I joke when I come inside.

Ruth, who sits at the kitchen table, gives me that disapproving daughter look. Her arms are crossed. She wants to talk about something serious, and for backup, I suppose, she's brought along her brothers, who are rifling through the fridge. Maggie joins them.

"Hey, girl, where've you been?" Alex asks the dog.

"Are you two done in there?" Ruth asks her brothers. "I've got to leave soon. Gregg has the baby."

Her brothers shut the fridge door and dutifully join Ruth at the table.

"What's up?" I ask as I take a chair.

Ruth glances at her brothers.

"Matt heard about what those Beaumonts did the other day, how they almost ran you off the road. That was dangerous, Mom, and I, uh, we don't like it one bit."

"The Beaumonts did scare me a little, but they're not going to bother me anymore."

"How can you be so sure?"

How do I explain Dave Baxter to my daughter? I'll guess I'll give it a try.

"If they do, they'll be banned from the only bar in the hilltowns that will let them drink. I have the owner's word. That should do it. You don't look convinced."

Alex and Matt are stuffing their faces with food, so I expect Ruth will do all the talking or rather scolding.

"I don't understand why you are working on this case," she

says. "The last one was bad enough, but at least you knew the people involved, and it was in our town. But this one? It's way the heck out of the way. You're dealing with junkyard owners and drug dealers."

I hear the concern in my daughter's voice. She is definitely speaking out of love for me.

"The junkyard owners are actually nice people. But if it's any consolation, you're not the only one to question this case."

"Grandma?"

I tip my head.

"Actually, no. Grandma's okay with it. It was somebody else. Jack Smith." Now I'm expecting a lecture about Jack, so I ramble on. "Just so you know, this case doesn't seem like it's going anywhere. I'm giving it one week, and then I'm calling it quits. I was ready to quit today, but Lin Pierce, the P.I. that I work with, said to give it a little bit more time."

I see Ruth's resolve melt a bit. She relaxes those crossed arms.

"One week."

"Uh-huh. I just told Annette, the woman who hired me, the same thing. Being a P.I. is harder than I thought. But I said I'd give it my best shot, and I still have a few things to look into for her. Okay?"

Ruth sighs. She glances at her brothers, who haven't stopped chowing down.

"We just don't want anything bad happening to you like what happened with Eleanor Smith," Ruth says with a quiver in her voice.

I pat her arm.

"I promise you three I won't do anything that puts me in danger. I will be more selective about the cases I decide to take on. All right?"

"Yes." Ruth whips her head toward her brothers. "Thanks a lot, you two."

The boys shake their heads.

"You're welcome," Alex says with a full mouth.

"Any time," Matt says.

The Rivalry

As planned, Jack shows up after closing the Rooster. He surprises me at the door with flowers, a real big bouquet and not just carnations. I'm surprised and amused. It's obvious he made a trip to the city earlier today to buy them because none of the stores in the hilltowns carry flowers, including the Conwell General Store. I get a smooch as he hands me the bouquet.

"These flowers are absolutely beautiful." I take a sniff. "Oh, stargazer lilies."

"They're almost as beautiful as you."

I feel my neck and face flushing. I'm doing that insane giggling.

"Oh, Jack," is about all I can muster before I kiss him back.

I shut the door, and while Jack gives the dog, Maggie, a couple of pats, I'm in the kitchen searching for a vase in the cupboards. I fill one with water as Jack strolls toward the table. He grabs the flowers Dancin' Dave gave me and tosses them in the trash.

"You won't be needing these anymore," he jokes as he sets the empty vase in the sink.

I place the flowers Jack brought me on the table.

"I guess not."

He grins as he wraps his arm around me.

"You guessed correctly, ma'am."

Reporter's Notebook

The landline rings while Jack and I finish our coffee the next morning. As usual, I made him pancakes, and when he protested, I reminded him that he needs to keep up his strength if he's going to keep up these nightly visits. That sure got him chuckling. Jack's a cinch to please.

I glance at the phone to see if it's worth answering or leaving for voice mail. The call is from Sean Mooney. I pick up right away.

"Isabel, guess what? I found that notebook," he says.

"That's great news, Sean. Uh, can you read your writing?"

He chuckles

"Barely. But just enough to prick my memory. It seemed there were a number of townspeople who gathered at the junkyard when word got out about Mr. Waters' death. They stayed out of the way of the cops and firefighters. I paid attention because I was looking for anyone who might be willing to talk. I kept striking out. Except for a couple of guys, nobody wanted to speak to the outsider reporter. I just stayed back and studied the group."

"Smart. Were they near the spot where you found the blood?"

"No, they weren't. From my notes, there were two guys who looked like brothers. One had a scar on his face and the other, a mustache. Real local boys. They didn't seem that broken up over Mr. Waters' death. Actually one of them made a joke about the old man being... "

"A crispy critter?"

"How'd you guess? Naturally, I didn't use that in my story."

"Those were the Beaumont brothers, high on my list of

231

suspects."

"No kidding."

I glance toward Jack, who is listening to my end of the conversation. I blow him a kiss.

"They're the ones who stood out from that crowd. And there was a woman who was crying."

"Crying? The woman wasn't Annette Waters?"

"No, somebody else. I think I wrote her name, but that part of the page got torn off. Actually, the notebook is in rough shape. Looks like I dumped coffee on it. Sorry. I've gotten neater about my notes."

"Don't worry about it. I'm surprised you still have the notebook."

"Anyway, she was pretty bundled up. It was damn cold that day. She had a wool hat pulled down low and she was wearing one of those puffy coats with the hood up, so she could've been fat or skinny. She was wearing sunglasses, too. I couldn't even tell you her hair color." He takes a breather. "I did try to talk with her, but she just stared back at me and shook her head. That's what I wrote down anyways."

"Was she alone?"

"It was hard to tell. The cops made everybody keep out of the way. There was maybe twenty of so. They were in one group. One of the guys was the owner of the Pit Stop. I did get a quote out of him later at the store."

"Maybe the woman was a relative. Thanks anyway."

"How's the case going?"

"Eh, not so good. I'm giving it one week more. Actually, now six days. The clock is ticking. Too many dead ends."

"Well, keep me in mind if you do break the case."

"I'll call you after the cops and my mother."

I give Jack the lowdown about Sean and his part in the case. I feel free to tell him anything, well, except about the Beaumont brothers' stash of dope in the Corolla. I keep my promises even with scumbags.

"Six days, eh?" he says. "You'd better get going, Isabel."

"Yes, I'd better. I don't want to fail on my second attempt at being a P.I. So, I'm kicking you out and heading to

Sinclair's Junkyard." I laugh. "My life these days is spent mostly in junkyards."

"What are you doin' there? I thought Al had an alibi."

"That he was home with his wife? That's not very airtight, is it? I have some questions about his boys. I figure I have an in since I'm delivering that watch to one of his boys, the one he lost at that poker game you told me about."

"It belonged to Junior. How'd you get your hands on it?"

"Annette found it in the garage. She asked me to return it."

Jack hums.

"You're gonna make that kid happy."

"We'll see after I question them. Maybe I'll ask him and his brother a few questions about the Beaumonts since they used to be buddies," I say. "Will I see you tonight?"

"Try keepin' me away," he says, grinning.

The Return

Al Sinclair studies my mother's car as I pull into his junkyard. I bet he's wondering if I'm some old lady who got lost, or maybe he thinks I'm some religious nut trying to convert junkyard owners. One eye is cocked when he steps closer to inspect my mother's heap. I shut the engine. The watch is in the pocket of my jacket. I pat it just to make sure.

"Hey, Al, remember me?" I say as I get out. "Isabel Long."

"Yeah, I do." His voice is flat. "Didn't recognize the car. Not your style as I recall."

"It belongs to my mother. Annette says I shouldn't let it sit so much."

"Annette. I see."

"Are your sons here?"

His eyes sliver into slits.

"Junior and Roy? What for?"

"I have a gift for one of them. I believe Junior."

"Gift? What kind of gift?"

"Let's say it was something that belongs in your family, and one of them lost it in a poker game." I pull the watch from my pocket. "This was your father's, wasn't it? It says Eben Sinclair on the back. See?"

For the first time, the man's features relax. His mouth hangs open for a moment, but then he catches himself.

"Be right back."

I slip the watch back into my pocket and take a gander while I wait, presumably for the return of Al and his boys, or rather men. Just like at Rough Waters, the junks, except for the newer additions or the ones they need, are locked in snow. I haven't heard from Annette about Abe's progress, but I don't plan to bug her about it. I wouldn't put it past her to do it

234

herself if the kid doesn't get the job done.

The garage door opens. Al and his sons stroll my way. I recognize them from the Rooster. Both have their father's facial features and about his height. I could joke that he would have lost a paternity suit, but Al doesn't seem like a guy who would appreciate my irreverent sense of humor.

"This is Isabel. Junior, she's got somethin' you lost."

"Lost?" Junior asks.

"I believe it was at a poker game a few years back," I say.

I hand Junior the watch.

"Grandpa's watch. I don't believe it." He turns it over to read the engraving. His brother moves closer to get a better view. His head is up. "Thanks. I thought it might've burned up in that fire."

"No, Annette said she found it in the garage on one of the work benches when she was cleaning up. I was there yesterday and volunteered to bring it over. I heard from Jack Smith what happened that night at the Rooster."

Roy snorts.

"Did she find the money he cheated out of us?"

"Uh, no, but Jack told me he gave you both some cash that night to make up for it. He also said you, Junior, went outside to get a gun, but he talked you out of using it."

Both sons are red-faced. I hear a bit of low stammering.

Their father smirks.

"You boys didn't tell me that part," he says, but then he recovers. "Doesn't dismiss Chet Waters cheated at cards and, pardon my language, was a complete asshole."

"Al, I heard you and he got into it over a poker game at the Rooster just before he died. I was told you were pretty ticked off."

"Yeah, but I got over it. I still don't buy that story somebody killed Chet, but if someone did, it was probably over some bad business deal."

Thank you very much, Al Sinclair, for that opening in this conversation. I clear my throat.

"Now that you've brought up that topic, I'd like to ask your sons about their association with Gary and Larry

Beaumont back then."

I see frowns all around.

"What'd you mean by that?" Al mutters.

"Once, when I had a sit-down with the Beaumont brothers, they told me they used to have, uh, an arrangement with Junior and Roy concerning the extras that were stowed in some of the junks from a certain business in Springville."

"What about it?" the younger Sinclair brother, Roy, mutters.

Ouch, I hit a sore spot I see. I will play it cool.

"I'm not here to get you into trouble. But it was my understanding a certain car, a '78 Corolla, went to Chet Waters' place instead of here."

Al holds up his hand.

"I know what you're gettin' at. I put a stop to it. I want nothin' to do with those jackasses or that business. I'd be more than glad if you found out they're the guilty ones, and they go to jail for good. Everybody in this town would be better off."

"Did Chet figure it out?"

Al spits on a muddy patch.

"Course, he did. He might've been one mean son of a bitch, but he wasn't stupid. He even had the nerve to show up here. I can see that smug look on his face as if he had somethin' over me and my family. He even threatened to call the cops."

"Did he?"

"Nah, he died before that happened, I guess."

Al and I give each other a long, hard stare. We both realize the implications of what he just said. And if it's true, I'm in a bad spot. But I've come this far. I'm not backing down.

"You have anything to do with that?"

"Like I told you, if I wanted to kill Chet Waters, I would've done it years ago."

"How can you be so sure?"

"Cause he did that kind of shit all the time." He snorts. "I gave it back to him. Like when I heard somebody was suing him for sellin' a real lemon, I made sure to push his buttons. It was the way we didn't get along."

I eye the Sinclair boys.

"You remember where you were the night Chet Waters was killed?"

Both nod.

"Shit, I was on my honeymoon," Junior says before he turns toward his brother. "Can't forget somethin' like that. You?"

"I was with Mom and Dad," Roy says. "I was still livin' at home. Right, Dad?"

Al nods.

I don't respond. Both are using a woman near and dear to them as an alibi. Do I think the Sinclair boys are killers? I didn't suspect Eleanor Smith of being one. Six days, I remind myself. Six days.

"Mind if we talk privately?" I ask Al.

"Sure," he says before he turns toward his sons. "Get back to work, boys."

I wait until Junior and Roy leave, which gives me enough time to either lose my nerve or figure out what I'm going to say. I went over it in my head on the drive here. Al Sinclair waits.

"Some folks told me about a tragic accident. Chet Waters was at the… "

He raises his hand.

"Yeah, I lost my sister in that one," he says. "Would I have killed him because of it? I sure felt like it at the time, but forty or so years later? Nah. We were kids. Stupid kids. It could've happened if I was the driver. He and I were drunk that night. But it was the end of any friendship between us. Chet didn't even go to her funeral. Do you believe that?"

"That's awful," I say. "Maybe he was too ashamed to show his face. Didn't he go into the service around that time?"

"Maybe."

"How would you have felt?"

"Like shit, but I would've gone to the funeral. It would've been tough, but I would've done the right thing."

"I bet you would," I say. "Well, I should get… "

Al's face lights up a bit when a van rolls into the yard. Two

237

women are in the front seat.

"Hold on," he says. "I want you to meet my wife. That's my daughter-in-law, Linda, driving her. Junior's wife."

The side door slides. The woman at the wheel pushes her mother-in-law's wheelchair over a ramp.

"Was your wife hurt in that accident?" I ask.

Al shakes his head.

"No, no, Kate's got MS." He purses his lips. "Terrible disease. But Linda is real good about comin' over and giving her rides. So's our other daughter-in-law, June, the one who's havin' the baby. Come meet them."

"Watch out for the mud," Al tells Linda. "There you go. This is Isabel Long. I told you about her."

Kate Sinclair gives me the once-over.

"You're the one," she says. "Heard my Al gave me as an alibi. Well, I can vouch for him that night. I only let Al out once a week, when one of my son's wives comes over to help me. As you can see, it's hard for me to get around by myself."

"Do you remember the night Chet died?"

"Of course, I do. We all do. It was a horrible thing to happen to that man. Whoever says they don't is probably lying."

"You've made an excellent point."

Then I remember the reporter Sean Mooney saying the Beaumont brothers were at the fire scene that morning. But they told me they didn't remember what happened the night before. What liars. Damn it, I wish I had solid evidence to nail those guys. Maybe I'll find it at Rough Waters.

Chief Dutton

Minutes later, when I reach Caulfield, I spot the town's cruiser parked in the rest area off the main drag. Maybe Chief Nancy Dutton is trying to catch speeders and make a little money for the town. I pull off the road. Chief Dutton gets out right away. I join her.

"Hey, it's you, Isabel," she says with a laugh. "That's not your usual car."

"It's my mother's."

"Going under cover?" she jokes.

"Something like that. My mechanic says I need to take the car out more."

"How's your case going?"

Ah, the eternal question I hear these days, and now I give the eternal answer.

"Not so good. It was only three years ago, but I just can't seem to make headway past the Beaumont brothers. I still don't have any hard evidence to link them."

She plants a hand on her hip.

"I believe those two would be capable of doing something like that. I hear they're up to no good, probably selling drugs, but I have nothing to nail them." Her head bounces a bit. "Yeah, I hear you. Hard evidence is necessary. I just don't have the budget or the time to put a surveillance on them."

"I'm giving this case a week, actually now I'm down to six days."

She turns her ear toward the cruiser.

"Sorry, I thought I heard my radio," she says. "Six days?"

"I'll give it my best shot until the last one. Speaking of which, I had a conversation with the reporter from the Berkshire Bugle who covered Chet's death. He called me after

239

he found his notebook. He mentioned a crowd of local folk had gathered that morning at the fire scene and how one of the women was pretty distraught. Do you remember that?"

Chief Dutton doesn't answer. The radio insider her cruiser is squawking. I hear the words "two-car collision" and "head-on." The chief does, too.

"Sorry, I gotta take this," she says as she sprints toward her car. The radio keeps going: "Injuries." She turns briefly. "Catch up with you later."

I lean against my mother's car as Chief Dutton rips out of here with the siren blaring and lights flashing on her cruiser. She certainly has more important business to attend to than answering my questions. I shake my head. This is the way things have been going. Isabel, you might not be cut out for this P.I. business.

But as I ponder my possible failure, I hear the honk of a pickup truck and watch as it makes a u-turn on the road then rolls into the rest area. I recognize the truck and the man behind the wheel. Dancin' Dave cranks down his window.

"I almost didn't recognize you with that car," he says. "You broke down or somethin'?"

I go around to the driver's side.

"It's my mother's. I was just talking with Chief Dutton, but she got a call."

"Yeah, I saw her tear outta here."

"I guess there was a bad accident."

Dave shuts the engine of his truck. I am careful not to lean against his door although I stand close enough to be friendly but not too darn friendly. Then I remember the good manners my parents taught me.

"I can't thank you enough for helping me the other day," I say, which cranks open a big smile on Dancin' Dave's face. "I heard you warned the Beaumonts about not bothering me."

He chuckles

"You did, eh? I tried to scare the crap outta those two. I believe the threat of a lifetime ban from my joint did it. Nobody else is gonna let 'em drink in their bar."

"That was mighty sweet of you to defend me like that. I

haven't heard a peep out of those guys or even seen them."

"Sweet. I like that. Say, wanna stop by my place? We can talk some more. I'll buy you a drink and whatever else you want."

Shoot, that guy doesn't give up. I'll give him that.

"Sorry. Can't. I've got stuff to do at home. But I am looking forward to our date Sunday."

The word "date" slips out of my mouth. I immediately regret it. Dave obviously doesn't.

"Date, eh? I like that. Well, I sure am. Hey, if you change your mind, come by. For you everything's on the house."

I blush, smile, and thank him in that order.

Catching Up with Ma

My mother finally calls me at around ten that night. She's maintaining her habit of staying up late at my brother's house. She's often the last one up in that household, even later than my brother's teenagers, but then again, they have school in the morning.

We've been playing phone tag for a couple of days, so Ma's voice is gleeful when I tell her the story about Annette's remorse over the pocket watch and then my returning it to Junior Sinclair. She, of course, is interested in my encounter with Al Sinclair and his wife. Al definitely has slipped from the suspect list, but he was a long shot anyway. So have his boys. I didn't see killer instincts in either of them.

"I would have liked to have been there for that," she says.

"You're missing out on all the fun being at Danny's," I joke.

"I see I am. I'll be back Monday." She laughs. "Any new clues?"

"I finally got a call from Sean Mooney. Remember him? He's the reporter from the Bugle. Anyway he found his old notebook. Get this. He says there was a woman bawling her eyes out at the junkyard that day."

"Not Annette?"

"No, this woman was with the group of nosy locals who gathered. She was bundled up because of the cold, so he couldn't describe her. He didn't know anybody anyways. Besides, everybody was concentrating on Chet's death." I pause. "I asked the chief about it today. She got called away for an accident before I could get anything out of her. It could be nothing. Maybe old Chet had a girlfriend. Annette said he had lady friends. Maybe there were some people in town who actually liked him." I laugh. "The only one I've met so far though is his daughter and that woman at the Pit Stop. Oh, and get this. The Beaumont boys were at the scene of the fire that morning."

"I thought they didn't remember anything about the fire."

"Yup, that's what they said."

Ma doesn't speak for a while. I hear CNN on a TV in the background.

"So, how's your love life?"

"You're too much, Ma," I say. "Oh, wait a minute. Jack's knocking at the door. I would say it's pretty good these days."

"Then you'd better hang up and let the man in."

Old Farts and the CIA

Jack leaves early the next morning to hightail into the city to buy groceries. Carole, the Rooster's cook, gave him a list of what to buy. He should've done it yesterday, he says, but he had a plumbing problem on Fred's side of the house that took most of the day to fix. A new band, the Hayseeds, is getting a tryout tonight. Naturally, he made sure "Good Hearted Woman" is on their playlist.

As I watch his pickup leave my driveway, I call Maggie in from the woods.

"I need to pay a visit to my friends up the road," I tell the dog. "You haven't met the Old Farts, have you? Sorry, no dogs are allowed in the backroom of the store."

The five regulars are in their usual spots when I arrive. Of course, I get a warm greeting and that joke about the espresso machine. The Fattest Old Fart pats the empty spot beside him. These guys sure like to make me feel welcome.

"We hear you have less than a week to go on this case," the Fattest Old Fart tells me with his fat face beaming as if he won something big.

His buddies hum and nod their heads.

"Uh, five days now," I say. "How did you know? Oh, never mind. You guys missed your calling. You should've worked for the CIA."

The Serious Old Fart smirks.

"Who says we don't? CIA stands for the Country Intelligence Agency by the way," he jokes, which makes me wonder if I should change his name to the Wittiest Old Fart.

"You guys are on a roll today," I joke back.

The Old Fart with Glasses clears his throat.

"Heard you had a scare with those Beaumont boys the

other day," he says.

The other Old Farts give him an appreciative stare. It's been unusual for the Old Fart with Glasses to bring up something new. By the smile on his hairless face, he feels awfully damn proud of himself. Everybody's eyes are on me.

"Yes, I did."

The Fattest Old Fart leans toward me, so his arm presses against mine.

"Inquiring minds want to know, Isabel," he says.

I turn toward the Old Fart with Glasses.

"This inquiring mind wants to know what you've heard."

I swear his chest puffs out.

"My sources say," the Old Fart with Glasses begins while I try hard not to roll my eyes. "The Beaumont brothers tailed you for miles. They were probably hoping you'd get nervous and run off the road. I guess they underestimated you." He licks his lips. "Course, I heard you got a little help from a certain gentleman who owns a bar. I believe his first name is Dave."

"Dave Baxter?" the Serious Old Fart says. "What else you got on Isabel?"

"Isabel ducked into the bar and this gentleman got really hot under the collar. And being a real gentleman, he followed her home to make sure she got there safely. Heard he gave the Beaumonts the riot act when they came in later that night." The Old Fart with Glasses smiles. Damn, he's feeling proud of himself. "Am I right, Isabel?"

The attention is back on me.

"So far so good," I say. "Anything else?"

The Fattest Old Fart chuckles.

"Somethin' going on with you and Dave? Everything okay with you and Jack?"

The Skinniest Old Fart coughs. It's his turn.

"I believe so. I heard his pickup has been parked overnight at Isabel's most nights this week."

I get to my feet.

"I believe you guys have had enough fun at my expense. I'll let you know how I make out with my case, or maybe you'll all tell me since you seem to have spies everywhere. See ya, fellas."

The Old Farts protest, but I leave anyway with a smile and a wave.

Third Degree at the Rooster

When I show up at the Rooster, Jack and one of the True Blue Regulars are dragging the pool tables to one side to make room for the dance floor. A few of the tables and some of the chairs will get stacked outside. Jack will reward the guy with a free beer or two for the assist.

"Be careful of the mud out there," Jack tells his helper. "Hey, Isabel, long time no see."

I grab the clean apron Jack stowed beneath the counter and walk toward him as I wrap the ties around me.

"Need any help?" I ask.

"Nah, we're almost done here."

He reaches for a quick kiss on the lips. Jack has been more open about his affections ever since Dancin' Dave showed up that night. Maybe Ma is right. A little competition doesn't hurt.

"Nice to see you, too, boss," I say.

After I visited the Old Farts, I just hung around home, cleaning and doing laundry because Ma is coming home Monday. I took Maggie for a long walk. Then I spent some time in my office going over my leads, adding some new info, but nothing popped out at me. No ah-ha moments. I still haven't heard from Annette, but I'm not going to call and remind her. That woman has a mind like a steel trap. She'll get after her son until he's finished the job.

The night goes well, first the wave of diners, plus those who planned to come early and stay late. It's a full house tonight. Spring, real spring, can't come fast enough for this town, and people are just sick of the snow although now I see clearings of dirt and grass in the fields. The common complaint tonight is muddy roads. When Sam and I built our house, we made sure we lived on a paved road. No axle-sucking mud for us, thank you.

The next wave comes before the band starts, filling in the holes made by those who left early. The Hayseeds, new to the Rooster, are revving up the local favorites, the usual danceable blend of Skynyrd, Alabama, and an assortment of country and western stars. I'm pouring beer. Jack is clearing. At one point we switch jobs when I ask.

"Need to move my legs," I tell him.

He glances down at my skirt.

"Go ahead and move them for me."

His cousin, Fred, who's sitting at the counter within earshot groans.

"Stop it, you two."

Jack punches Fred's arm.

"You're just jealous," he says.

"You betcha."

And so, the evening goes with lots of good-natured joking and foolhardy drinking. I'm on the floor gathering empties when I hear my name yelled across the room and above a rather gutsy version of the Stones' "Brown Sugar." The song takes the dancers by surprise for a moment, but then they crowd the floor, ponytails bouncing on both the men and women.

I glance back, trying not to drop the tray to see who's hollering my name. I might've guessed. The Floozy and Tough Cookie have arrived. They hustle across the floor as I set the tray on the counter.

"Your best buddies," Jack jokes.

"They are these days."

Marsha and Annette crowd to my right and left. I smell they've had a few beers already. Of course, there's a bit of BO, too, from Marsha. I wonder how her boyfriend, Bobby, stands it, but maybe he likes his women a little on the ripe side.

I am happy to see these two women. They're loud and don't hold back now that they know me better. I certainly admire their work ethic. And better yet, they make me laugh.

Annette punches my arm.

"Guess what, Isabel?" she asks.

"Uh, you won the lottery?"

Another punch.

"You're a scream, Isabel. If I won the lottery, do you think I'd be drinkin' in this dive?" She nods at Jack. "No offense, Jack."

"None taken," Jack says.

Ouch, Marsha jabs my other arm.

"Sure she would, but she'd buy a round for everybody," she says.

Annette's head tips back as she makes a full-throttle laugh.

"Yeah, yeah, that's what I'd do."

I escape behind the counter, so I don't get punched and jabbed again. My head is up as I drop empties into the box below. I swear I could do this part of my job one-armed and blindfolded.

"I take it you didn't win the lottery after all," I tell Annette.

She gives her cousin a jab.

"Listen to her," she says. "Nah, Abe finally finished the job today. It took longer. That snow was kinda tough. Besides, my boy has to learn how to work harder."

My gut tells me Annette's focus has shifted to making her boy a better man, an admirable trait these days. I want to solve this case for her, but maybe she'll be somewhat content that someone, especially a newcomer, took her seriously. As I pledged to her at the start, I will give it my all until the last day.

"I made that special delivery for you," I tell Annette.

The Floozy goes, "Huh, huh," before her cousin jabs her.

"The watch I told you about," she says.

"Ah."

"So, what did that little punk say?" the Tough Cookie asks.

"He was grateful," I say. "Oh, I did have that talk with Al and his boys. I'd say they're off our list."

"Figures."

"But I'm not giving up just yet," I tell Annette. "How about I come over tomorrow to dig around?"

"That works for me. Make it early afternoon, say one or later, after the sun hits that spot for a while. Make it easier."

She smirks. "Besides, I'm expectin' company tonight."

"Anyone I know?" I ask.

"Not sure. Haven't picked him out yet."

"We've got a full house, so your chances are good."

"Yeah. And if I ain't as picky as you."

That gets Jack laughing.

"I'm glad Isabel isn't just settlin' for just any old guy," he says. "What can I get you two babes?"

Marsha snorts.

"Babes?"

Of course, the Floozy and Tough Cookie order Buds before they bump their way through the crowd to the other end of the room.

"What'd you think of the band?" Jack asks.

"By the looks of it, the Hayseeds are a hit. People are bopping all over the place."

Jack grabs a tray.

"Get ready to dance, Isabel." He fills four shot glasses with bottom shelf whiskey. "I predict I'm gonna be ringin' that cowbell pretty soon."

I almost give him a playful jab, but instead, I pinch his cheek.

"Sure enough, boss."

Something Good

"Will I see you tonight?" Jack asks while he ties his boots in the living room.

He's sitting in what used to be Sam's favorite chair, one of the pieces he built. Jack looks natural there.

"Uh-huh," I say. "I'm doing the usual Saturday stuff this morning before I head over to Annette's junkyard."

"You really think you're gonna find some clue on the ground?"

I shrug.

"I felt so sure before, but now, eh... "

Jack stands.

"Aw, Isabel, don't be so hard on yourself. You've done more than the cops ever did."

"I suppose."

After Jack leaves, I hit the Conwell triangle: the dump, store, and library. Mira, the librarian, called to tell me she's put aside new books for my mother. Ma will be glad when she gets back Monday. Her stash of steamy novels was getting low. I decide to take my mother's car, so I don't get any grief from Annette when I see her later today.

I reach Rough Waters at around two, just as one of Annette's lover boys is pulling out of the driveway. I recognize the pickup. One of the Rooster's True Blue Regulars got lucky last night. I hope his wife, who's out of town visiting her mother, doesn't find out. Yeah, yeah, I hear everybody's business at the Rooster. But my lips are sealed.

Abe did a decent job clearing the snow around the old Ford. The sun helped, too. Annette, who's decked out in a bathrobe and boots, joins me when she sees me rifling through the trunk of my mother's car for my bucket of garden tools. I decide on a claw and spade.

"Need any help?" she asks.

"No, but thanks for putting Abe to work."

"Somebody has to," she says with a bit of scorn in her voice. "I'll leave you to it. Gotta take a shower. Just holler if you need me. By the way, I'm glad to see you took your mother's car out for a spin."

I shut the trunk.

"Yes, ma'am."

I stand near the cleared area, figuring the best way to search. It's a bit muddy beneath the thin layer of snow, and I don't want to step in the parts I haven't searched yet. The area is about ten by ten. My plan? I'll gently probe the mud in one-foot strips and then advance forward.

"Come on, Isabel, find something good," I tell myself out loud.

I'm about halfway through the mud, and so far, all I've found are beer bottle caps, the lid to a Skoal chewing tobacco can, and an assortment of screws. Annette checks on me after her shower. So does her son, Abe, who mumbles something after I thank him for clearing the snow. One of his buddies dropped him off at the gate. He's got a roll of heavy chain on his shoulder.

"We'll be right back," Annette tells me. "We gotta tow Abe's car back here. It broke down last night. At least it happened in his driveway."

"Okay, you know where to find me."

After Annette and Abe leave in her pickup, I get back to work. I am methodical, using the claw slowly, and when I hit something, I grab the spade to dig it up. I keep moving. I'm glad I'm wearing my old boots and have a fresh pair in the trunk, so I don't dirty the floor of Ma's car. This is definitely my last shot, a rather desperate one I will admit, unless the Beaumonts come clean. Fat chance on that.

I concentrate on my task, but as usual my mind wanders to the people involved in this case. I don't want to let Annette down. I've grown to like that scrappy gal and her cousin. I think of the others I've met, her brothers, Al Sinclair and his family, Dancin' Dave, even those Beaumonts. It's an interesting cast of characters.

So far, I've found nothing that resembles a clue. I take a break from squatting so long. It'd be easier on my legs if I could kneel, but then I'd be covered in the mud from the knees down. As I walk around the junkyard, I don't spot any life in the trees around the junkyard, which now is down to mud in parts. It's without a doubt the ugliest time of the year here in the hilltowns.

I check the open gate. There's still no sign yet of Annette and Abe. Okay, Isabel, back to work.

I am about three-quarters the way done when the claw's tip catches something that isn't a bottle cap, Skoal lid, or a screw. It's something small and rather delicate, and when I wipe it with a rag in the bucket, I realize what I've found. Barbie Woodrell's missing earring is on the palm of my glove.

I stand. The earring is definitely hers. I don't even have to see its twin. I've stared enough times at that necklace to recognize the artful twist in the gold and the amethyst's color.

This has to be the clue I thought was here. But what does it mean? I slip the earring in my pocket. Now what to do? So many questions. It's time to find out the answers.

Barbie

I split from Rough Waters before Annette and her son return. I stick a note in the garage's side door: **I THINK I FOUND SOMETHING. CALL YOU LATER.** I dump everything in the trunk, change my boots, and after I get my mother's car outside the yard, I return to close the gates before heading to the Pit Stop. I'm hoping Pete isn't there, and just my luck, the first I've had in a while, I see him leave in his pickup and drive in the opposite direction. If he checks his rearview mirror, he'll just see some Ford anybody could be driving instead of my Subaru. I slow the car and wait until he's completely over the road's hill before I turn into the Pit Stop's lot.

Barbie greets me with a big sunny smile. Her arm is out of the sling, but there are bruises around her wrist. My guess is they weren't made by a fall but by Pete's big fingers.

"What's up, Isabel? You just missed Pete."

No, Barbie, I'm not missing Pete. Yeah, it's a bad joke, and one that I keep to myself.

"I believe I found something of yours."

"Mine?"

I pull the earring out of my pocket.

"Isn't this your missing earring?"

Barbie's eyes widen. She's blinking hard and bringing her fingertips to her lips.

"Where'd you find it?"

"At Chet Water's junkyard." I hand her the earring. "I have a question for you. How did you happen to lose it there?"

Barbie is tearing up.

She's silent.

At this point, I don't have the patience for any softball

questions. I'm getting right to it like a reporter at a five-minute news conference. Answer my questions, damn it.

"I have a few more to ask you. My next is when did you lose it there?"

Barbie doesn't answer that one either. Instead, she splits for the backroom. And without another thought I follow her into what appears to be the Pit Stop's storage area and an office of sorts. It's not hard to find Barbie. She's backed against the door that leads outside. Her hand is clenched, presumably over the earring.

"Stay away." Her voice trembles. "Please."

"I'm not going to hurt you. I just want to hear what you've got to say."

She shakes her head.

"But he will."

"Pete?"

"He'll be comin' back." Tears run down her face. "He's gonna kill me if he finds out."

Yes, my suspicions that Barbie is a victim of domestic abuse are right on. I'm figuring how I can help her when my cell phone rings. I slip it from my pocket. I'm only going to answer it if it's somebody important and it is. Chief Dutton is calling. I press the red circle.

"Hey, chief."

"Sorry, it took so long for me to get back to you, but I remember who the woman was that was crying. It was Barbie Woodrell."

I keep a watch on Barbie. She hasn't moved.

"I'm right here with her. Chief, I think you should come over to the Pit Stop right away. I believe she needs your help."

With a bit of a shriek, Barbie charges forward. She tries to wrestle the phone from my hand. I don't want to hurt her, but I'm not giving up that phone. I glance at the screen. Crap, I've lost the chief.

"You've ruined everything," Barbie wails.

She's still fighting me. I shove her backwards although not hard enough for her to fall. She backs toward the door. I stay right in front of her.

255

"Pete beats you, doesn't he?" I soften my voice. "Barbie, the cops don't have to catch him doing it anymore to arrest him. They changed the law a long time ago."

She's pressed against the door.

"You don't understand," she sobs.

Damn, now I get it.

"You were there that night. You saw what happened to Chet Waters."

She makes a deep stuttering breath.

"Please, I'm beggin' ya."

A couple of scenarios are possible. I honestly don't believe she'd be capable of killing Chet on her own. What would be her motive? It's got to be Pete.

I start with one scenario.

"Did you and Chet have an affair and Pete found out? Then he caught you there with him?"

Her head swings back and forth.

"No!"

"Oh," I say, suddenly feeling even sorrier for her. "Chet was trying to help you."

"Yeah," she sobs. "He was gonna help me get to my mother's in Ohio. He even bought me a bus ticket."

"And?"

"Pete was supposed to be at Baxter's with a couple of buddies that night. But he came home early. He found the letter I left him. I didn't write anythin' about Chet, but he figured it out." She gulps air. "Chet was always extra nice to me. It made Pete jealous and sometimes he accused me of foolin' around with him. It wasn't true, but Pete gets things in his head... "

I touch Barbie's upper arm.

"You're doing good."

"Chet picked me up, and we went back to his place cause he forgot the bus ticket. I was waitin' in Chet's truck when Pete showed up and dragged me out. He started hittin' me hard. That must've been when I lost the earring. Chet heard my screams. Then he and Pete went at it. Pete wacked him hard in the head with a shovel."

256

She sobs.

"Go on."

"Chet fell to the ground. He didn't move or make a sound. Pete checked and said he was dead. He said we had to cover it up."

My brain is going fast. If Annette said it looked like her father tried to crawl out of the fire, he didn't die right away. But Pete Woodrell killed poor Chet either way.

"Were you there when he started the fire?"

Barbie makes stuttering sobs.

"He dragged Chet's body in the house and put him in his chair. Then he made the fire. He dropped a lit cigarette onto a pile of papers at his feet. He made me watch. He said… "

That's when the bell on the Pit Stop's door jingles, and Pete Woodrell hollers, "Barbie? Where are ya?"

Barbie's eyes grow larger.

"Let's get outta here," I whisper.

"He'll find me."

"Not if I can help it."

I grab Barbie's hand. We are out the back door and I hold on tight to make sure she doesn't run back. I make like hell for my car, half-dragging Barbie with me. I get the passenger side door open and shove her inside, and then slam it shut. I have my key out and ready when I take my place. I punch it into the ignition.

"Get your seatbelt on," I say as I fix mine.

She's fumbling with the belt as I hit the gas. Pete Woodrell races from the store's back door.

"You bitch, get back here," he yells.

Pete rushes toward my car, but I manage to dodge him and pull into the road without hitting him or bothering to check too hard to see who might be coming. Barbie's got her hand on the dashboard. Her cry is more like a scream.

When I check the rearview mirror, Pete is running toward his truck. He's not going to let us get away. I push the car forward faster.

"Hang on," I yell.

Minutes later, Barbie's head whips around.

"He's right behind us!" she wails.

A quick glance in the rear-view mirror confirms it. Pete's truck is getting closer fast. I press the gas pedal.

I should be scared to death and, God's honest truth, I am, but right now I'm a bit thankful the Beaumonts chased me on this road. It was good practice. But while those guys may have been fooling around, Pete isn't. If he would kill Chet Waters, and there is no doubt in my mind he did and set that fire, he'd kill Barbie and me, or at the very least, me.

"Why didn't you tell anybody?" I ask Barbie.

"Pete said I was an accomplice cause I saw what happened. I could go to prison. He said I couldn't say nothin' in court cause we were married."

"He was wrong on both counts." My cell phone rings in the right pocket of my coat. I'm driving too fast to risk it with one hand. "Grab that phone. See who it is."

Barbie does as I ask.

"It's the chief."

"Answer it," I snap. "Put her on speaker phone."

"Where are you?" Chief Dutton asks. "I'm at the Pit Stop. There's nobody here and the door's unlocked."

"I'm driving on the main drag, and Pete Woodrell is chasing me in his pickup. He's the one who killed Chet. I've got Barbie with me."

But before the chief can answer we hit a curve and a dead spot for cell service.

"She's gone," Barbie says.

"Don't worry. She'll find us."

Barbie twists around.

"Oh, no, he's catchin' up with us."

The speed limit sign says fifty. I'm going sixty-five. Sam would be proud of me. He said I drive like an old lady. Move it, he would say. Pete's big pickup handles this road better than my mother's big car, so now there's only ten feet or so between us. How long can I keep this up?

I'm figuring my options. I'm not about to turn off on one of the side roads. Most of them are dirt anyways and likely axle-deep in mud. I'll aim for Baxter's like I did when the

Beaumonts tailed me.

I press the pedal. We're going seventy.

"What happened to Chet's dog?"

"He attacked Pete and bit him hard on the arm. He killed the dog when he broke its neck. Then he dumped it somewhere." She looks over her shoulder. "Oh, no, Pete's right behind us."

"Uh, Barbie, any chance Pete carries a gun?"

"Gun?"

"Yeah, like a handgun?"

"He keeps one under the seat."

"Shit."

"What are we gonna do?"

"Well, I'm hoping Chief Dutton catches up with us, but we might have to make a hard right into Baxter's. We're gonna reach it soon. We'll be safe there."

Pete's pickup is close enough I see him sneering behind the wheel. I don't believe I can drive much faster on this winding road, but I believe I have no choice. I'm doing eighty. A pickup coming the other way blasts its horn but stays in its lane. Where in the hell is that police chief?

We make it around one steep curve and halfway around a second, when the front bumper of Pete's pickup hits the back of my mother's car. I push the car forward, but Pete does it again harder.

It's then I know we're not going to make it, and the car careens off the road, barely missing a tree before it heads into a snowy field, rolling over and over like it will never stop, but it does, on its wheels, mercifully. Barbie and I are screaming our heads off. The air bags deploy.

Beside me, blood streams down the side of Barbie's face. She's crying. I feel sharp pains in my shoulder and ribs.

I try to open the door, but I can't.

"Barbie, you okay?" I ask her.

She whimpers when her hand comes away bloody from touching her face.

"I dunno. I think so."

I hear a siren. Finally.

259

"Where's that fucker?" I ask out loud.

But a painful look to my left gives me an answer. Pete Woodrell's pickup is on the side of the road, wrapped around that tree my mother's car barely missed.

I glance up when somebody knocks on the windshield. Holy crap, it'd better not be Pete.

Instead, I hear a man's voice I'd recognize anywhere. Gary Beaumont is talking.

"Isabel, what the hell you doin' in there? Is that Barbie with ya?"

"Yeah, it is. I can't open the door." I turn toward Barbie, who tries to open hers. "Barbie can't either. We're kinda stuck in here."

Gary whistles sharply.

"Hey, Larry, run up and grab a crowbar from the truck. We gotta get 'em outta there."

Gary wanders around the car, checking out the damage. When I turn toward the road, I see the flashing lights of the chief's cruiser. Cars and pickup trucks are stopping.

This is likely my last chance to talk with Barbie before she meets Chief Dutton, who surely has to press charges against Pete Woodrell for harassing and forcing us off the road. Maybe he'll be charged with attempted vehicular homicide or something like that. At the very least, driving to endanger. I'll insist.

But I want to be certain where Barbie stands. Too often, I've learned, abused women just can't break that forgive-and-forget cycle.

"Barbie, I want to say something. Pete's gonna have to answer to what he just did to us. But it's up to you that he's found responsible for what you said he did to Chet Waters. The man tried to help you, and he lost his life because of it. You owe it to him."

Her bottom lip quivers.

"But Pete... "

I don't let her finish. I'm not up for being polite and understanding.

"Oh, he'll post bail and get out after they patch him up.

Think about that. He knows you told me. You think this is gonna get any easier? He's hurt you before. What do you think he'd do to you this time? Where are you gonna hide?"

Barbie makes a stuttering sigh. Tears pour down her face along with the blood. So, Barbie what'll it be?

Outside the car, Gary yells for his brother to hurry up. Chief Dutton knocks on my window.

"You all right in there?"

I turn toward Barbie.

"What should I tell her?"

"Tell her yes."

The Aftermath

The town of Caulfield has only one ambulance, so Chief Dutton makes the right call and lets it take Pete Woodrell, who's in rough shape, to the hospital. That's what you get when you drive eighty miles per hour to terrorize two women and you don't wear a seatbelt. Yeah, I'm not being sympathetic. Why in the hell should I be? I'm hurt. The EMTs, all local guys, including one who's a Rooster True Blue Regular, have checked me over. They suspect I may have a broken left collarbone and a few bruised ribs.

I told the True Blue Regular, "How am I supposed to pour beer with one arm?"

"Aren't you right-handed?" he replied. "Piece of cake."

Now I sit in the cruiser's backseat with the door open, Chief Dutton insisted, while I watch the EMTs load Pete's stretcher into the back opening. His wife, Barbie, who seems to have survived the crash with only a nasty cut on her forehead and maybe a broken or badly sprained wrist, stands beside the ambulance. She bites her lip. I'm wondering what's going through her head. Will she conveniently forget everything she told me when we were stuck in my mother's car? I hope not. Her scumbag husband doesn't deserve to get away with it.

Then Barbie looks my way. She raises her head and gives me a nod. I believe Barbie's going to do the right thing after all.

Naturally, a crowd has assembled along the side of the road. News like this spreads fast on the hilltown network. It's a Saturday after all, so most folks aren't at work. One of Caulfield's part-time cops directs traffic and keeps nosy bystanders herded on the road's shoulder.

Gary and Larry Beaumont stick around. I laugh to myself that of all the people living here, they were the ones who hauled ass down to the field and got us out of the car. They were feeling proud of themselves when they finally pried open the doors and dragged us out of there.

"You okay, Isabel? You okay?" Gary kept saying as if we were best buds.

Larry made a goofy laugh.

"We passed you on the road back there. Looks like you were goin' a hundred miles per hour," he says.

"Nah, only eighty."

I thanked him and his brother a million times. You should have heard them go "Aw shucks, Isabel."

Yeah, I've had a change of heart about Gary and Larry. They aren't the only ones in this case. As it turns out, Chet Waters wasn't the complete son of a bitch most said he was. Yeah, the man had his faults, but he tried to help Barbie Woodrell when nobody else did. And he died because of it. Annette should be proud of her old man. Maybe her brothers will be, too.

Speaking of Annette Waters, I turn when I hear the Tough Cookie holler my name. She sweeps through the crowd with her son, Abe, trailing several feet behind.

"Isabel, thank God, you're alive!"

I raise my hand.

"Yeah, I'm alive. Got some bruised ribs and I might've broken a collarbone. Other than that, I'm okay. Not much you can do for them. That's what the EMT told me, but they want me to get checked out at the hospital just in case."

Annette peeks over her shoulder before she lowers her voice.

"Is it true what I heard?"

"What did you hear?"

"That Pete Woodrell chased you in his truck and ran you off the road."

"Yeah, he did. Looks like he and his truck got the worst of it. Same goes for my mother's car. See it down there? I believe it's totaled."

263

"Holy shit. What an asshole. Why'd he do something like that?"

I glance around at the crowd. The chief is busy, so I get to my feet slowly.

"Come with me."

Annette dutifully follows me to a place that's away from everyone.

"What's going on?" she asks. "Abe and I came back and saw your note."

"I did find something. One of Barbie Woodrell's earrings."

"Huh? What the fuck was… "

"Shh, please keep your voice down. Barbie told me your father was going to help her get away from Pete that night, but he caught them. She told me it was Pete who killed him and set the house on fire. I was trying to get Barbie outta there when he showed up."

"Shit, I don't believe it."

I grab her arm.

"She confessed to me. But the only way Pete will answer for it is if Barbie testifies in court. She said in the car she would, but I'm not sure if she'll go through with it. Her telling me isn't enough to put him away. I've already talked with Chief Dutton."

Annette forgets what I told her earlier. I yelp in pain as she hugs me.

"Sorry, sorry. I'm just excited. You did it. Shit, I can't believe it."

"You're going to have to sit tight and keep this to yourself. No Marsha. Do you understand? It's important. Let the chief do her job. Hopefully, Barbie's conscience will do the same."

One of the town cops asks us to move out of the way of the wrecker. Annette whistles as it uses a winch to haul my mother's car from the field.

"I bet your mother's not gonna be too happy about that."

"Eh, she was okay with it when I called. She said it was easier to replace a car than a daughter."

Annette folds her hand into a fist for a playful jab but catches herself.

264

"Your mother cracks me up. Hold on. I'll tell 'em to take it to my junkyard."

Yes, I called Ma, who was concerned, of course. I talked with Ruth, too, but downplayed the seriousness of the chase and crash. I was expecting a lecture, especially after the recent sit-down, but instead she said she and the boys would meet me at the hospital's emergency room. Eventually, she'll learn the truth, and then I'll be in for it.

I left a message for Sean about the accident. I don't feel in good conscience I can share what Barbie told me, but the owner of a local business running his wife and a P.I. off the road might make a juicy story to start. I suggested he contact Chief Dutton.

As for Lin, I'll call him from the hospital.

The chief approaches.

"Isabel, I thought I told you to stay in the cruiser," she jokes. "I'm going to take Barbie to the hospital. You can come along, but I've gotten several offers to drive you there."

"Huh? Like who?"

"Gary and Larry for two. Some old guy who says you know him from the Conwell General Store." She jabs her thumb over her shoulder to where the Fattest Old Fart is talking with a few of the locals. Of course, he's already gotten the scoop from me, so he can have something over the other Old Farts in the backroom. "Then there's this guy."

This guy turns out to be Dancin' Dave, who's face is awash with concern, as he marches through the bystanders.

"Isabel, you okay?" are the first words out of his mouth.

"I believe so. Just a little banged up."

He snorts.

"I heard what happened and came right over. You're one tough lady. I don't think Pete Woodrell knew who he was messin' with."

I'd laugh if it wouldn't hurt so much.

"Guess not."

"I always suspected he wasn't good to Barbie," Dave says. "I give it to you for tryin' to help her get away from that jerk."

That's not the whole story, but for now, the official one will have to do.

"Uh-huh."

"I suppose we'll have to postpone our date tomorrow night."

The guy's a real country gentleman, I'll give him that. But I'm also betting he's not going to give up so easily. He won't forget. He won't let me either.

"If you don't mind. We can do it some other time."

He moves in closer.

"How about I drive you to the hospital?"

But before I can respond, Annette is back and as usual, she doesn't miss a beat.

"No way, Dave. I'm takin' Isabel. I already said I would."

Annette is fibbing, but I'm grateful. I bet she wants to talk some more.

"Looks like your friend beat me to it." Right then, Dave bends toward me and plants a sweet kiss on my right cheek. "See you soon, Isabel. Now you take care of yourself. I'll call to make sure."

Annette and I watch Dave Baxter leave. She makes a hissing giggle.

"I actually can't drive you. I'm towing Abe's Mustang with a chain on my pickup. But I bet somebody else would. Maybe somebody like him."

Annette jerks her thumb behind her as Jack Smith makes his way through the crowd.

"How did he hear what happened? I didn't call him."

She snorts.

"Well, I did. He's puttin' his cousin and that cook in charge of the Rooster tonight."

Jack picks up his pace. He smiles at me. I'm smiling back.

"Hey, Isabel, I've come to spring ya," he says.

"Jack, you're just in time."

Fantastic Books
Great Authors

CROOKED
CAT

Meet our authors and discover
our exciting range:

- Gripping Thrillers
- Cosy Mysteries
- Romantic Chick-Lit
- Fascinating Historicals
- Exciting Fantasy
- Young Adult and Children's
  Adventures
- Non-Fiction

Made in the USA
Lexington, KY
10 December 2019